C0000257935

Jacky Dahlhaus

Jacky Dahlhaus was born in Australia and grew up in The Netherlands. She checked out Adelaide, the city of her birth, for half a year after high school, before studying in The Netherlands to become a veterinarian. After a short career in the UK and a move to Western Australia with her husband, she changed to an even shorter career as a science high school teacher. She worked a few years as an office manager before giving up on employed work. Dedicating her time to her two children and exploring various hobbies, she finally found her niche in writing. Jacky now lives in Scotland. *Living Like A Vampire* is her first novel.

www.jackydahlhaus.wordpress.com

Books written by Jacky Dahlhaus:

Living Like A VAmpire
Raising A Vampire

Out soon:
Killing A Vampire

Sign up for news on the Suckers trilogy at:
www.suckerstrilogy.wordpress.com

SUCKERS
Book 1

Living Like A Vampire

Jacky Dahlhaus

Jacky Dai

The content of this book is copyrighted © by Jacky Dahlhaus

Published by Jacky Dahlhaus Publishing
First publication: January 2016
Second publication: October 2016
Printed and bound by Ingram Spark
ISBN 978-0-9956719-0-4

Book cover design by David Williams

All rights reserved. No part of this book may be used or reproduced in any manner without permission of the author, except in the case of brief quotations embodied in critical articles and reviews. The unauthorized reproductions or distribution of this copyrighted work is illegal. No part of this book may be scanned, uploaded or distributed via the Internet or any other means, without the author's permission.

This book is a work of fiction. The names, characters, places, and incidents are products of the writer's imagination or have been used fictitiously and are not ￼e construed as real. Any resemblance to persons, ￼or dead, actual events, locale or organizations is ￼coincidental.

Contents

Black October

Like everybody else's, my life changed forever during the 2004 event that became known as Black October. All of a sudden they were there. Vampire-like creatures who were once normal humans but now bitten by the infected. The infection made them UV-sensitive, giving them an epileptic seizure if they came into contact with sunlight. The infection also made them drink human blood to stay alive. As they swarmed the world in packs, they sank their teeth into as many humans as possible. If they didn't drain you, you lived, and you would change into a sucker yourself.

That was the name we gave them. Suckers. At first we called them vampires and it was funny how the media adopted vampire terms from modern books and movies. If only these monsters glittered in sunlight and were vegan. A bioscientist interviewed on TV had explained that these so called 'vampires' weren't the living dead. He used the term 'succedaneums' for them, meaning 'substitutes.' From then on everybody called those who had been bitten and now sucked blood 'suckers.'

It was surprising how fast the pandemic spread. As suspected, airplanes transported it around the globe and once earthbound it spread like wildfire. Suckers attacked the big cities first, leaving only death behind and taking their 'newborns' with them to attack the surrounding countryside. On the news they compared it to a fast spreading virus, like the common cold. Within the first week they had established it was indeed caused by a virus, but its origin was then unknown, as was any other detail about it. Whatever was causing the infection, it was exponentially worse than any other that anyone had ever seen in history.

The media had little time to give us more information on the outbreak as within the first week the suckers managed to overrun communication networks. All information updates ceased, the only form of communication left unaffected was via CB radios. In other words, suckers didn't seem to be mindless hordes. They were on a mission and had a plan. Unlike the people in my new home town.

There seemed to be three types of people here. The first type believed the stories they heard and fled as soon as they could, as far away from the cities as possible. The second type believed that something was happening, but weren't ready to leave their homes. They boarded up their houses and raided the food stores. It was as if they were expecting a hurricane to pass through. The third type thought it was just another form of mass hysteria, caused by none other than the media. They continued their lives as well as they could.

All of us became cut off from what happened in the rest of the world and it was as if we were living in the dark-ages again. Everybody was fending for themselves, trying to do what they thought was right. It didn't take long before the threat of suckers reached Bullsbrook, Maine, where I lived.

Friday Evening - Deciding To Leave

On Friday night, October 15th, 2004, Sue, Charlie and I, three new teachers at Bullsbrook high school, sat in The Celtic Frog, the local bar. We occupied the corner booth that we made our own since we had arrived in town two months ago. The bar was the only place that appeared to continue as usual since the start of the sucker pandemic a week ago. The bar owners, a couple called Abby and René, still served drinks and the usual patrons hung off the bar or sat in their usual seats. There were, however, a large number of new customers. They were refugees escaping the city. They first arrived six days ago, but their number had steadily grown. We didn't think anything of it at first, just an unusual time of the year to get vacationers. However, as the news reports became increasingly scary, more and more arrived and today the biggest wave hit. Their conversations were hushed and anxious. We could hear snippets of horror stories about people being chased, herded like cattle, and slaughtered. We too sat huddled in our corner booth, whispering, discussing what to do next.

All of a sudden, we heard a commotion. I had heard a man talk loudly, but now people shrieked and cried.

The three of us looked up to see what was happening and I could see a cluster of people had gathered around one of the newcomers.

"They're watching a camcorder," Sue said.

I pushed her to move as I wanted to see what was on the camcorder that would make people cry like that. "Come on," I said, "get going. I want to see it too."

She stood up, followed on her heels by me. Charlie got up as well and followed us to the wailing people.

"What's up?" I asked.

"Oh my god," said Abby, wiping tears from her face with one hand, she grabbed my shoulder with the other. "You'll have to see it to believe it."

She pushed me to the front of the crowd. An old man, I guessed in his sixties with a rather saggy build, was holding a camcorder with its viewing screen out. More people tried to see the recording, but the ones who had already seen it were reluctant to move. They apparently needed to see the footage for a second time to convince themselves what they had seen was not a figment of their imagination. The old man backed up the recording and restarted it. What I saw shook me to the core.

It started off with a younger couple in a happy pose at a restaurant. The camera was then handed, I presumed by a waitress, to the man of the couple. He continued filming the woman. It must have been her birthday or some other celebration as the man gave her a present and, after a big hug to the man, she began unwrapping it. I couldn't hear what was being said.

From that one scene of happiness, it turned into one of chaos and slaughter. Suckers stormed into the restaurant, their fangs clearly visible, grabbing customers and waiters alike. The lucky lady who had been unwrapping the present screamed when one of the suckers grabbed her arm and tried to pull her away. She struggled. The camera movement became erratic, as if it was being used to hit the attacker of the woman. I saw the arm of the sucker move in the direction of what I think was the camera man's neck. The camera then followed the movements of the man's hand as he fought to get the arm off himself. You could see the sucker laugh, he actually laughed, before pulling the woman he was still holding close. Her eyes were glazed over, she was in shock. The sucker then sank his teeth into her neck, watching the man as he did it. The camera movements became more erratic as the sucker dropped the woman and turned his efforts to the man holding the camera. We couldn't see what happened next as in the attack the camera was launched and landed on one of the other tables, in a plate full of pasta. Over the top of spaghetti, I saw the people in the restaurant become the dish of the day.

"Where did you say you found the camera?" someone in the crowd yelled.

"Two days ago in Needham, halfway down the road to Portland," said the old man loudly. "I was looking for food and found it lying there, in the pasta. Nobody but dead bodies there anymore, the suckers had already left."

"Why didn't you stay there? How'd you get past the suckers?" asked someone else.

"With a big, fast car," he replied abruptly. "I was lucky to have missed the sucker attack, working in my cellar and my hearing being bad, but my family didn't survive." There were tears in his eyes now. "I've come to warn you. I've lost my loved ones, but you still have a chance to save yours. I want people to know what's coming for them. Y'all have to get outta here! They're coming!" His voice was thick with emotion, his eyes wild, as he frantically looked around the gathered crowd.

I looked over my shoulder at Sue, then at Charlie standing beside me. They were as shocked as I was. More questions were called out to the old man, but I wasn't interested in them. I'd heard enough. We returned to our corner booth, too traumatized by the images to speak for a while.

School had been suspended until further notice earlier today. Most people had taken their children out of Bullsbrook during the past week anyway. So far the threat had seemed far away and we all thought it would be dealt with before it spread. These people and these images told a different story. It wasn't going to be safe here for much longer.

"We've got to get out," I said. "We have a better chance of survival getting away from the crowd."

"Are you sure? Wouldn't it be better if we stayed here?" Sue shifted in her seat. Her dreadlocks bounced as she spoke.

I scanned the bar's customers again. "You saw the tape."

So many new faces. So much fear.

"I think," Sue said, her southern accent thicker than usual, "that we have a better chance if we stand with the people from the town. More manpower."

My eyes went back to Sue again. I let her words sink in. I pursed my lips.

"I don't agree. What do you think Charlie?"

Sue and I both turned to look at Charlie. Being a dwarf didn't diminish his presence and, being ten years our senior, I gave his vote more weight. The low lighting cast dark shadows on his face, accentuating his dark mood.

"I agree with Kate. Even if all the people in town worked together we could never stand up to the numbers that the suckers must have gathered by now. Let the army take that fight. We need to get out of here and hide until this is dealt with by the authorities." I followed Charlie's stare and waited for Sue to respond. Finally, she nodded, dreadlocks bouncing again.

"You sure?"

"Yeah, he's right. Better to hide than to fight."

"Okay, so where do we go?" Charlie asked.

I stuck my thumb into my mouth as I'd bitten too much skin off next to my nail while was listening to Charlie. I shut my eyes to deal with the pain and the image of my parents and sisters flashed by. I still didn't know their fate. Last night I'd hardly slept, being tormented by nightmares of possibilities, and the resulting tiredness didn't make me think any clearer. There was nothing I could do for them at the moment, so I tried to concentrate on deciding where to go. Even though Charlie, Sue and I'd lived in Bullsbrook just over two months now we still didn't know it, or the surrounding area, well.

"Hey, maybe we can go to the campground!" Sue burst out. Charlie and I raised our eyebrows at her.

How in heaven's name does she know a campground? She's not what you call the camping type.

"I'd asked around about where to find an affordable place for my parents to stay. They want to come and visit me over the Christmas break," she explained. "My neighbors told me about it. They said it's along the river north of town. It has cabins for rent at reasonable prices and a small cabin could easily sleep the three of us."

My face lit up. "That's a great idea. They might have a camp store too, with long-lasting food supplies."

My thoughts drifted to movies with underground fallout bunkers. God only knew how long this sucker pandemic was going to last. When my attention came back to the conversation I realized both Sue and Charlie didn't comment on my practicality. They were too excited about the campsite.

"Yeah. Best of all it's off the main roads," Charlie said, staring into his own private universe. Then his eyes snapped back to us. "We better go there as soon as possible. We probably aren't the only ones who came up with this idea."

"Are we going right now or tomorrow morning?" Sue asked. She shifted in her seat again.

I hadn't thought that far ahead yet. Suddenly I felt a surge of fear gripping me. It was as if a giant hand squeezed my insides, pushing adrenaline into the far corners of my body. This was really happening and it wasn't a figment of my imagination. The idea of leaving Bullsbrook, my beautiful, new hometown, made the whole dreadful situation so much more real. However, Sue's question was valid and a decision had to be made right now.

"I'll sleep better if we leave tonight," I said.

Suddenly, Charlie slammed his hands flat on the table. Sue and I jumped.

"Okay. Let's go home, pack our stuff and meet at Kate's. She's the only one with a car." He stared us down until we both agreed. "And only pack the essentials!" he added as he leaned forward towards Sue. I turned my head to see Sue's reaction.

"What?" she asked innocently, shifting her eyes from Charlie to me, seeking back-up against his insinuation.

"Don't get carried away, Sue," I said. "My little hatchback may have five doors, but that doesn't mean there's a lot of space in the back."

Sue opened her mouth in protest, but she couldn't find any good excuses. Charlie chuckled.

The two of them hurried to finish their beers while I left mine untouched since I was going to be the driver. We paid our bill and went on our way.

Friday Evening – Mrs. Babcock

As I walked back home from the bar I decided to ask my neighbor Mrs. Babcock to come with us. I felt I couldn't leave the old woman all on her own. I walked up to her front door. Before I knocked I saw the curtains twitching.

"Mrs. Babcock, can I talk to you for a second?" I called, trying not to disturb anybody else in the street.

No answer. I took a step towards the living room window.

"Mrs. Babcock, it's me, Kate, your neighbor. I know you're there. Please open the door."

I saw the curtains move again and after a few seconds of silence, I heard her shuffling towards the front door, sliding the security chain in place, and opening the deadlocks before the door opened a few inches. Mrs. Babcock was wearing a pink nightgown, her long, white hair, which she normally wore in a huge bun on her head, cascading over it like a waterfall in moonlight. Her right hand gripped a baseball bat she was trying to hide behind her tiny frame.

"What is it, dearie?" she said, her eyes darting into the street behind me.

"Mrs. Babcock, you must have heard about what's happening. Suckers will come here soon and my friends and I are leaving town to hide from them. You can come with us if you want to."

Her wary face turned into her familiar smile as her kind eyes focused on me.

"Oh, sweetie," she said, "I'm not going anywhere. I can take care of myself." She proudly held up the wooden baseball bat as if to demonstrate her invincibility.

How can she lift that thing with arms as skinny as cotton swabs?

"Are you sure? There's enough space in my car..."

I'd no idea if this was true, not knowing what Sue was bringing yet, but where there was a will there was a way and I didn't want not having enough space being the reason to leave Mrs. Babcock behind.

"You're very kind to offer, love, but you do what you have to do. I've never left Bullsbrook in my life and I'm certainly not going to leave it now."

Her smile was as sweet as candy. I felt my jaw drop. I rushed to shut it so I didn't come off as insulting.

A bunch of bloodthirsty suckers is coming this way and she's going to fend them off.

"Are you sure? It's okay, you know. We've got plenty of space," I tried again. "We're going to a campground north of here." I tried to find more words to persuade her, but one look at her told me that anything I could come up with would be a waste of time.

"Don't worry about me, Kate. You go with your friends. I'll be perfectly all right here."

"Okay, if you're sure."

"I'm sure, love."

I left, but before I stepped off her porch I turned around and said, "If you change your mind…"

"I won't, dearie." Another smile.

I fought the urge to sigh out loud. "You take care then, Mrs. Babcock."

"You too, Kate. You too."

As I walked back to my home, I heard her put the locks back on the door.

Will I ever see you again?

Friday Evening – Leaving

It was 11pm and I stood in my cozy bedroom. I looked around. What to pack? 'Just the essentials,' Charlie had said. But what essentials do you pack when fleeing from suckers? A mirror, maybe?

No, aren't vampires. What's the use even if they had no reflection? You put a mirror around the corner and you see nobody. You then turn the corner and bang, you're face to face with a sucker. Forget the mirror.

Fortunately, memories of my Girl Guide camp experiences kicked in. I'd needed warm clothing for cold nights, toiletries (don't forget the toothbrush), extra pairs of socks, hiking boots, a water-tight jacket and pants, layers of clothing, a first-aid kit, and a whistle.

Skip the whistle. Don't want to draw attention to myself with suckers around.

Light! I remembered them saying suckers were light-sensitive, so I need light. I dug deep in my closet and found my big Maglite. As I held it, I realized that battery-light wasn't the same as UV-light.

Oh well, if I can't make them have seizures with the battery-spawned light, I can always clobber them over the head with it.

I balanced the flashlight in my hand while I weighed up the pros and cons of lugging the item with me. Four DD batteries made it heavy. It also made it a handy tool to get around a campsite, so I decided to bring it. I put it next to the backpack on my bed and started packing the usual overnight stuff and as much dark clothing as I could find. There was a pretty big chance I'd have to provide Sue with dark clothing as well, since most of hers made her stick out like lights on a Christmas tree in a pine forest. Her preference for bright colors wouldn't help if we needed to hide in dark corners to avoid any suckers finding us.

I sat on the edge of my bed, lacing up my walking boots, when there was a knock on the front door. Grabbing the Maglite, I hurried into the living room and peeked through my curtains, aware I was imitating Mrs. Babcock. Sue and Charlie stood illuminated under my porch light. Charlie carried a leather duffel bag. Sue had a huge, red weekend bag hanging off her shoulder and was leaning on the handle of a cabin suitcase. She looked around nervously, her eyes wide at every sound she heard. I lifted my Maglite above my shoulder, opened the door with a swift move to let them in, and shut it immediately behind them.

"Wow. Aren't you just ready for action," Sue said as she fumbled while trying to rest her weekend bag on the top of her suitcase.

"Well, my landlady just gave me a good example of how to be prepared. She's got herself a baseball bat."

"Did she clobber you over the head with it?" Charlie said with a twinkle in his eyes.

"Of course not. Duh! But she's gonna defend herself with it." I made a swinging action with my Maglite.

"Not coming with us then," Charlie said, the twinkle gone and his heavy eyebrows frowning.

"No, unfortunately not." My shoulders slumped. "I did offer, but she wouldn't have any of it. Poor lady, she has no idea what's coming."

Sue let her weekend bag drop on the floor and flopped into one of my chairs. I knew she liked Mrs. Babcock too.

"We don't really know what's coming either, but I'm not going to hang around to find out," Charlie said. "Let's awaken that mechanical beast of yours and get out of here."

He padded Sue's shoulder. She gave him a weak smile and got out of the chair again.

As I got behind the wheel of my little hatchback, Sue took the passenger seat and Charlie sat in the backseat. All of our luggage fitted in the limited space in the back, which surprised me, but it meant that

Charlie had the whole backseat to himself. However, Sue pushed the passenger chair right back to fit her long legs in and Charlie had no choice but to sit behind me.

When I turned the key, the starter sounded like it was choking itself out. It didn't start. My heart skipped a beat. The car had never given me any trouble before. I looked at Sue and her eyes met mine, mirroring the anxiety I felt.

"Try again," Charlie said from the back as I felt him pull himself forward by my seat. I couldn't help but notice his breath on my neck. It made my heart pound faster.

I turned the key a second time. The car revved and started normally. I let out a big sigh of relief. Charlie slumped back in his seat and I smiled at Sue.

"Phew," she said and pretended to wipe her brow.

I backed out of my driveway and we were on our way. Sue guided me to the highway we hoped would lead us to safety. I had to dodge shopping carts and waste bins lying in the streets. The town scenery was so different from the previous few months.

Bullsbrook used to be the most wonderful place on earth to me. The people who lived here cared for it. There was no litter, no graffiti, and flowerbeds colored the front gardens of people's homes. What I liked best was that people exchanged greetings when passing each other in the street. That was so unheard of in Portland, where I was born and raised.

After I'd finished my teaching degree in June I received a position as a science teacher here in Bullsbrook. I'd been so thrilled that I was chosen to teach in this idyllic country town. I counted myself lucky as usually only a limited number of positions were available. That I landed a job here right away had been like winning the lottery. Fellow teaching grads had offered to trade places with me, which I of course gracefully declined.

Now, in the dark of night, the town looked even more dreadful than during the day. Shop windows were broken, showing as dark, black holes in the facades. Houses, boarded up and half covered in plastic sheets, had loose planks rattling in the wind. And there wasn't a soul in sight. Bullsbrook looked more like the slumps than a pretty country town.

We were out of Bullsbrook quickly and quietly. The campground was not too far from town and the road was pretty straightforward. My thoughts went back to Mrs. Babcock.

She said she would defend herself with a baseball bat. Suckers are coming... and she'll fight them with a baseball bat. Tiny, fragile, sweet Mrs. Babcock.

I had an awful feeling in my gut and I felt my perspiration going into overdrive.

Did I pack my deodorant?

The conversation with Mrs. Babcock kept running like a looped video in my mind. Had I made the wrong decision? I knew I wouldn't have been able to persuade her to come, but still my conscience kept telling me I should have tried harder.

Maybe I should have hit her over the head and kidnapped her?

My mind was coming up with ludicrous ideas now, so I focused on the road in front of me, following the yellow lines.

I feel like I'm Dorothy in The Wizard of Oz, following the yellow brick road, but instead of going home I'm fleeing from it.

I glanced sideways at Sue and tried to find Charlie in the rear view mirror. I wondered which one was the lion, the scarecrow, or the tin man. Sue had closed her eyes and Charlie was staring out the side window. He was lost in his own world.

I better not start singing 'Follow the yellow brick road.'

Friday Night - The Campground

It wasn't long before I saw the signs to the campground called 'Piney Creek' and turned off the main road. The approach wound through a forest of pines and birches and their foliage cut out the light from the moon. The glow of my car's high beams was the only light illuminating the way.

The entrance to the campground was blocked by a boom gate. I drove up as close as I could before putting my car into park.

"Keep the motor running," Charlie said as he beat me getting out of the car.

"What's he doing?" Sue asked. She'd only stopped snoring a few minutes before.

"He's going to lift the boom gate."

"It doesn't work automatically?"

I looked back, but I didn't see a pole with a button on it.

"Nope, this one is manual. Did your neighbors say how old this place was?"

Sue remained silent, answering my question.

As Charlie struggled to push down the boom's counterweight, Sue opened her window and called out to him. "Be careful!"

"Don't worry, my lady" Charlie called back, "I won't drop it on my head."

I smiled, but Sue was annoyed he hadn't taken her concern seriously.

You may lose your job, jester Charlie.

While Charlie kept the boom gate vertical, I drove the car to the other side. I kept an eye on him and the forest through my mirrors. Since watching the video in the bar I kept expecting sucker attacks at any moment. Charlie dropped the boom and hurried back to the car. We drove on for a short distance before reaching the visitor parking lot. Apart from my car, it was empty. There were no trees nearby and the moon now lit up our surroundings. We could see an office building with what looked like a dwelling attached, along with a separate camp store and a building I assumed housed toilets, showers, and launderette. We saw the light in the reception area was on, but nobody came outside to greet us. After I killed the engine I tensed but couldn't see or hear anything suspicious.

No evidence of anyone being attacked by suckers.

Charlie and Sue didn't move to get out either. We waited a few seconds for something to happen, but when it didn't I stepped out of the car, followed by Sue and Charlie. As soon as we were all out, the door of the reception cabin was opened and a man appeared. He held a shotgun aimed in our direction. The three of us shot our hands up, holding our breath.

"What do you want?" the man shouted. The tone in his voice was stern, but somehow not with deadly intent. I gathered that if he wanted to kill us he would have done so already. I took him in to try and find out what his intentions were. He had short hair, red-veined cheeks, wore a black and red checkered shirt, and brown corduroy pants. He looked like a lumberjack.

Not sure if he's okay though.

I bit the inside of my lip, suppressing a smile.

This is not the time to be funny, Kate!

My eyes darted to the others and I got the impression that Charlie was also trying very hard not to laugh.

"Well?" the man asked again.

"We're here to get a cabin, sir," Sue said, "j-just for the three of us." She gestured towards Charlie and me and flashed a smile. Her stutter made me realize Sue thought the situation was scarier than I did.

"Keep your hands up!" he shouted again as we dropped our arms in the assumption that things were okay now. We shot them up again.

Okay, so he doesn't fall for the pretty lady routine...

"We can pay for it. We've got money," I offered.

As the man's eyes shifted in my direction with noted interest, I took my chances and pulled out a few bills from my pocket.

The man's demeanor changed at once and he lowered his gun. "Ah, okay, that's good to hear."

Awkward smile. "Please come in and I'll write you a receipt." He turned around and disappeared into the office.

We stood there with our hands half in the air, looking at each other, wondering if this was for real.

"You guys got any cash on you?" I asked. "I don't know if I have enough." I showed them the few twenty-dollar bills from my pocket.

We gathered up all the cash we had on hand and went into the office to pay for a cabin. The room was small and dingy. There were no seats for waiting customers, no toys to keep children busy while moms and dads did business with Mr. Lumberjack.

"I'm sorry for that reception," the man said as he gathered some paperwork. "I've been hearing disturbing stories from customers and one can't be too careful enough. Is any of it true?"

"I'm afraid so," Charlie said. "We haven't seen any trouble ourselves, but we've seen video footage. Seemed legit."

"They're coming this way," Sue added. Mr. Lumberjack looked up from what he was doing.

"Well, we're hoping they're not coming here," I said. "We're hoping they stay on the main road."

Mr. Lumberjack made a guttural noise and proceeded to give us the prices of the cabins. We asked for a two-person cabin, as Charlie was happy to sleep on a couch. But Mr. Lumberjack insisted that the insurance company would be on his back if he let us. I got a hunch that he was more interested in renting out a bigger cabin and receiving a higher price as he was clearly disappointed when we then decided to only pay for three days instead of a full week. We would have to find an ATM if we decided to stay longer, especially since I was sure the sucker threat wouldn't be over quickly.

Once Mr. Lumberjack handed over the keys to our four-person cabin, No.8, he highlighted its location on a copied map, which he gave it to us. We hopped back into my car and drove slowly along a lantern-lined path. The light cast an orange glow on the tarmac. Cabins were on one side of the path, campers on the other. Most looked occupied. We could see lights on in several of them, but every single one had their curtains drawn. Now and again I saw a curtain move and somebody peek out. As soon as I'd look in their direction, the watcher would withdraw. In contrast to Mr. Lumberjack, who seemed more weary than anything, these campers were scared.

When we arrived at our cabin, I parked next to it and we got our luggage out. I held the screen door open while Sue fumbled with the key to open the front door. Charlie and I followed her inside. We stood in a living room/kitchenette, with two doors on the left and two on the right. Charlie inspected the bedrooms while Sue and I checked out the cleanliness of the bathroom and toilet. They would not live up to my mother's standards, but after having lived on my own for nearly three months my standards had dropped considerably. I could live with it.

"First dibs on the big bed!" Charlie yelled.

Sue and I hurried over and threw appreciative glances into the dark, mostly brown-colored, roomy bedroom. It had mirrored closets and a double bed.

Not my favorite color scheme, but the bed looks comfy.

Charlie lay spread-eagled on his back on the orange-brown checkered bedspread. Sue and I checked out the other room. We nearly got jammed in the doorway trying to get into it. It was a very narrow room with bunk beds taking up most of the space.

"Oh hell no!" Sue yelled back to Charlie. "We can't possibly fit in this tiny cupboard, so you are sleeping in here, mister. We get the big room."

"Not fair..." he muttered as he lifted himself off the bed, dragging his duffel behind him.

"Sorry, Charlie, but you're better sized for that small room," I said as we passed each other switching rooms, and I dropped my backpack where he had been on the bed.

"No argument there," I heard him say as he chucked his duffel onto the bottom bunk bed.

Friday Night - First Night at the Cabin

It felt as if we had traveled back in time as I looked around the cabin. It had a decided 70's look. Brown carpet, wooden paneling and orange curtains everywhere. It made me think of the photos of my parents when they were young. Mini-skirts and high hair. The cabin didn't smell of cigarette smoke though, which was a relief. We made ready for bed, putting our toiletries in the bathroom, laying out our pajamas, and closing the curtains. I saw Charlie checking out first the refrigerator, then the cupboards.

"Who's up for a nightcap?" he asked, holding up a six-pack of beer.

"Good find, Charlie!" I took out three different-sized glasses from a wall cupboard in the kitchenette.

Charlie handed me two cans, pulled another one out of the plastic rings and put the remaining three in the refrigerator.

"I don't need a glass, so you girls can take the bigger ones," he said as he pulled the lid from his can. He sat down on one of the orange, retro-looking chairs and took a sip.

Sue joined us. I finished pouring the beer into the two glasses and looked forward to some mindless chatter to stop my thoughts from rambling on about what 'could have,' 'should have,' or 'would be.' I gave Sue her glass of beer.

"So... what did you guys bring as weapons?" Charlie asked. As much as I liked Charlie, I despised him that moment for bringing up 'the subject' again.

Party pooper.

Sue and I sat down on the two-seater opposite Charlie. We both dropped lower than expected, spilling our beers, due to the foamy seating being extensively worn below the tatty fabric. We both laughed.

"You girls already drunk? Must be the lukewarmness of the beer," Charlie said.

"Oh, shut it, Charlie, we haven't had a drop yet. And you know us. It takes more than one glass of beer to get us giggly," Sue responded.

"You may not want to taste this horse piss, it's disgusting." Charlie pulled a face while looking at the can.

"Weapons?" I said, after uselessly trying to wipe the beer of my shirt.

"Yeah, weapons," Charlie repeated. "Things to defend ourselves with against suckers. Like the guy with the gun." His free hand waved towards the reception building. "I'm assuming you don't have fold-away pitchforks in your bags."

Sue and I glanced at each other.

"I thought we were hiding here so we wouldn't have to fight any suckers," Sue said. She liked Charlie's idea as much as I did.

Charlie leaned on the side arm of his chair. "Gotta be prepared for everything. If suckers can get to Needham, they can get here too. It's probably just a question of when."

A scout is always prepared... Too bad it's been a long time since I was a scout.

"What did you bring?" I asked him.

"A blowtorch."

"That doesn't give off UV-light. It won't stop them," I said. I thought about my Maglite and how ineffective my weapon would be.

"Maybe not, but it'll sure as hell burn them!" He chuckled and took another sip of beer, followed by scrunching up his face again.

'Sure as hell burn them.' Nice word choice, Charlie!

Sue wrinkled her nose. I wasn't sure if it was because of the beer or her following words.

"If it's all the same to you I don't want to get that close, thank you very much."

"I brought my Maglite," I said to her.

"I hope you aim for their teeth with it," Sue said.

I haven't thought about where to hit them at all!

I pretended to hit a sucker with my Maglite and imagined the pieces of teeth flying. As my imagination got me carried away, I wobbled my lips weirdly, exposing my teeth, which made Charlie chuckle. He was having more fun than Sue and I were and I wondered if his apparent happiness was caused by being on edge. Whatever it was, I didn't think there was anything funny and took another sip of the awful tasting beer.

Suddenly I wished I owned a gun, despite the fact that I'd been dead against them my entire life. This was one of the reasons I wasn't good at keeping in contact with my older sister Maxine and her Navy career husband. I'd always been of the opinion that if there weren't any armed forces, there wouldn't be any wars either. The desire to hold a gun in my hands shocked me. Considering the current situation, I sat back and argued the pros and cons of this unexpected violent wish.

Why would I want a gun?

Because I am exceptionally attached to my life and want to defend it by any means possible.

What if I accidentally shoot myself, or Sue or Charlie? Would I be able to shoot a person intentionally?

There were too many 'ifs' involved in handling a gun, so I forced myself to stop thinking about it for now.

Fortunately, I don't have one to begin with anyway.

I noticed nobody had said anything after Sue's remark. We were all seemingly lost in our own thoughts. We finished our beers in silence and went to bed. None of us brought up keeping watch as we were all exhausted from the excitement of the past week. I said goodnight to Sue and turned off the bedside table light. She was asleep in no time and I followed her into dreamland shortly after. Even Charlie's snoring couldn't keep me awake. I must have felt safe.

Saturday Morning - Meeting the Neighbors

The next morning I woke to sounds and smells coming from the kitchen. At first, I thought I was back at home with Mom and Dad again. The thought felt warm and fuzzy. But as soon as I opened my eyes I had a shock. I was staring at myself in a huge wardrobe mirror and it was not a pretty sight. I didn't have a clue where I was, I couldn't move one of my legs. I let my gaze wander around the room and reality hit. Turning my head I found that Sue was sleeping next to me, realizing it was one of her long legs pinning my leg down. I managed to slip from under her and get out of bed without waking her. I pulled on my skinny jeans and went into the living room. Charlie was standing in front of the stove, frying bacon and eggs.

I love a man who can cook...

"When did you get those?" My voice was still groggy.

"Hey, you're up, you hungry?"

"Like a horse," I said and yawned. "I thought you didn't eat meat?" I got cutlery out of the kitchen drawer.

"That's right, I don't, but I know you two do."

Now that's thoughtful.

"Thanks, smells great."

After I had the plates and glasses out, I stood beside him for a while, looking at the eggs and bacon as he moved them around in the pan.

"Do you think we should wake Sue?" I asked.

My stomach grumbled and I tried to hide it by wrapping my arms around myself.

"Is she still asleep?"

"Yeah..."

"Then no," he said, "let her sleep for a while longer. You never know how little sleep we'll have the coming night."

Man, you sure are the party pooper!

I kept hoping for a normal day without talk of suckers and doom and death.

"There's OJ over there," and with his spatula Charlie pointed to paper bags on the floor.

Following his direction, I found a carton of orange juice in one of the bags. I filled two of the glasses I'd put on the table. As I put the carton in the refrigerator, toast popped out of the toaster. I buttered them and Charlie let the eggs slide from the pan on them.

"You want Sue's egg?" he asked.

"No thanks, too much cholesterol for me. You have it." A yawn escaped my mouth again and I stretched. I still wasn't fully awake.

"I don't count that stuff," Charlie muttered as he shoved the last egg onto his plate. I took out half of the bacon and Charlie put the pan back on the benchtop. We sat down and had breakfast together.

"How is the bunk bed?" I asked him before stuffing the egg yolk into my mouth. The yellow liquid sloshed around in my mouth and I savored the delicious taste. At the same time, I felt rather guilty about Sue and me shoving Charlie into that small room.

"It's okay," he said.

Whether he was telling the truth or not, I couldn't say.

I got dressed and after Sue woke I draped a few of my black clothing items over the bed for her to pick and choose. Sue didn't see the point though.

"Why would I want to wear *your* clothes?" she asked me.

"Look, we may need to hide in the shadows and *your* outfits just won't do," I explained. "You might as well wear a banner with the slogan 'Bite me' on it." She stared at me. "Your clothes are too bright, Sue..." I hoped she understood I was talking survival here.

She took a bit of convincing, but in the end agreed to wear my over-sized black Imagine Dragons hoodie that, only just, didn't show her belly button. She couldn't fit her big butt and long legs into any of my skinny jeans, so we agreed she wore her own dark purple chinos.

When we got out of the bedroom together, Charlie was doing the dishes. He flashed a huge grin in our direction.

"Are you going to share with us what's so funny?" I asked him.

Without a blink he replied. "Oh, it's just that you girls took so long getting dressed that for a moment I thought you must have been killed by suckers."

"So why didn't you come save us?" Sue dared him, taking the bait.

"Because I knew the fashion police was in control of the situation."

There was a micro-second of communication between Sue and me and in unison we grabbed the couch cushions and pummeled Charlie with them. In return Charlie splashed us with the dishwashing water. It felt wonderful to have a good laugh.

Charlie hadn't unpacked the groceries he had bought yet, Sue and I finished this together. Charlie had bought as much long-life food as he could get his hands on: lots of canned food, energy bars, orange juice and long-life milk, and, of course, more beer.

We'd just put everything away in the cupboards when there was a knock on the door. Sue and I looked at each other, expecting the other to know who it could be. Charlie was the one to realize that because it was daytime there couldn't be any suckers out there trying to recruit our souls. He opened the door and there were a man and a woman standing on the doorstep.

Don't tell me you are Jehovah's Witnesses...

The man was casually holding a shovel. The woman stuck her hand out to Charlie, but kept it outside the cabin. Charlie had to open the screen door and lean forward, into the light, to shake it. The woman smiled.

"Hi, we are your neighbors, from cabin No.7," she said, and the man pointed to the left. "My name is Moira," the woman continued. "This is my husband Paul and these are our kids, Fiona and Patrick." The kids had been standing out of view and the woman called them over to come and shake hands with Charlie. But as soon as they came within distance Paul pushed them behind his back. So instead they waved to us. The three of us returned the wave.

I was perplexed. We were here in hiding and intent on not staying any longer than was absolutely necessary. I hadn't thought that this warranted us to introduce ourselves to our neighbors. Nobody said something.

Awkward!

My manners kicked in after a few seconds. "Eh, do you perhaps want to come in and have a cup of coffee?"

"No, no, that's fine," Paul, said. "We have stuff to do, dig holes and such," and he indicated the shovel he was holding, as if we hadn't noticed it before. Moira shot him an angry look.

"Oh, okay," I said. "Actually, I don't even know if we have coffee." I couldn't remember coming across it as we had unpacked the bags, but maybe Charlie or Sue had unpacked it. "Do we?" I turned to Sue, then Charlie.

"Eh, no, we don't, I forgot to get coffee. Sorry," Charlie replied. He wiggled the door while shuffling one foot nonchalantly. He knew he was in trouble, because he knew Sue and I always drank coffee at our morning break at school. He then looked at the family and shrugged his shoulders.

"Well, it was nice to meet you anyway. We won't keep you any longer," Moira said and ushered her family back to cabin No.7. As they walked away we could hear her say to her husband, "See, they aren't suckers at all. You were worried for nothing."

Charlie closed the door and, as one, we laughed.

"How awkward was that," I said.

"Yeah, no coffee," Sue grumbled as she shot a menacing glance at Charlie and started throwing couch cushion at him again.

"I said I was sorry, my lady," Charlie joked while defending himself. "You can lock me up in your dungeon if you want to punish me!"

"You are so lucky they don't have dungeons here..." Sue said after she was sure Charlie had repented with enough sincerity and had offered to go to the camp store again to get coffee.

Saturday Afternoon - Checking Out the Campground

After Charlie returned from the camp store and Sue and I had a coffee, we checked out the campground. It was light after all and safe to do so.

Piney Creek appeared to be a decent size campground. I counted ten cabins along the path from the reception building. Apart from these, we walked past lots of RV's and camper trailers parked on both sides of the winding paths that crisscrossed the site. Quite a number of these mobile holiday homes had permanent-looking furniture in front of them.

Why would people want to go to the same holiday spot, year in, year out? It seems so boring.

I always felt compelled to check out the world and see as many places as possible, meet new people.

We now crossed an empty field along the riverside. The wind blew across it and gave me a chill. A few light green patches in the grass were evidence there had been tents here recently.

Who wants to camp in October?

Most of the tent field was level, with only the last third slightly sloping down to the river. There were a handful of canoes tied up to a jetty and a metal dinghy lay upside down on the riverbank.

"Hey guys, you wanna go canoeing?" Sue asked. She pointed to the sign that said we had to contact the office to use the canoes. Charlie and I both shook our heads.

Too cold, Sue!

Instead I hooked my arm through Sue's and smiled at her. She smiled back at me. The wind picked up and I pulled my jacket's collar up to keep the wind out. The three of us walked on without talking. I wasn't in the mood for chitchat as I couldn't shake the worry for my family.

I wondered who Charlie's loved ones were. Sue was an only child, though I knew she had an extensive family back home - with lots of uncles, aunties, nieces, and nephews. She was worried for all of them. Charlie didn't seem lonely or sad. He once told me his parents had died in a car crash, years ago and that he was a single child. He only had one distant aunt and no pets. So I wondered who he cared for.

When we neared the back of the camp store I spotted a playground. A sprinkle of childhood sentiment overtook me. I let go of Sue and ran to the swings. I planted my bum on the little wooden bench, pushed off, and tried to swing as high as possible. Sue followed suit and together we giggled like toddlers. Charlie smiled at us and jumped on one of those turning platforms. His smile seemed to get bigger every time he came round. When I was at the highest point of my swing, the chains slacking, I let go and jumped. I almost lost my balance, but managed to stumble to the turning platform and gave it a big push as I joined Charlie on the opposite side. Charlie kept stepping to keep the platform spinning and we had to hang on to the metal bars for dear life if we didn't want to fall off. As I was swinging around and around I took in the playground. It wasn't much, but I guessed it would keep the little ones busy. Not that anyone was venturing outside.

I closed my eyes. The cold wind on my face and through my hair felt like freedom. The rush of the moment was amazing! I opened my eyes again and saw that Charlie was laughing too. For a moment I wished time could stand still. Sue had stopped swinging and walked over to us. I realized that the turning platform was going too fast for her to jump on, but I didn't want to let go of this delight. So I clung to the metal bar a bit tighter.

"Ugh, I need to get off this thing," I said after another few rounds of growing guilt. "I think I'm going to puke!"

At once, Charlie slowed the platform by dragging his foot on the ground and I took my chances. Of course I fell over due to the fact that we were still going way too fast to get off safely and the centrifugal forces kept on playing havoc with my balance. I laughed as I rolled over the grass, but Charlie jumped off the platform nevertheless. He ran towards me in his spin-off, miraculously staying afoot, and asked me if I was okay. He leaned with his hands on his knees to stay upright himself. I noted that his face was as green as mine must have been.

"Yeah, yeah, I'm fine," I said a moment later after my head had stopped spinning. I sat up. After Charlie got his full bearing back, he offered me his hand and helped me get up. "Let's go back," I said.

"Yeah, good idea," he replied.

"Aw, spoilsports." Sue moaned. She had stepped onto the merry-go-round and was spinning around slowly. "I wanted to have a go too!"

"Oh, you can have a go if you want, I don't mind," Charlie said, waving his hands. "But I'm not going back on that thing again, because I probably will return my breakfast if I do."

"In that case, forget about it, I'm not into recycling that much," Sue said. She jumped off the platform again.

"Okay then, let's go back." I put one arm over Charlie's shoulder and my other around Sue's waist. Considering the situation I felt pretty good at that moment. It was as if we just had had a good Friday night at the bar in Bullsbrook and were half-drunk on our way home, as per normal.

Saturday Night - First Shift

We didn't meet anybody else during our little expedition, but we knew there were other people around. Like last night, now and again you saw a curtain move, heard voices or snoring. The closer we came to our cabin, the more I realized how many people were here. I didn't think this wasn't normal for the time of year. It also didn't make me feel any safer. The place was supposed to be a hideaway, not a take-away for suckers.

Back in our cabin we played games of cards with two packs Charlie had thoughtfully brought along. After lunch he suggested we try to sleep as we had decided it would be a good idea to take turns to stay awake during the night. We all went to lie on our beds and I didn't have a problem falling asleep at all. Lunch had been plentiful, which helped me combat my insomnia of the last few days as soon as I lay my head down.

In the evening we agreed to each take two-and-a-half hour shifts. I took the first shift as I was the one who'd slept the longest that afternoon and was feeling the most awake. Sue didn't sleep at all during the afternoon and was rather tired by midnight. Charlie and I were happy for her to take the last watch. Charlie was okay with taking the second watch and having his sleep interrupted. I knew I'd never be able to cope with that, so I was very relieved when he said he didn't mind.

Keeping watch was boring. There was no TV and no radio. I did try them, just in case, but had no luck. I struggled to stay awake after a while. I'd learned you can only do so many games of solitaire before you get fed up with the odds of making it to the end. The only things that kept me awake were the sounds coming from outside. There was an owl hooting and pigeons cooing.

I thought pigeons slept at night.

I could hear the leaves of the trees being rustled by the wind. They dappled the moonlight on the curtains and their shadows moved as the leaves swayed with the trees. It was a welcome distraction from the drab and still interior of the cabin.

At 2:30am I woke up Charlie and he took the next shift. When I got into the big bedroom I found Sue had completely taken over the double bed in her sleep.

My, girl, you've got long arms and legs!

I didn't want to wake her so I grabbed my pajamas and decided to sleep on the top bunk. As I tippy-toed into Charlie's room, I heard him flush the toilet across the living room. It hadn't taken much to wake him. After I closed the door I got into my pajamas, climbed up the steep ladder, and slid under the blanket. At that moment I was so glad we had taken the four-person cabin. I was asleep in no time.

Sunday Morning - Passing Time in the Cabin

Long after the sun was up we were woken by Sue shouting 'Breakfast is ready!' in her cheery voice. I yawned, rubbed my eyes and sat up. I hit my head on the ceiling and fell back onto the bed again.

Ouch! Who dropped the ceiling?

I opened my eyes and realized I was on the top bunk. When I opened the curtain of the little window above the bedhead I had to blink a few times against the rays of sunshine.

"Guys, breakfast is getting cold!" Sue yelled again.

"Yeah, yeah, hold your horses. I'm coming." I climbed down the ladder of the bunk bed.

"Good morning, legs." Charlie said from the bottom bunk bed.

I looked down and realized that the pajama shirt I was wearing only just covered my panties.

Oops...

"Good morning to you too, Smu...dge," I stuttered as I changed my words mid-syllable.

"Hey, I'm not a little, blue... blurred mark?"

"True, but I'm not fully awake yet, so everything's still very blurry." I grinned, glad I found an explanation for my sudden change of word choice. I knew he didn't like people making remarks about his small stature, so calling him a Smurf would probably not be appreciated.

I picked up the clothes I'd left on the floor when I'd gotten undressed and nearly stuck my bum in Charlie's face as I bent over. It was a *very* tiny room.

I know you noticed that too, Charlie.

I hurried to the other bedroom to get my jeans on. Sue noticed me slipping from Charlie's bedroom into the other. She raised an eyebrow, but I didn't make a comment.

Please don't think what I think you're thinking.

Through the gap of the bedroom door I saw Charlie walk into the living room, still dressed in his pajamas.

"Good morning, Charlie," I heard Sue say.

"It certainly is a good morning, Sue," he said and I could just imagine his face smug with that voice.

"Oh, and why's that?" From Sue's voice I knew she was as eager as I was to hear Charlie's reply. I paused getting my pants up to not miss it.

"Because I rarely wake up with a woman on top of me," he beamed.

The cheeky bugger!

I grabbed a pillow from the bed and hopped into the living room, holding on to my jeans as I did.

"In the top bunk, Sue, I was in the top bunk," and I threw the pillow at Charlie, who was laughing his head off.

Sue squinted at us at first, but then smiled and told us to sit down at the table as the breakfast she had cooked for us was getting cold. I hoisted up my pants properly while Charlie picked up the pillow and threw it back on the big bed before we all sat down for breakfast.

I was so glad Sue didn't make one of her Mississippi meals. Sue's cuisine differed greatly from what I was raised with. My mother's cooking had been extremely bland, to keep Dad happy. Sue's dishes included lots of things I'd never even heard of. Words like gumbo, boudin and tasso were all new to me and Sue had taken it upon herself to introduce me to each and every single one of them. I found none suitable for breakfast and was glad she had served us scrambled eggs.

We decided to stay inside, but after a few card games we were rather bored. None of us had thought of bringing a book or any other game.

"We could play strip poker," Charlie suggested. He wiggled his eyebrows.

"In your dreams," Sue muttered without even looking at him.

"Yeah, go play with yourself on your bunk bed with the door shut please," I added. Sue high-fived me.

Charlie pretended to be hurt, but didn't make too much of a fuss over it. I gathered he hadn't really expected us to say yes to the game. The next suggestion he came up with was to play 'Truth or Dare.' As we were really, really bored, Sue and I agreed. How bad could it be?

Charlie immediately stood up and took three cans of beer out of the refrigerator. "Okay, as I was the one that came up with the idea, I'll start with the first question."

I took the can that Charlie offered me, feeling like a queen being waited on as I occupied the whole of the two-seater with my tiny frame.

Interesting concept, drinking beer before lunch, and probably not a good one while playing 'Truth or Dare,' but what the heck!

Charlie walked around the couch, handed the second can to Sue, and sat down again.

"You want a glass?" I asked Sue.

"No, it's okay. I'm happy to drink from the can," she said, opening her can.

"Good, because I wasn't going to get you one," I said as I popped mine open.

Sue, quick as a dart, grabbed behind her and threw one of the little cushions at me. I caught it before it hit my can and immediately threw it back at her. She caught it too and put it back behind her back before sticking her tongue out to me.

"Okay, serious stuff now, girls. Truth or dare, Kate?" Charlie said, as he leaned forward, seated on the edge of his chair.

I'd little experience with this game, but remembered the first questions were normally harmless. "Truth," I dared him.

"You're brave, woman," Sue said.

Charlie built up the tension by being silent before he asked his question. I had to admit I began thinking Sue was right as Charlie's stare intensified.

"What's your favorite color?" he asked.

Phew!

I let go of my breath.

"Oh my god, I thought you were going to ask me for my credit card pin code for a second." Sue and I laughed.

"The answer's easy, blue." There was no hesitation whatsoever. It had always been my favorite color, so I didn't even have to think about it. I turned to Sue to ask her my question and just before my eyes left Charlie I saw this peculiar look on his face. I paid no attention to it as I had to think of a question for Sue.

"My turn," I said, "Truth or dare?"

"Truth," Sue said. "Remember I have access to your toothbrush though."

What in heaven's name could she do to my toothbrush?

Forget it, I don't think I wanna know!

"Okay... Who was your first love?"

"Right," she said, positioning herself on the chair as if she were going to tell her life's story. "His name was Ben and he was in my 6ᵗʰ grade..."

Charlie choked on his beer. "You did it in 6ᵗʰ grade?!" he blurted out, spilling beer all over.

"No! Of course not," Sue said. "I was in love with him. That was the question, wasn't it?" she asked, turning to me for help. She held the beer can to one of her cheeks to calm down her blush.

"Yes, that was my question, Sue. And you, mister," I said while pointing to Charlie, "have a dirty mind."

"That's what you get when you wake up with a woman on top of you," he said, focusing on his attempt to wipe up his spilt beer.

The cheeky bugger, he's still thinking about my legs and bum.

"Smudge!" I threw a couch cushion at him, missing him by a long shot.

At that, Charlie's face became serious. "That's it!" He set his can of beer on the side table, got up and made straight for me. Maybe I'd gone too far this time. When he reached me, however, he had a huge grin on his face and started to tickle me. "Don't call me Smudge!" he yelled, "Surrender or die!"

Over my dead body was I going to surrender, so I kept calling him Smudge again and again. The torment increased. He kept asking me to surrender, alternating his tickling with pillow bashing. I tried to keep saying

Smudge, but I could hardly breathe, I was laughing so hard. Charlie was laughing as well.

"Guys, I think you should get a room," Sue said all of a sudden.

Charlie stopped manhandling me. I shot upright and we both stared at Sue, tears of laughter still streaking my face.

"Just a thought," she said, and smiled one of those knowing smiles.

Holy moly, she didn't think that Charlie and I...last night...?

"Don't worry, I'm not into Smudges," I managed to say after catching my breath while trying to wipe my face dry.

Charlie turned his head to me and made one more sudden move in my direction. I shrieked, pulling my arms in to protect my vulnerable sides. But he went to sit in his chair again and I straightened up.

The game continued innocently after Sue's remark. I chose 'dare' every time Charlie asked me a question as I was afraid he would ask me why I wasn't interested in Smudges, or what it would take to get me interested. I prevented him asking as I didn't want to let him down. Charlie was my friend and a very good one at that. I didn't want to lose what we had.

Sunday Afternoon - Letting Emotions Go

After lunch we tried to get some sleep again. The six or so hours of last night's rest were not enough for me and I soon fell asleep. It wasn't a pleasant sleep, with very vivid dreams. I dreamed of vampires, of people having convulsions, and of blurry characters chasing me.

When I woke, Sue wasn't there. I got up and found her in the living room, asleep and drooped over the two-seater. I must have been tossing and turning a lot to make her flee the comfort of the big bed. I heard Charlie snoring in his room so I went back to the big bedroom and sat on the bed. The bed head had an uncomfortable edge, so I popped up the pillows to soften it. When I finally got comfortable I thought back on what had happened in the past few days.

It was just over a week ago when the three of us sat in our local bar. Charlie had just gone to order another round of drinks for us when we heard of the sucker problem for the first time. Sue and I were watching the TV news when Charlie returned from the bar, carrying three pints of beer.

"Listen to this," Sue said to Charlie.

"Give me a hand with these first, my lady, before I drop something. Then I will do your bidding." We took the beers out of Charlie's hands and the three of us turned our attention to the TV screen. The newsreader just ended her sentence with '...disturbing images.' We were shown footage of what was apparently happening in the big cities. We saw people chasing others and it looked like they were biting them in the neck. The images were extremely vague and grainy as it was all filmed in the dark.

"New vampire movie coming out?" Charlie asked.

"No! This is for real. This is really happening, man," Sue said.

"You're kidding me," he replied.

I glanced at him and it was clear he didn't believe her.

"It's true," I said. "Otherwise they wouldn't show it on the news now, would they?" I took a big gulp of beer.

The drunk-one has spoken.

Charlie just stared at me, then at Sue.

"You're kidding me," he repeated.

I could understand his disbelief. The footage had seemed so unreal and far away, like some fantastical imaginary war in some far away country that didn't affect us. Sue and I both stared at Charlie with big eyes. He finally sat down.

"Wow! That's spooky. Is it bad?" He looked at the TV again, but the newsreader had moved on to the next topic.

"Only if you get killed apparently," I said. "If you live, you get to be a vampire and suck blood."

"Cool!" he grinned, "But I'm sure you mean 'if you die, you get to be a vampire.'"

"No, that's not what they said." I frowned.

"Yeah, that's not what they said," Sue agreed.

"But you only get to be a vampire when you get killed by a vampire, not when you not get killed by a vampire," Charlie said.

I thought about it for a moment, comparing what the newsreader had just said and what Charlie was saying. "That's confusing," I concluded.

Both Sue and Charlie laughed.

After we all did a bit of contemplation while sipping our beer, Sue spoke.

"Would you get to live forever you think?"

"Well, that'll be awkward, with the shortage of housing everywhere already," was my quick reply.

Sue and Charlie burst out laughing again.

"What?" I asked them. "It's true, isn't it? There's a housing shortage."

"You always look at things from a practical point of view, don't you?" Charlie said as he punched me playfully on my arm.

The conversation drifted to the housing problems our college friends were having in the big cities. That topic seemed so much more important at the time.

The three of us didn't watch any more news that weekend as we were too busy making and tweaking teaching plans and strategies for the coming week. When I arrived in the staff-room on Monday morning I was surprised to find it was buzzing with news about vampires, chaos and death. Mrs. Sloan, the old history teacher, who was giving Charlie such a hard time because he was given the Arts & Crafts teaching job she had hoped her nephew would have gotten, was crying and snottering while others were trying to calm her down. Apparently she couldn't contact her daughter, who lived in Portland, anymore. Other teachers were standing in little groups, whispering, as if in conspiracy about something. Charlie wasn't there as he always went straight to his classroom in the morning. His excuse was that he needed time to set up equipment for the first lesson, but I knew better.

When Mr. Finkle emerged from his office, everyone became quiet and looked at him, waiting for him to speak guiding words. He was a small man and not particularly handsome. He was more of a weasel, really, and as such didn't entice much respect from his looks. However, as he stood there with his hands on his hips looking at everyone, he knew that we would all listen to him. He was after all the principal, the puppeteer holding the strings. From the grin on his face it was obvious that this was a position he quite liked. His face became more serious and he spoke with a loud voice, to be heard by all in the staff room.

"I know there's talk of a grave situation going on in the world. However, we must think of the children. We shouldn't worry them with grown-up problems." He looked around the room again. You could hear a pin drop. "Therefore we will continue teaching as usual and not talk about it at school at all."

The majority of teachers nodded in agreement, telling each other 'not to worry the children.' Mrs. Sloan began another crying session, her morbidly obese frame shuddering with every sob.

My mind was blown.

This is such old-fashioned ostrich policy! I can understand not talking about it with the children, but why can't we discuss this amongst ourselves?

I raised my arm to protest, but Sue grabbed it before my hand went past my head and held it down. I yanked my arm out of her grip, frowning at her.

"It's no use," she whispered, "nobody will listen."

I looked around and saw that everybody was already leaving the staffroom, as if nothing had happened.

"We'll talk at lunchtime," Sue said as she, too, left for class.

Over the next few days news reports of sucker attacks came in from all over the world. It became clear the epidemic was actually worldwide, a true pandemic. New images of these so called suckers remained grainy and dark. The news reader mentioned the number of victims rising steeply.

This terminology of victims is very inappropriate. These suckers don't seem in the least bit disabled, physically or mentally.

When we weren't teaching, Sue, Charlie and I were glued to the TV screen, hungry for more information. We heard suckers had their own form of 'kryptonite'; sunlight. They appeared to be extremely UV-sensitive and when exposed to sunlight would instantly have an epileptic seizure, causing muscle spasms. We laughed about this. We envisioned endings of movies where vampires had epileptic seizures when exposed to sunlight, instead of disintegrating into piles of dust. I pointed out they would have to clean up whole bodies now, instead of using a brush and dustpan.

On Thursday, the day before the three of us left Bullsbrook, the situation came too close to home for me and so much more real; I couldn't contact my parents anymore. They lived in the one of the outer suburbs of Portland. They didn't pick up the phone, weren't online, and didn't answer my texts messages. I'd told them to come to my place earlier in the week, but they were adamant it was just a fad and that it would soon fly over. Now I was afraid for their safety. I wanted to jump in my car and drive home. Sue and

Charlie had had to physically stop me, arguing it would be senseless as the army had closed off the roads into and out of the cities in an attempt to contain the situation. I frantically tried to contact my sisters, to find out if they were okay and if they had heard anything from Mom and Dad, but this had no result either. Maxine lived on a naval base which was probably in lock-down. I felt relief in the thought that at least she would be safe. Julie, however, lived in a country town not too far from me and I worried immensely about her.

Sue also couldn't get a hold of her family, but driving to Mississippi would be way too dangerous.

Charlie didn't even know where his aunt lived.

By Friday most communications had stopped. During the week, one TV station after another had ceased to broadcast. Then the radio had gone silent. The internet had still worked, so to speak, but there were no broadcasts, no news flashes. Fewer people had been trying to contact one another. CB radios seemed the only form of communication left. Those giving out locations of safe places had soon stopped communicating and we could only speculate that suckers had followed their directions.

By this time most of Bullsbrook had been in chaos. There were some people who still pretended nothing was wrong, but most others had been rampaging through town. Some had tried to fortify their houses and plundered supermarkets for food. Others had taken advantage of the situation, looting as much as they could, as if a large flat screen TV could save them from suckers.

As I sat on the bed, hoping we were safe in the cabin, I thought about it all. So much in the world had changed in such a short time. It was hard to take in. My vision of having a worry-free, suburban life in a dream town had vanished. People were being hunted, killed even, and the world would never be the same again. My life would never be the same again.

Would all the kids from school be okay? Would Mrs. Babcock still be alive? What has happened to my parents and my sisters? Would I ever see any of them again?

Sunday Night - Hunted

This mortal fear for the welfare of the people I knew gripped my insides, tried to mush them all up in a tight ball. I felt so helpless. I wanted to save them, but there was nothing I could do. Tears ran over my cheeks. I didn't want to cry, it just happened. I didn't make a sound but the tears kept coming. Unable to stop them, I didn't make any attempt to dry them either. I could feel their wetness on my T-shirt after they fell from my jaw-line.

I became aware of Charlie standing in the bedroom doorway. I turned my head towards him, but didn't move otherwise. I knew he could see my tears, but I was not ashamed. He just stood there and looked at me with his sorrowful eyes. It was as if we had a connection without speaking, without words, only emotions exchanged between us. There was a tranquility I never experienced before. His presence soothed me and brought me out of the vortex of my desperate thoughts. I liked it and didn't want it to end. I didn't move or say anything, afraid that this would break the spell. Charlie also didn't move.

"Come on, let's make dinner," he said after a long while.

We agreed to keep the same watch-shifts as the night before and so I was up late again. After a few games of solitaire, I sat on the couch listening to the animals outside. My thoughts haunted me with memories of the past days. It was all so unreal. The first TV announcement in the pub, Mrs. Sloan's shaking body, Bullsbrook being rampaged by looters, Mrs. Babcock with a baseball bat, the campground owner aiming a shotgun at us. Trying not to go down that rabbit hole again, I thought about the life I'd led so far.

Have I made the most of my life? Should I have chosen another profession? Did I become the person my parents had hoped I'd be?

There were so many questions. Certainly, there were some aspects of my life I wasn't proud of. The choice of boyfriends I'd had, the occasional smoke without my parents knowing, my cheating during one of the tests at college. Sometimes, after a bad day at school, I'd wished I hadn't become a teacher. Overall though, looking back at some of the great interactions with the children during my classes, I was sure I'd made the right choice. I hoped I'd achieved what my parents wanted for me. If they were disappointed, they'd certainly never let it show.

All of a sudden I realized I couldn't hear any animals outside. No birds, no insects, nothing. Plucked out of my self-absorption, I sat upright.

This isn't good.

The crack of a gunshot reverberated through the campground.

"Shit," I said under my breath and jumped up to wake Sue and Charlie. Sue was already clambering out of bed when I opened the door and Charlie came out of his room as I turned around.

"Did you see anything?" he whispered.

I shook my head. "But I didn't look either."

Sue and Charlie got dressed as fast as they could, we were ready to flee. Charlie got out his blowtorch and I my Maglite.

Sue looked at us with despair. "What should I get?" she whispered.

I scanned the cabin in a hurry and spotted the table lamp with its ceramic base on the little corner table. I unplugged its cord and removed the light bulb to get rid of the lampshade.

"Here, clubber them with this," I said as I handed the lamp base to Sue. The cord was dangling down, but she wound it around the base of the lamp.

I joined Charlie at the window and peeked outside. There wasn't much to see. The lights from the lane were blinding my night vision. All of a sudden we heard lots of screaming down the little street. Fearful, we waited, hoping this was just a single attack. When new screams arose closer and closer, it became obvious the suckers were going from cabin to cabin.

"Let's get out of here!" said Charlie.

He opened the door and shimmied along the wall of the cabin in the opposite direction of the screams. I followed him, Sue was behind me. We tried to be as quiet as possible. Then the screen-door of our cabin slammed shut. Sue had forgotten it had a spring-closer. I saw it had trapped the plug from the lamp as it had become half-uncoiled. I nearly screamed as Sue continued to move away from the door. I saw the lamp slip from her hands and shatter on the concrete porch. The three of us froze and stared from the crash site to the row of cabins. Someone stuck their head out of a door and yelled to the people inside, "They're trying to escape!"

That was the cue for us to run.

"To the river!" Charlie yelled and we dashed in between the RV's and camper trailers, taking the shortest route.

We could hear at least two people following us in hot pursuit. I was worried for Charlie and his short legs, but boy, could he run. We didn't have much of a head-start and our pursuers were soon gaining ground. I heard loud swearing and threw a glance backwards. One of the pursuers had tripped over a piece of heavy furniture in front of one of the camper trailers.

Thank you so much, boring person!

We kept on running until we reached the tent field. The field lights lit up an eerie scene that gave us the scare of our lives. There was a whole bunch of suckers here, herding humans together while more and more were being added. Those suckers hadn't seen us yet so we continued our sprint for the jetty. Sue was in front, her long legs giving her the edge. For some strange reason she ducked under the upturned dinghy.

"No! The canoes!" Charlie and I both screamed at her.

I tried to reach for her as Charlie grabbed my arm. At that same moment the closest chasing sucker caught up with me. He seized the same arm Charlie had a hold of, the one I had the Maglite in, and I couldn't fight the sucker off me. Charlie didn't waste any time thinking as he swung round and planted the bottom of his blowtorch right in the suckers face. The shock made the sucker lose his grip on my arm. I again tried to get a hold of Sue but Charlie pulled me towards the canoes.

I followed him, running onto the jetty, and we jumped into the furthest canoe. Charlie worked frantically on the cord to get it loose. It was old and broke, allowing him to push all the canoes away from the landing stage. As he did this, I noticed Sue hadn't followed us. She must have stayed under the dinghy. My gaze was drawn by movement from the center of the field. Some of the suckers there had spotted us and were running towards the jetty now. I knew they would never be able to reach us in the canoe, as we were already more than a yard away from the jetty. I searched again for Sue and saw that the second chaser had caught up with the first one, who was clutching his nose. My heart stopped as number one pointed to the dinghy and number two then dragged Sue from under it.

"Sue!" I screamed, fear pulling on every nerve in my body.

Sue also screamed. It had no effect as they dragged her struggling body with ease towards the center of the field. A man from the crowd tried to free Sue from her captors. Was it Paul? I couldn't believe what I saw next. One of the suckers, not an overly big one, picked the man up above his head and threw him away from Sue, away from the pile of humans.

This is unreal, superhuman, movie stuff.

At first I thought I hadn't seen it right and blinked.

"Did you see that?" Charlie said.

I turned to him and nodded. We looked back to the tent field. More and more victims were added to the crowd of prisoners. Like Sue, they hadn't escaped the hunt.

The suckers who'd run onto the jetty halted. They had realized they'd never be able to catch us and turned to return to the tent field.

Charlie and I watched as all the suckers gathered around the humans. What happened next chilled me to the bone. As one, the suckers fell on their victims. It was a feeding frenzy. People were screaming, fighting, clawing, desperate to escape. But the suckers were stronger, their hunger was great, and the resulting bloodbath was like a scene from a horror movie.

"No! Sue!" I screamed again at the top of my lungs, nearly tipping the canoe over. "Sue! Sue! Sue..." I looked at Charlie and back to the field again.

I was frantic, panicking. I had never been so scared in my life. I wanted to help those people, to help Sue, but I couldn't do anything. I wanted Charlie to do something, but of course he couldn't either. Charlie and I were safe in the canoe and they weren't.

"Sue..." I said again.

This time I felt like someone wasn't simply grabbing my insides, but was ripping them out. I had to fight for breath, to stay conscious. I became lightheaded and within a moment I felt myself fall forwards.

A strong hand grabbed me by the scruff and pulled me back. It was Charlie. He embraced me and turned my head so I couldn't see what was happening on the tent field. I could still hear the screams and wailing, even though we were slowly getting further and further away from them.

"Deep breaths," Charlie said in between his own sobs, "deep breaths..."

Slowly the current of the river had us drifting away from the campground and eventually the screams faded into nothing. We sat in the canoe hugging each other for what seemed like an eternity, both of us crying for the loss of Sue's life, for the loss of all those lives.

Sunday Morning, Early - Going Back to Bullsbrook

The canoe followed the river, which wound and bended like a slithering snake. I huddled at the front end of the canoe, Charlie sat at the back. As we meandered along, my memories drifted back to when I first met Sue.

I had met her in the hardware store, where I was looking for paint to do up my new home. We bumped into each other trying to grab the same can of paint. She was the most colorful person I had ever met. When we started chatting, I found out she was the new English teacher at the high school. We got on really well and from that day, we spent most of our time together, helping each other painting and decorating. Then school started and our time was spent teaching long hours in the classrooms as well as at home preparing lesson plans.

How I wished I had spent more time with her those last few weeks. How I wished I'd saved her. How I wished I still had my friend.

We drifted for hours. When we got too close to the shore Charlie pushed us off with a branch he'd broken off from an overhanging tree. We didn't talk. We didn't want to be heard by any onshore suckers.

Besides, we didn't have anything to say to each other. Sue was gone, people were dead, what was there to say?

If I hadn't given her that lamp we might have all escaped together.

If I had run faster she would have followed me to the canoes.

If I had turned to fight the sucker we could have helped Sue get free.

I went through all the possible scenarios over and over in my mind. I couldn't stop it. It was as if my mind had a subscription on repeats lately. Though my brain knew I couldn't change what had happened, my heart seemed to refuse that fact. It kept telling my mind to try and find a loophole to undo past events.

When the first sun rays climbed over the horizon it created glittering sparkles on the water's surface. Birds had already begun singing earlier and life seemed to continue as if nothing eventful had happened.

Charlie spoke all of a sudden.

"It's not your fault."

I was facing him, but didn't look him in the eye. Silently I pondered his words for another minute before answering.

"Yes it is. If I hadn't given her the lamp she'd still be alive."

"You don't know that." His voice was devoid of emotion. Calm, if anything.

"Don't give me that bullshit about Karma." My breathing sped up a notch.

Charlie sighed. "Look, if you want to blame somebody, blame me. I was the one that grabbed and saved you instead of Sue."

I finally looked at him and saw his sad eyes.

OMG, he thinks he's to blame for Sue's death!

"It's not your fault either," I said.

He didn't reply, which was on par with my verbal refusal. We let the silence linger. There was no use wasting our breath on words that had no bearing on changing the situation. I let my arm drop outside the canoe, fingers gliding over the water's surface. The cool, little waves lapping against my hand were all I had to keep me from drowning in my sorrow.

We had no idea how far we had drifted down the river. When houses began to appear, we could only guess we'd reached Bullsbrook. We got off at the first jetty we came across and moored the canoe.

I felt like a fugitive as we walked through the town, dashing from house to house, huddling against the walls. We stopped at every sound we heard as we didn't know if there were any suckers here, and we didn't want to find out either.

Before we got out of the canoe we had decided to go to the school. There was a ribbon of pure magnesium in the science storeroom. I had explained to Charlie that magnesium, when you set it on fire, gives off an extremely bright light, including UV-light. I knew it was only a tiny piece, but Charlie agreed it might be our only chance to escape from a sucker attack in a dire situation. The school buildings might offer a safe place to hide too. Who would want to go back to school?

It took us a while to find out which part of town we were in, but we soon recognized where we were and set off for the school on a more direct route. We arrived there without incident and went straight to my science classroom on the second floor of the main building. Bullsbrook High was the only high school in the area. As it also housed the only local adult education facilities, hence the school wasn't a small one.

Sunday Morning - Magnesium

At the front of the classroom was the door that led to the storeroom. We hurried to it and I searched the boxes on the shelves for consumables from top to bottom. Charlie let me get on with it. In the meantime, he examined pieces of equipment, like beakers, cylinders and clamps.

"Gee, you need to do some dusting in here, Kate." I saw him wipe his fingers over the surface of an Erlenmeyer, before wiping his hands.

"Yeah, I meant to, but I haven't had the time for it yet. I've been having too much fun with the light equipment."

I continued my search. The shelves boxes were almost empty, so it didn't take me long to find the one I wanted.

"Ah, got it," and I showed Charlie the small, silvery piece of ribbon in a little zip-lock plastic bag filled with oil. The magnesium strip was about five centimeters long.

"Is that all?" Charlie said.

"Yes, unfortunately." Even though I had known it wasn't much, I was disappointed too.

"How long is that going to last?"

"To be honest, I have no idea. If I remember correctly not long, but I don't want to waste it trying." We both looked at it a while longer. "Let's cut it in half, so we each have a piece." I put the package on the desk and opened a desk drawer.

"Are you sure it's a good idea to make it even smaller?"

"Where's a zip-lock bag when you need one?" I rummaged through the contents of the drawer.

"Wouldn't it be better to keep it whole, to keep it burning longer?" Charlie tried again.

I stopped my search to think about that. "Yes, but what if we're attacked from two sides? We need to be able to ward them off from different directions."

"Hmm, you've got a point there. But if we are attacked by hordes we won't get out anyway. At least, it'll be very unlikely."

"Ah, but you're forgetting this stuff will make them have seizures and we can just step over them to get away." I continued my search for a small zip-lock bag when Charlie didn't have a parry for that one.

When I finally found one, I took a pair of scissors from one of the wooden blocks on the shelves. I took the ribbon of magnesium out of the bag and I cut the silvery piece in half. The metal was soft and pliable. I carefully poured half of the oil into the new bag and dropped a piece of ribbon into each one. I closed the seals and held out one bag to Charlie.

"Don't lose it through a hole in your pocket," I said.

He took it, looked at it for a moment and put it in his pocket. I turned around and rummaged some more through the desk's drawers.

"What are you looking for now?" he asked.

I turned around and held up two lighters. "These!" I said triumphantly. "We need to be able to light them."

He smiled and held up his own lighter, retrieved from his pocket.

"Got one already. Need one to light my blowtorch, remember?" His face had a smug look as he picked up his blowtorch which he had set down for the time being.

I looked at the cheap-looking lighters in my hand and again at the silver-colored, engraved lighter in his hand and dropped my arms.

"You win, your Schwartz is bigger than mine," I conceded throwing one of the lighters back in the drawer and pocketing the other.

"Sorry," Charlie said, but he was still smiling.

I leaned against the desk. "You'll have to scratch the surface of the material before you light it to get rid of the oxidized layer, otherwise it won't light. Actually, I don't know if my lighter will do the trick as we normally use Bunsen burners in the classroom."

Charlie gave me another smile, cheeky this time, and held up his blowtorch again.

"I'll try and stick to your side," I yielded again. "Oh, before I forget, once it burns, water won't stop it. It will only fuel it."

"Great stuff for a campfire on a rainy day." Charlie's face lit up.

"No, no, no! You can't look into the flame! I nearly forgot to mention that. The light will be so bright it'd be like looking into the sun. Remember it emits UV-light. So don't look into it unless you want to give your retinas a tan. Sorry."

Charlie's smile faded. He took the little piece out of his pocket again and looked at it.

"As long as it burns the suckers, I can live with that."

Sunday Morning, Late - Mr. Finkle

We decided to go to the staffroom. We had agreed it was a good idea to get some sleep on the comfy couches there. I wasn't sure if it was the physical discomfort of the canoe or the emotional drain of last night that made me so tired, but I wanted to lie down and sleep. When we entered the staffroom we were surprised to find a man lying on one of the couches with a newspaper over his head.

Charlie pushed me behind him and sneaked up to clobber the stranger. I followed him and as we came closer I recognized the tweed jacket and stopped Charlie just in time. Charlie turned around to me with a surprised look and I mouthed Mr. Finkle's name to him. Charlie sighed and seemed reluctant to lower his blowtorch.

We watched Mr. Finkle and waited for him to notice us. When nothing happened Charlie cleared his throat, but it still didn't wake Mr. Finkle.

"Mr. Finkle," I said quietly. No response. I moved a bit closer. "Mr. Finkle," I said a bit louder and shook his shoulder.

He scared us to death when he suddenly jumped up, waving his arms and scanning the room in total disorientation. The newspaper that had been on his face drifted to the floor, an old article about the sucker attack in the city on the front page.

"It's okay, Mr. Finkle," I tried to calm him. "It's only us, Charlie and Kate."

"Oh, you two. What are you doing here?" He adjusted his tie and tucked his shirt back in.

"We could ask you the same question," Charlie said.

Mr. Finkle looked down at Charlie. "I am here to protect the school from looters, what else?" he stated.

"Yeah? You and what army?" Charlie sat down on one of the chairs opposite the couch.

"What do you mean?" Mr. Finkle asked. When Charlie didn't reply, the head teacher looked at me.

"We better sit down," I said.

Mr. Finkle sat down on the couch again and I took a seat in one of the chairs next to Charlie and told our story. Mr. Finkle listened with bright eyes, he didn't interrupt me. When I had finished, he sat back taking it all in.

"That is one hell of a story." He nodded his head. "It is obvious that you have seen too many sci-fi action movies," he added as he folded his hands and pointed his index fingers at me.

My jaw dropped. He looked at me as if I had told him a fancy fairy tale.

Mixed emotions welled up in me, one after the other; disbelief, frustration, anger.

"Sue is dead, Mr. Finkle!" I shouted at him as I rose. I put my hands on the low table between us and leaned over to him. "And many more people have lost their lives! This is really happening, don't you get it?" I pointed at the newspaper on the floor.

Mr. Finkle looked at the newspaper and chuckled.

I straightened up and ran my hands through my hair.

"People lifting other people above their heads and throwing them about as if they were mannequins," Mr. Finkle said. "Come on, Kate. You must have had a bad dream, that's all."

I turned to Charlie for help, but he looked at Mr. Finkle in disgust, refusing to come to the rescue. The situation was so frustrating.

Charlie, you've got to help me out here!

I suddenly realized that this was how Charlie had felt before, when he had gone to Mr. Finkle for help about his problem with the other staff. When Charlie had just started at Bullsbrook High, certain teachers had been roused by Mrs. Sloan's hatred for him. She had taken offense that Charlie had been offered the job of Crafts & Arts teacher, not her nephew, and took it out on Charlie. She had coerced her teaching friends to call him names. Not too long ago it had progressed into hurting him, bumping into him on purpose and stating they hadn't seen him. Charlie had gone to Mr. Finkle for help, but he had pretended the issue wasn't there, that his most respected teachers wouldn't stoop so low.

Pun not intended.

Not such a dramatic issue compared to the current one, but I now understood how frustrated he must have felt. I looked at Charlie again and this time he did return my stare. His expression told me two things. One was 'I told you he was in idiot,' the other being 'Sorry, I can't help you.' I slumped down in the chair again.

"Okay, fine. Think what you want to think then, Mr. Finkle."

I gripped the armrests until my knuckles where white. Nobody said anything. I forced myself to take deep breaths, remembering Charlie's words in the canoe. I felt my heartbeat slow down slightly.

"Do you mind if we stay here though? We're tired and would like to sleep on the couches."

"Yeah, sure, be my guest, the more the merrier," Mr. Finkle said cheerfully. After all I had said, it appeared he still didn't understand the seriousness of the situation.

Charlie and I got up without a word, picked a couch each, and fell asleep.

Sunday Night - Attacked Again

Charlie and I woke up later that afternoon and we were very hungry. We checked the staff refrigerator, full of hope, but it was as good as empty. There were only some green sandwiches that were about to walk off by themselves.

Mr. Finkle didn't let us raid the snack machine in the canteen and we didn't want to vandalize it against his will. He lent us some money, but it was only enough for one snack each, as it was 'against his principles to lend money to colleagues.' We didn't dare go check out a supermarket, so we had to listen to our stomachs rumbling the rest of the afternoon.

To keep our minds off food, we spent the rest of the day reading old newspapers. It was scary to recall how the pandemic had started in the cities and how little had been done to stop it from spreading.

We had a sense of security in the big building. Mr. Finkle had told us that he hadn't seen nor heard of any sucker attack in Bullsbrook, but he also admitted he hadn't talked to anyone over the weekend.

Early in the evening, Charlie and I went back to napping again, so we could stay awake and be vigilant during the night.

I woke up a few times, plagued by nightmares, and I tossed and turned on the narrow couch. Finally, I drifted off to sleep again.

I had no idea how much time had passed when I woke up, fully awake. A cold chill rippled through my skin when I saw the darkness around me. I looked for Charlie and Mr. Finkle. I was relieved when I found Charlie still asleep on the other couch. I craned my neck to see over the back of the couch and scanned the rest of the staffroom, but Mr. Finkle had gone. I rolled off the couch, crouched my way to Charlie and woke him gently. He didn't need a lot of rousing and looked alert from the moment he opened his eyes.

"Mr. Finkle's gone," I whispered.

"Good riddance," he said, sitting up and rubbing his face.

"Charlie, we can't leave him on his own. He's got no idea what's coming. We've got to find him." I got to my feet.

"I know, I was just kidding. He may be an idiot, but he's still a human, blah blah blah..."

I put one hand on my hip and opened my mouth, but refrained from replying.

I better not say anything to keep him in this frame of mind if we want to save Mr. Finkle.

"He's probably on patrol through the school," Charlie said, "making sure nobody steals a pencil." He stood up too and stretched.

I shot Charlie my patented 'teacher-not-approving-of-student-behavior' look.

"What?" he said, "It's probably what he's doing, isn't it?"

Okay, touché.

Charlie grabbed his blowtorch and I my Maglite and we went into the hallway. The main school building had a U-shape, with the staffroom at the center of the first floor and staircases and entrances on the inside of the two corners. The decor was old, with little yellow tiles on the floor in the hallways and green, marbled linoleum on the classroom floors. The sound of our steps in the hallway echoed through the building, so we tried to tiptoe. We were almost at the stairs when we heard footsteps above us. We stopped in our tracks, listening intently. It sounded like only one person and we assumed it had to be Mr. Finkle. Continuing up the stairs, we peeked around the corner and saw Mr. Finkle walking away from us three quarters down the length of the hallway.

"Mr. Finkle," I called and he turned around.

"Ah, you're awake again. No need to join me, everything is okay."

As he was talking, something caught my eye. From our position, I could see the schoolyard and noticed something moving. I stepped towards the window and became paralyzed with fear. Suckers were running across the schoolyard coming in our direction. My eyes went wide and I suppressed a scream by jamming a hand over my mouth. Instinct kicked in and I moved away from the window as fast as I could. Seeing my initial reaction, Charlie had glanced out of the window too. He, too, shied away from the window as fast as he could.

"Mr. Finkle, you really need to come with us now!" he yelled.

By the time Mr. Finkle stepped towards and looked out of the window, the suckers had already disappeared into the building. He saw nothing suspicious.

"I'm not having any of your charades. Go back to the staffroom if you want to, or leave, but let me do my rounds." He turned again and walked away from us.

"Mr. Finkle, please come," I pleaded.

He waved a hand without turning around.

At that moment the group of suckers appeared from the stairs in front of Mr. Finkle. Stupidly, he started to lecture them about trespassing, but didn't get a chance to finish his sentence. The first sucker to reach him hit him in the face and threw him over his shoulder. It all happened so fast. The suckers surged towards us. Charlie and I turned on the spot and ran down the stairs. We skipped as many steps as we could, but as we hit the main floor we heard them reach the stairs above.

We continued running the length of the hallway, desperately looking for a place to hide. By the time we neared the end of the hallway and the other set of stairs, we could hear the suckers closing in behind us. Since we couldn't keep running in circles, I motioned to Charlie to follow me to the exit, thinking there'd be a better chance of escape outside the school. Thankfully, it seemed Charlie agreed as he ran outside after me without hesitation.

Sunday Night - Chased

After crashing through the doors, we ran into the schoolyard only to halt abruptly with shock from the scene we encountered. I thought I was having déjà vu.

Hungry suckers were chasing screaming, horrified people. The suckers had already gathered a group of people in the center, like they had on the tent site. Some people were fighting back, with guns and shovels, but most of them were just trying to run away. It was a scene of chaos and despair.

I scrambled to think of what to do next. There were too many suckers here and no time to come up with a plan. We needed to get away from the schoolyard but couldn't turn back. We were stuck between a rock and a hard place. And the rock was approaching rapidly.

I dashed along the side of the schoolyard, avoiding the thick of the confusion. I hoped to reach Charlie's classroom in the auxiliary building where we could pick up something more deadly to defend ourselves with.

I'd run about ten steps when I realized Charlie wasn't following me. I turned to look for him, but couldn't see him in the turmoil. We were separated. My heart skipped a beat, my mouth went dry and I faltered. I started to call out to him, but I couldn't make a sound as my throat closed up from terror. One of the chasing suckers had set his eyes on me.

The hairs on the back of my neck rose as I made eye contact. The sucker was stocky, with curly-hair, dressed in a knitted sweater.

I never liked men in knitted sweaters.

His eyes held intent for a hunger that was more than blood alone. The aversion to this man gave me a boost to make me speed up again and go that little bit faster. The sucker raced after me and in no time was within an arm's length away. He reached out and I could feel him touching my jacket. I curved my back to prevent him from grabbing me. I didn't know if I was about to go down or get another chance to live. Willing my legs to carry on after a brief stumble, I dared a quick glance backwards. The curly-haired beast had fallen, but was already getting up again. I had no time to think about him as there were other suckers to dodge.

The auxiliary building was now a no go as I saw two suckers chasing a young man into the building. I decided to go around the corner from it, as far from the crowd as possible. Mr. Ugly Sweater was getting close again.

A woman crossed my path, forcing me to reverse direction to avoid getting in the way of the sucker chasing her. I veered to the left, but the pursuing sucker, in his own attempt to avoid me, had also changed course in the same direction. We collided, crashing to the ground, rolling over each other. We ended up with him lying on his back and me half on top of him.

Our faces close, I looked into his eyes and my surroundings disappeared. His eyes were a beautiful dark brown, darker than I had ever seen, and they were all I could look at. I was alone in the universe with this beautiful soul. His gaze didn't waver either and instantly I knew I had found my soulmate. For these few seconds neither of us moved, lost in this eternal moment. The chaos that surrounded us didn't matter. What else was there beside my love for this man?

My survival instinct kicked back in when I blinked and I registered his fangs. My feelings of love were exchanged for fear of near same intensity. I had to get away from this killer. I jumped up and tried to run away, but he grabbed the corner of my jacket, halting my movement.

At that moment Mr. Ugly Sweater crashed into me and knocked me off my feet. My back hit the ground hard. His heavy body crashed onto mine. I saw triumph in his eyes and realized I'd been wrong to think my disgust for him couldn't get any worse. I thought I was done fore when my brown-eyed, sucker soulmate, Mr. Perfect, grabbed Mr. Ugly Sweater's fist and twisted it behind his back, forcing him off me.

As the heavy body was taken off me, I took the opportunity to escape. I shuffled backwards a little distance before turning over to get up in the opposite direction. I came face to face with two black, fake-leathered, high-heeled boots standing in front of me.

How do people walk in high heels like that?

As I scrambled to my feet I saw two long, black, skinny legs in fake-leather, skin tight leggings above the boots. The legs went up and up.

These legs look like they belong to a black widow spider.

I was still moving forward in a half-crouch as my eyes went further up. The legs were attached to a long, slim body, also clad in black plastic. The person was surrounded by a long, black, plastic-looking coat.

On top of the body was a face. Not a particular beautiful face, but definitely a face that made you look twice. The features were even, the skin smooth, and the lips full, painted a dark red. The attractive but stern face was surrounded by a black bob hairdo.

That's definitely a wig.

When I was finally upright, the long arms, attached to this long, skinny woman, threw me aside with ease. For the third time within the last ten seconds I hit the ground.

I am really getting tired of being thrown about.

My knees scraped the rough playground concrete and my pants were probably torn through. My hands were certainly sporting grit-in-flesh wounds, but weren't sore.

Don't you worry, Kate, the pain will come.

I whirled around. Ms. Black Widow didn't seem intent on grabbing me though. Instead she calmly walked over to Mr. Perfect who was in a stand-off with Mr. Ugly Sweater.

"You take care of him," Mr. Perfect said to Ms. Black Widow, after she put her hand on his shoulder. Ms. Black Widow stepped forward and pushed Mr. Ugly Sweater away. Mr. Perfect turned to me.

I gasped and kicked myself for not using those precious seconds to get further away from these killers. Jumping up, I ignored the burning sensation in my hands and knees, and started to run away. But Mr. Perfect easily caught up with me and by putting his arm around my waist directed me in a one-hundred-and-eighty degree turn that took away my speed. My arms were still free, however, and I aimed a swing at his head. Unfortunately, I had dropped the Maglite when I collided with him earlier.

He laughed, sporting perfect white teeth, and easily blocked my arms. He grabbed my wrists and thrust them behind my back, pulling my body into his as he did so. I had no option but to look into those beautiful eyes.

Here I go again...

Again, I drowned in those deep, dark, brown eyes. I would have lost my footing if it wasn't for Mr. Perfect holding me up.

"Resistance is futile, you know," he said, almost whispered it. He smiled and I could hardly drag my eyes away from those kissable lips.

Just to make sure he wasn't kidding I tried to break free from his grip.

"Ah, a feisty one you are," he said, tightening his grip on my wrists.

You should have said that in a little, green alien's voice... And no, I am just somebody who is very attached to her humanity!

He must have seen what I thought from the look on my face as he laughed. He had the cutest laugh.

"Let's go," he said. He let go of my wrists and grabbed me by my upper arms. Turning me round, he held me by one arm, walking me back toward Ms. Black Widow.

I tried to break free again, but his grip was just too tight.

"I really don't know why you're even trying," he said. He looked at me with this grin on his face, his fangs only showing a little. He saw me looking at them and said, "Don't worry, I am not going to bite you...yet."

"What does that mean?" I sneered. "Am I going to be the snack for on the road?"

Another cute laugh.

"Now that's an idea, I'll have to think about that one."

I wasn't sure if he was serious or joking with me. He sat me down on one of the benches in the schoolyard.

Ms. Black Widow had apparently gotten rid of Mr. Ugly Sweater in the meantime, as he was nowhere to be seen.

"He won't bother us again," she told Mr. Perfect. Her low female voice had a Russian accent, perhaps Polish, something Eastern European for sure.

"I hope you ate his sweater too," I said.

She turned her head abruptly towards me, making her fake bob oscillate.

Mr. Perfect laughed before he said to her, "This is a funny one, Sasha! We may have to keep her..."

So Ms. Black Widow's name is Sasha. What would his name be?

Monday morning, early - Caught

Most of the chasing had ended by now. I was sitting on the bench close to where the toilets were in the auxiliary building. It was never a popular place due to the smells wafting from the little windows. I could hear the occasional scream as more and more people were herded into the schoolyard. My back was turned to the larger area of the yard around the corner, where a lot of whimpering and sobbing was coming from.

Now was the time the suckers would feed on their victims. I remembered how they had caught Sue, how they had dragged her to where the others were gathered, and how the whole pack had fallen on their victims. Memories of the massacre made a lump well up in my throat. I assumed I was going to be added to the gathering pen as well. I was going to end up just like Sue.

Sasha stood with her arms folded in front of Mr. Perfect. "So what do you want to do, Caleb?"

His name is Caleb. Nice.

But Caleb was looking away from us, not moving or making a sound. He appeared to be in deep thought.

Maybe he's seriously contemplating taking me with him as a snack for on the road.

I studied my captor. He wore sneakers, jeans and a long, dark-blue, fisherman's coat. He was handsome. He had a gentleman's haircut; short at the sides and back, and a wavy lock of hair on top that had fallen partially over his forehead, very stylish. His face was long, but not too long, and complemented by his strong nose and chin. I knew his eyes were the darkest brown, even though I couldn't see them right now.

I like the way he had looked at me with those gorgeous eyes.

OMG, did I just think that?!

This was my captor, the guy who was going to kill me, or, perhaps, the one who would stop me being the person I was.

How can I 'like' anything about this guy?

A shiver went through my spine. I was repulsed by my feelings for him and tried to think of reasons for feeling this way.

I've heard of people falling in love with their captors, it is called the 'Stockholm syndrome,' but can this happen within a few minutes? I sincerely doubt that. Otherwise they can put me in the Guinness World of Records book for the fastest Stockholm syndrome case. Whoopdeedoo, lucky me...

I scrapped the Stockholm scenario, which was very unlikely.

Then what? I know I like handsome-looking guys, but I am not so shallow I'd fall for the first good-looking guy that bashes his eyelids my way. I do have a brain, you know, and it knows that there are more qualifications than just good looks to pass the bar for being a possible partner.

For heaven's sake, I'm not even looking for one.

My continued reasoning didn't stop me from liking this guy. Why was I reacting so weird? More questions flashed through my mind.

Why am I so attracted to this killer? Is this a secret skill of suckers that the media forgot to tell us about? Do they hypnotize people to do their will?

Then my mind took a U-turn and told me the opposite of what I should be thinking.

If you have to get 'turned' by somebody, then why not by this guy?

Fortunately my conscience got the better of me.

Oh, don't you listen to that! You don't want to get 'turned' by anybody!

It tried to mentally slap myself in the face to shake me out of this reverie for this handsome stranger. My efforts were aided by Sasha, who grabbed me by my shoulders.

"Why don't you just finish her right now?" she said, looking straight into my eyes.

Title adjustment; Ms. Impatient *Black Widow.*

As I returned her stare I froze. Her eyes were as cold as liquid nitrogen.

Am I glad your stare can't kill.

I don't know what I had done, but it was clear she didn't like me. I would have to be blind as a bat if miss seeing the hatred in her eyes.

There's something else going on here and I don't know what.

Only now it struck me how tall she really was. Much taller than me and maybe even taller than Sue had been. Her short, black hair was swinging forward on both sides of her face, making her face long as well. That hair was way too neat to be real. It had to be a wig, fake. Just like her plastic top and her plastic coat and those fake-leather leggings and boots. They were all black and fake and unreal. In contrast to the threat she represented.

Maybe it was the fact that she interrupted my thoughts about Mr. Perfect or the way she suggested Caleb should kill me this very instant, but something about her made the hair on the back of my neck stand up.

I really *don't like this woman.*

"No, I won't," Caleb said. "You keep her here, I'll be back for her," and with this he walked off, leaving me alone with Ms. Impatient Black Widow.

I wasn't so sure this was a good idea. I moved my arms closer to my body to fend off another chill.

To my surprise Sasha didn't touch me, she let her gaze follow Caleb, who disappeared around the corner. I glanced at the empty street that ran along the school for a second but decided not to make a run for it as I refused to give Sasha the satisfaction of giving me a beating. I knew she would outrun me easily with those long legs.

Even in those heels.

She didn't say anything to me until Caleb was gone from sight. "Great, leftovers for me again tonight." She almost spat the words out.

"You could always drink a bit of my blood," I offered, trying to keep the situation light, hoping that her drinking my blood would make Caleb so angry he would punish her...severely...kill her even...maybe.

OMG, did I just wish somebody dead?

Hey, she just wanted to have me killed!

Sasha looked at me as if I'd just asked her to turn herself into a goldfish.

"He said he would be back for you," she said. "Your turn will come."

I was surprised by her resolute answer and my mind started fast-tracking.

Why are you so sure he will do that? Did you mean turn-turn or kill-turn? If you really don't like 'leftovers,' why won't you eat me? I wonder what spell he has on you. Would it be the same spell that he has on me? Uh oh, I hope you don't see me as competition. This is not making me feel any better...

We continued waiting in silence until we heard the screams rising from around the corner. We listened to it for a few minutes. Then I couldn't take it any longer.

"So," I said, starting a new conversation with Ms. Impatient Black Widow to keep myself from freaking out. "How does it feel to kill everyone you meet?"

She didn't respond. I didn't think she was going to dignify me with a reply.

"We don't kill everyone," she finally said, still staring in the direction Caleb had gone.

That took me by surprise. "Oh, I thought you did. Aren't you the 'undead'?" I asked, for a second completely forgetting the 'suckers' explanation.

She gave another derisive snort. "Of course not, we are 'turned,' changed into a better version. We aren't dead. Dead people can't walk around. That only happens in movies." She looked down at me and made me feel like the dumbest kid in class.

I couldn't help myself and pushed my luck to get as much info out of her as possible.

"But you do kill people, I've seen it myself. What makes you decide who gets to live and who dies then?"

I made myself hold her stare. I felt my palms go sweaty at this direct question and sincerely hoped she couldn't hear my heart pounding away in my chest. I could tell she was struggling with the question too. It seemed she was contemplating whether to tell me the answer or not. I gathered she decided I was going to find out anyway, or maybe she was just passing the time, but she started explaining it.

"Most of us just feed on anyone, killing them in the process, leaving no one behind alive. They turn the strong ones, to make the pack bigger and stronger. Caleb doesn't agree with their killing strategy. He doesn't touch children, nor their mothers if they're really young. As for the others, he does pick out the strong ones to live as well. There's no other choice."

"That's so nice of him, not killing the children," I sort of said to myself.

"They're a burden to the pack with the amount they sleep and feed. And we need to keep the blood supply up for the future," Sasha said as a matter of fact.

She had a knack of making me feel very stupid and crushing my positive feelings for Caleb.

Another title addition; Ms. Impatient Black Widow, Party Pooper.

"What do you mean 'there is no other choice.' With picking out strong ones?" I asked.

My mind had taken me back to the tent site where they had devoured everyone but hadn't touched the man that had stood up for Sue. I couldn't help it, I had to know.

Sasha clicked her tongue and sighed, but she did answer. "We tried to turn everybody in the beginning. That was a disaster."

"Why?"

"For a star, we became very hungry. We need to drink a lot at first. The worst thing was that most newborns just couldn't handle it. They killed themselves or they started killing us. They just couldn't accept being one of us. You can see it in their eyes at the gatherings. That's how we choose who gets to live and who doesn't. We look into their eyes."

Well, that shut me up as I'd no idea how I could fake the eye thing. I had no clue what she was talking about.

Enough food for thought for the time being.

Monday Morning, Early - Hooked

Caleb finally returned from doing whatever he thought was more urgent than turning me. Our eyes met for half a second and again there was this pang of something. My heart skipped a beat and I got this sensation of happiness and hope.

What is this stuff? Is this love? Does he feel it too?

If he does, he certainly doesn't give it away.

I couldn't tell if Caleb was feeling the same. The suspense was killing me, so to speak.

"You go and feed now," he commanded Sasha. As he did he turned his face and I could see blood smeared from the corner of his mouth.

Well, that's the same effect as having a cold shower.

I nearly forgot that Mr. Perfect here was about to turn or kill me. I pulled my knees up and tried to make myself smaller.

You never know, he may not see me all of a sudden.

Yeah, right!

The eastern sky was turning purple when he finally faced me.

"It's your time now," he said in this husky voice, "You know it is, don't you?"

I nodded, I couldn't say anything as my voice seemed to have skipped town for the moment. He held out his hand and helped me up.

Why did I take his hand?

He pulled me a few steps away. His grip was firm but not painful. Still, I surprised myself by letting a sound escape from my throat. He looked at me in alarm.

Did I just see concern in his eyes? Is he worried he hurt me? Do you really care?

"I'm okay," I said, not sure if I'd said this to him or to myself.

"Just turn her, Caleb," Sasha said, interrupting, impatient, still there.

I really, really *don't like her.*

Caleb looked around at her and snapped, "I thought you were hungry?" He dragged me further away from her.

Good, he doesn't like her either!

I wished I could gloat in her direction, but Caleb pushed me into a corner of the school building and put both his hands on my hips. I couldn't turn away from him. I should've felt petrified, but somehow I wasn't. He moved his face close to mine, our foreheads almost touching. His closeness made me feel warm and fuzzy. I was surprised by the heat I felt radiating off him. Then I remembered again that suckers weren't 'undead.' They were alive, just like I was, with beating hearts and blood flowing. And I, too, would continue to be alive after I was turned.

How bad can it be?

"I am going to turn you now," he said. His voice resonated more feeling than I'd ever heard in any of my short list of past boyfriends.

"I know," I whispered and looked up into his eyes. His pupils were almost as big as his irises, which were almost as dark as his pupils.

"I have no choice," he said, and there was this hint of an apology in his voice.

No choice, no choice? Yes, you do, you just don't want to make the right one. It isn't as if I somebody is holding a gun to your head, geez.

There was no connection between what was going on in my head and what came out of my mouth.

"Will it hurt?" I said, surprising myself.

He moved his mouth closer to my neck, nuzzling my skin. He then pulled down the zipper of my jacket and pulled the collar away to expose more of my neck.

"Only a little, at first," he said.

I was feeling anxious now, excited by his warm closeness and fearful of what was about to happen. Unable to resist, I moved my head away from him, to give him better access to my jugular vein. He moved my hair back with his hand, his fingertips lightly stroking my neck. It gave me goosebumps. I closed my eyes.

His lips touched my neck and my heart began pounding like a maniac. When his lips parted I could feel his fangs on my skin. I could barely suppress a groan, this was so intense. Underneath his fangs, my jugular beat like a drum. Boom boom, boom boom. I wanted this moment to last forever. As he widened his jaws he gently put pressure on me with his wet fangs. My whole body stiffened from the pain when they pierced my skin.

"Caleb!" Sasha shouted from not too far away.

Go away, woman!

Caleb hesitated but decided to ignore Sasha. As he deepened his fangs a little more, Sasha shouted again.

"Caleb, you really need to come! Now!" Her voice was laden with urgency.

Abruptly he withdrew his fangs. "What?" he shouted annoyed as he turned away from me.

We both looked at Sasha and she stood there with a blank look on her face, as if frozen solid. Caleb looked at the sky and back at Sasha. Sunlight was already on her legs, creeping closer to Caleb by the second. He looked back at me and again towards Sasha.

"Shit," he said and he ran to grab her. His pull released her out of her pre-epileptic aura and they ran away in the opposite direction of the sunlight.

Monday Morning - Alone?

I was left alone, standing in the corner of the school building. My nostrils flared with my heavy breathing. I had to get oxygen to my brain as it wasn't computing. It was trying to figure out what had just happened, but couldn't get a grip. I was about to get turned by the love of my life, my soulmate.

But I was still here, alone, and still human. My hand went to my neck and I felt there was no blood gushing out, just the sticky wetness of the blood from Caleb's fangs piercing my skin. He hadn't gone all the way, hadn't pierced my jugular. I pulled my hand away from the stickiness. Still trying to get my mind around the situation, I sank down in the corner. After wiping my bloody hand on my jeans, I zipped up my jacket, collar and all, covering my neck. My arms then hugged my knees. I was alive! And, to my amazement, I was still a normal human.

My memory went back to the moment Caleb had looked back at me for the last time. What had I seen in his eyes? Was it love, pity, anger? I couldn't tell what his thoughts had been when he left me. I was such an emotional mess.

Why didn't he say something like 'I'll be back,' or even 'It was nice knowing you, babe, have a nice life...'? Anything. What was I to do now? Would I ever see him again? Should I go look for him?

Surely not, that would definitely get me killed. I can't walk up to the first sucker I can find going, 'Say, do you perhaps know a sucker called Caleb?' Ridiculous.

I didn't sit in the corner of the school building for long before the sun touched my face. The warmth of it made me smile. Again, I realized my luck of not being turned and that I should be glad.

I got up, got my panties out of my butt, and dusted off my pants. My hands and knees were in a terrible state, but I didn't care. I started walking, legs stiff from the grazes. I was still in a daze, happy to be alive, when I passed the schoolyard. There weren't any suckers there anymore, only a pile of human bodies-the remainder of the onslaught. I turned my head away. I was still in shock and didn't want to be confronted with dead people I had known. On automatic pilot, I turned into the shadows at the back of the main building. I was on my way home.

"Kate, is that you?" came an unexpected voice. It seemed to come out of the dark.

The air felt cold in my lungs as I inhaled sharply. No, I must have been mistaken.

But I knew that voice...

I lifted my head and I saw the silhouette of my sister Julie walking toward me. I thought I was dreaming. A group of young women followed behind her. I hardly recognized my sister as she was wearing a long overcoat, covering most of her body. For the last three years I had only seen her wearing the shortest of shorts, and skirts for that matter, much to our parents' annoyance. But her voice and overall posture were definitely Julie's.

"Kate, it is you," she was close enough for me to see her smile now.

After a moment of initial relaxation, a new wave of panic crept over me. Was she turned or not? I was confused about what to do. Flee or fight? If I had been an animal I would have probably started preening myself. Instead, I resisted the urge to pull up my socks.

As my sister and the women approached, I saw blood smears on their faces and on the necks of some of them. They were suckers.

I threw a glance back towards the sunlight that lit the ground past the building, but, due to my contemplations, my sister and her company were now too close for me to turn around and run. I put my hands in the pockets of my jacket and hitched up my shoulders in a sad attempt to protect my neck.

"Hi Jules," I greeted my sister, "they turned you too, eh?"

"Yes," she replied, "I didn't stand a chance, but doesn't it feel great?"

The other girls all exclaimed positive remarks in reply.

My eyes squinted as I took this in. I knew I had to go with the flow if I wanted to survive. "Yeah, never felt better," I said, copying the feeling of exultation in the group.

Suddenly Julie tried to pull my jacket collar down. My survival instinct kicked in and I pulled away from her, pushing her arm down.

"Ooh, touchy neck, sister?" She laughed.

"Yeah, you could say that again."

"Don't worry. Once your fangs have dropped the pain will stop."

Phew, now that's a convenient inconvenience...

"Right..."

She didn't persist trying to look at my neck, but her frown told me she wasn't totally convinced yet.

"It just happened, you know," I said.

"No shit? Then where is your pack?"

I had no idea what she was on about, so I just lifted my shoulders.

"Never mind, I've picked up a stray here and there along the way. Anyway," and she exposed two round scars in her neck, "you will be proud of your marks later, you know."

"Just give me some time. I'm sure the feeling will kick in shortly."

"That's okay, sis, I understand. I love you, you know. I'm so glad I found you." She stepped forward and gave me a big hug.

Those words and the hug combined suddenly overwhelmed me with emotion and I so wanted to hug her back right there and then, but I was afraid I would expose myself for the fraud that I was. Somewhere in the back of my mind, the memory of Caleb popped up, but I had no time to dwell on it. Survival was stronger than my emotions at that time.

Julie turned around and introduced me to the other girls. "Everybody, this is my sister Kate. Please make her feel welcome in the pack."

The other girls smiled, said 'hi', 'nice to meet you,' and some gave me pats on the arm, uttering more welcoming words.

I smiled back at them, "Thanks, guys."

Girls, Kate. They are all girls.

It seemed the girls all followed Julie as she took the lead. "Okay, ladies, let's go and find a place to sleep the day away."

That just sounds so weird...

There was no way I could get away from the group at this very moment, so I decided that helping them would be my best chance of survival, for the time being. As long as Julie didn't find out I wasn't turned, I reasoned I'd be safe. We were standing next to the back of the main school building and my science classroom was on the second floor. I told Julie the room had blackout curtains, to aid light experiments, and that the school very likely wouldn't be used in the foreseeable future - knowing that a gathering and feeding had just taken place in the schoolyard. Julie agreed it was a good location to make camp for the day. There was, however, the problem of how to get inside the building. The sun was rapidly rising and we couldn't go around the corner to get to the entrance without getting a bit of a suntan. I had always wanted a sun tan, but pushing for one now didn't seem like a good idea, health-wise, and the danger didn't lie in the sun's rays. My sister had said she loved me, but I still didn't know how much she *really* loved me. As for the other girls, I didn't know or trust them at all, and crossed my fingers they wouldn't smell my 'unturned flesh.'

I jumped when I heard glass shattering. One of the girls had picked up a rock and thrown it through a school window. It made everybody tense for a few seconds.

"Good thinking, Ellie," my sister said to the girl who had thrown the rock. Ellie, a short, plump, blond girl beamed a broad smile back at us. Julie began to clear away the glass from the window frame so we could climb through.

Never you mind, Ellie, it's only Mr. Finkle's room and I am sure Charlie wouldn't mind when I tell him you did this to his room. If I ever see him again.

Thinking about Charlie's fate made joy leave the building.

Once all the girls were inside I showed them the way to my classroom. This meant we had to pass windows letting through sunlight. Julie told all the new suckers, including myself, to keep our skin and eyes covered while walking past the windows to prevent us from seeing or touching any sunlight. Of course, I couldn't resist the urge to keep an eye on everybody, so I peeked between my fingers. To my surprise, some of the girls positioned themselves in front of the windows in the hallway with sunlight beaming through. They had their hoods over their heads, held their long coats open with gloved hands, and stood there with their backs turned towards the sun until the last girl passing pulled them along. I was actually glad they did this as seeing the sun-rays further up the hall hurt my eyes after spending a whole night in the dark like a bat.

When we made it to my classroom, I hit the button to close the blackout curtains and we all relaxed. We cleaned ourselves up at the sinks of the science desks. As I was waiting for my turn, my eyes fell on the door to the storeroom and my thoughts drifted off again. Only a few hours earlier I was here with Charlie...Thinking of losing Charlie felt like somebody dropped a brick in my stomach. Did he find a way to escape the sucker attack? Would he know I was still alive, and human? Would he still be alive?

My breath turned shallow and unconsciously I started picking the loose bit of laminate of the desk, something I always had to tell the kids to stop doing. I was rescued from my thoughts by one of the girls, who tapped me on the shoulder. She had a bag strapped over her shoulder. "Here," she said as she handed me something from the bag. "I bet you forgot to bring one."

I looked at the object in my hand and saw she had given me a roll-on deodorant.

That's not the brand I normally use.

I was lost for words so I just smiled at her and pocketed the deodorant.

Monday Morning - Explanations

Once I had cleaned myself up and used the deodorant. I sat down next to my sister, who sat leaning against the front desk facing the room.

"I'm afraid there's nobody in the building to feed on," I said to her. I hoped she didn't hear the tremor in my voice. As far as I knew I wasn't lying, but I wasn't sure I was right either. I didn't want her to go looking, just in case someone *was* hiding somewhere in the school that I wasn't aware of.

Possibly Charlie...

"It's okay, sis, we had a drink on the bus on the way over." Her own words made her giggle.

How can she live with herself?

I couldn't understand how an average, peace-loving person, like I knew my sister was, could turn into such a vicious killer. She had never hurt a fly. Sure, there had been the odd girlfriend bitchiness, but that was Julie for you. She never shied away from telling somebody what she thought of them. Most of the time she was right too. I couldn't figure out why she didn't have a problem with ripping somebody's neck open all of a sudden. Why did all these girls, who seemed so nice, have no objections to killing others? I had to know. As

I was too impatient to beat around the bush, I decided to be straight to the point. I figured I'd be safe with Julie being my sister and didn't think she would bite my head off over a question. I hoped she hadn't changed *that* much.

"Julie?"

"Yeah?"

"Why don't you have a problem killing people?" There, the question was out. I didn't know if I should have known as I was supposed to be turned, but I had to find out.

"That's quite a question you've got there." She didn't look at me at first, but after a few moments, she answered. "It's something to get used to for sure, but you have no choice, really."

I was relieved I hadn't given myself away with the question, so decided to push my luck. "What do you mean 'no choice'? Can't you just '*not* do it'?"

Julie stood up and for a moment I thought I'd blown it. But then she took off her coat and sat down again. All the while I could see the cogs turning in her head. "Once you're turned you're not the same person anymore. The hunger takes over and you have to do it to survive. At first, your mind doesn't want to, it's the thirst that drives you. You'll notice yourself when it kicks in. However, as soon as you sink your fangs into a neck and taste that sweet, sweet blood, it's so fucking good!" Her whole face lit up, erasing the gloominess that was there a few seconds before. "And then when you're changing you just *know* you are becoming a better person. The old you was weak and insignificant. We are a superior species, Kate." She almost sounded like a preacher, having reached her revelation.

No, you're not. You need a different number of chromosomes to be a different species.

It was scary listening to her. It was as if she was high on drugs. This drug, bug, or whatever was causing this pandemic, was changing rational thinking. It had to be. My sister had never believed in 'better' people. She had always gone by the motto 'live and let live,' and had been dead against those who thought they were better than others. I worked hard to get a smile on my face, to pretend I was looking forward to my change.

"Come, let me have a look at your marks," she said out of the blue.

I nearly died.

She smiled the sweetest smile at me and put a gentle hand on my arm. "Don't worry, I won't hurt you. It's just that I have to make sure you don't get an infection."

As it was clear from her voice that she wasn't taking no for an answer, I reluctantly resigned myself to the fact that I was surely going to be found out this time. But what else was I to do in this room crowded with suckers? From a pocket of her large coat, Julie retrieved a packet of sterile gauze swabs and a bottle of disinfectant. She told me to open up the zipper of my jacket. I was holding my breath as I turned my head so she could have a good look at my neck. I strained my eyes to watch her face, trying to detect the first hint of hostility.

"You were lucky, it looks like a clean bite," she said and she applied some of the disinfectant to my wounds. The sting of it made me gasp. "Alex there wasn't so blessed," she pointed to one of the girls in the far corner, "she nearly got half her throat ripped out by some idiot."

I looked at Alex and saw she had a bandage around her neck. I couldn't help thinking it was the result of an encounter with Mr. Ugly Sweater. He seemed to me a person who would make a wound like this.

While Julie was sticking two round Band-Aids on my 'marks,' I asked her why she was in Bullsbrook.

"I came looking for you, silly." She had a huge grin on her face. "I wasn't going to let you stay unturned now, was I?"

I smiled back at her. I couldn't help but feel loved.

"Thanks so much for thinking of me, but you were too late," I lied.

"Yeah, but at least I found you. I went to your house first and was afraid you had been taken when you weren't there. I'm so glad I've found you alive. And not with any of the other packs..." She looked uneasy when she let those last words trail. I didn't give it much thought. I was too eager to know more about how the girls were able to stand in the sunlight. As Julie prepared another disinfecting gauze swab, I asked.

"Jules, about this sunlight thing... I saw earlier that it was possible for some of the girls to stand directly in the light. Why didn't they get a seizure; isn't it true what they told us on TV?"

Julie treated my grazed hands and knees while she explained. I had to bite my lip not to scream out when she was putting the disinfectant on the wounds. Tears welled up in my eyes instead, but Julie was too busy to see it and kept wiping the graze with the gauze.

"Sunlight does have an effect on us, but it changes," she said. "At first you are very sensitive and you have a seizure as soon as you see daylight, you don't even have to touch it. But as time goes on, your body adapts and the effect gets less. The oldest of us, including me, are hardly affected by it at all now. When we get close to sunshine we slip into this aura and are slowed down, but it doesn't make us have a full seizure unless the sunlight hits our skin. It serves as a warning sign and lets you get away from wherever you are, away from the light."

My mind drifted off to Sasha and how she had just stood there, with sunlight on her clothing, frozen. I realized Sasha was one of the older suckers and that she must have stayed with us to warn Caleb of the coming sun, instead of going off to feed as she was told to do. Then Julie's words sank in.

"What? Wait. I don't get it. You say you're one of the older ones. But you live near here, don't you? Did you move to the city and forget to tell me about it?"

Julie's eyes flickered up reproachfully as she pulled one leg of my jeans down. "No, I didn't move. I was on a business trip in the city with my boss when it happened."

"Oh, sorry, I didn't know you made trips with your job..."

"Neither did I." She yanked the other leg of my jeans down. "And I also didn't know my boss had wandering hands. As soon as I was turned, I made sure they never wandered again. Not on me, not on anybody."

I could tell there was no love lost there and more to the story. However, it wasn't a story I was interested in now. I needed to change the subject. "Tell me more about the transition."

"There isn't much more to tell," she sighed. She sat down again next to me, leaning against the desk.

"Are you superwoman now?" I joked.

"Yes and no," she said.

I eyeballed her in disbelief. "Get out of here! You can fly?"

She laughed. "Of course not! At first, you will even be weak," she said. "Your body needs time to adapt and that's why you have to feed a lot. Your muscles will grow at a rapid pace and to do this they need nutrients, lots of blood. You will also want to sleep for long periods, but like the need for feeding it will wear off. I've taken over this system I've learned from other packs, where we hunt as a pack to provide for the young ones, who are too weak to hunt for themselves. We protect them during the day when they sleep to get stronger. I'm not sure when the transition is finished exactly, I'm still changing, but my body has adapted a fair bit. I'm as strong as an ox." She beamed proudly and pumped her biceps for me.

I was in awe of the size of her muscles. Julie was never one to hit the gym. "How 'old' are you?" I asked her.

"I was turned just over a week ago. I am not one of the oldest, but I am the oldest of this pack. I am the one taking care of these girls," she said. She let her eyes wander around the room with a look I'd never seen on her before.

"Why are there no men in your group, um, I mean...pack?"

She looked back at me and grinned. "Because I haven't met a man yet who will take instructions from a woman."

We both giggled.

She began to tell me how she was turned. How the suckers had stormed the office she was in and how she had tried to protect the other girls from the floor while the others just ran. I think it took less than five minutes before my mind wandered off. She was still the same sister with the same storytelling habits she'd always had, drifting into non-essential extras that made it hard to follow the storyline. It was another few minutes before she patted my knee.

"Go and get some sleep, I can see you need it."

"Thanks, Jules," I said, followed by a weak smile. She got up and I tried to make myself comfortable on the floor with my jacket under my head. My eyes followed Julie as she went through the room, making sure everybody was okay. A fuzzy feeling warmed my body. I felt proud she was my sister.

Monday Morning - Reflection

Sleep didn't come right away, even though I was exhausted. There's just no rest for the guilty. When I closed my eyes, I saw images of Sue and Charlie. Sue's smile morphing into a scream as she was being dragged away by suckers. Charlie tickling me, but when I turned around to laugh with him he wasn't there, which gave me a feeling of falling into a bottomless pit. I couldn't handle the images so I opened my eyes and looked around to escape them. I didn't dare to close my eyes again. Unfortunately, even awake, I couldn't escape the feeling of how I wished I could have saved Sue. Whatever I did, I was reminded of the fact that I had survived and she was gone.

I willed my mind to think of something else. So I wondered what had happened to Charlie. That didn't help. More guilt, more questions.

Why, oh, why hadn't he followed me? Why hadn't I followed him? Had he known a way out? Where is he now? Is he still alive? Would I ever see him again?

This brick in my stomach was getting really annoying. It also reminded me I needed food soon.

As I felt my limbs and eyelids getting heavy, I thought about the 'we' that my sister and Sasha had referred to. They didn't call themselves 'suckers.' They were 'we' or 'us' and unturned humans were 'the others,' 'them,' 'the opposition.' I was the one who made the distinction of suckers versus humans, which was silly of course as suckers were still human. You didn't lose or gain chromosomes by an infection...Or could you?

Could this be a case of extreme transduction, where new genetic material is introduced by viruses? I know it's possible in bacteria, but I've never heard of it being reported on this level.

Doesn't mean it doesn't exist.

I willed my tired eyelids up, to defy my overactive brain which wanted to drown me in my sorrows, and watched the girls get ready for sleep. As I studied them I realized not all suckers were as I had thought them to be. There had been stories told on TV of ruthless killers who brutally attacked humans, leaving mutilated bodies behind. They were supposed to have no soul, no remorse, no feelings... And here I was, head over heels falling for a sucker and adopted as 'one of the family' by a pack of them. They all seemed so *normal*. This was *so* not what I had expected.

And Julie, she was still the sister that I knew. She had even come for me and - what baffled me most - she had told me she loved me. I knew she had loved me when she was normal, but she had never, ever, told me directly. Nor had I ever told her I loved her. That was just not done. I knew she loved me, and I guess she knew I loved her, but we had never, ever said it out loud.

That's probably what shocked me the most. These suckers, these 'wild, savage killers,' had shown me more emotion than I had encountered in humans. Even bad emotions, with Sasha being a good example of those.

Thinking of Sasha brought my mind back to Caleb. I was baffled by my deep feelings of love for him in such a short period of time. Although I wasn't sure if that was exactly what it was. I had been in love before, yet this was different.

The first time had been little more than a crush. Josh was a boy in my seventh grade and he had never known that I had liked him. I had taken a photo of him with my brand new camera, he even posed for it. I had kissed that photo goodnight for weeks, never having the guts to tell him how I felt about him. After he moved to North Carolina I gave up on boys for a while. A few years later I fell for the attention I received from Eric, a fellow student. He made me laugh. We had kissed and made out for months before we had sex on an evening when his parents were away. It was exciting and we were good for a year or two until I went to college and he dumped me. How heartbroken I had been. During my university studies, I'd had a few more flings, but was never in love with those guys. Yet, whatever I had felt with all of these boys combined was nothing compared to the feeling I'd had when looking into Caleb's eyes. That intensity was like nothing I'd ever experienced before. When he had been about to bite me, his body so close to mine... It had been so thrilling and overwhelming. His teeth on my flesh had been so...so...

Okay, let's not go there now.

I embarrassed myself with my own thoughts. But I knew I'd die a happy woman now that I'd met Caleb, for I was sure I had felt love.

I finally fell asleep, dreaming of drowning in Caleb's eyes.

Monday Evening - On the Move

Julie woke me when the sun had just set. I couldn't believe I had slept the whole day.

"Hey, sleepy head, how are you feeling?"

"Like a punching bag," I said, rubbing my eyes. "I hope the sleeping arrangements will improve." I got up and stretched myself. My whole body literally felt beaten-up. All those falls and running last night added to the torture of sleeping on linoleum.

"One day it will, but for now we'll have to do with whatever we can find," Julie said, and she walked off again, waking the others.

Not being too pleased with her answer I looked around.

What are the other girls doing? How can I fit in?

I had to mimic the girls' behavior in order not to stand out. I remembered Julie's remark when we had met about 'fangs dropping.' My heart raced when I thought of how to explain this not happening to me. I made a mental note of making a serious effort not to laugh out loud in the foreseeable future. To hide my absence of fangs I would have to mumble.

No teacher's voice.

I grinned a big smile. Immediately I clamped my hands over my mouth. This was going to be trickier than I realized. The girl called Alex came up to me and I wondered if she had noticed my mistake.

"Here, some painkillers. Your fangs will soon be down and the pain will subside, but for now take them as often as you need to." She gave me a whole packet of Advil tablets. As I stared at her she showed off her long fangs. "Don't worry, I won't need them anymore," she said as she put a hand on my arm. I let out a sigh of relief, but not for the reason she probably thought.

"Thanks," I mumbled, and the girl walked away again.

My heart released itself from the grip of fear and I regained my composure. As I collected my cup from my desk drawer, I realized I had to be more vigilant of my actions. I got away with it this time, but I might not be so lucky in the future. I filled the cup with water, took two tablets from the packet and downed them with two large gulps. I had no toothache, but the rest of my body sure was sore all over.

"Okay, girls, is anybody hungry?" Julie asked loudly.

Out of habit, I put my hand up, but let it drop again as nobody else was doing it. Instead, the girls all cheered.

"Right, we will try and meet up with Duncan. He'd told me he'd help with the hunting again," Julie informed us. My mouth went dry. I couldn't do this. I couldn't chase a human being and open up a jugular. For my studies, I had cut open lab rats without a second thought, but the thought of sucking blood from someone's neck made my knees buckle. I always found that blood had an awful earthy, iron-like stench, which wouldn't entice me to drink it... or eat it... or whatever they called it. It became appeared I would need to eat something soon though, as my stomach rumbled loudly, reminding me I hadn't eaten for over twenty-four hours.

"Oh my, you are hungry," Julie smiled at me. "Don't worry, sis, we'll get you some blood soon."

"Great!" I said like someone with a toothache, meanwhile racking my brain to find a way out of this situation.

We waited until the last rays of sunshine had disappeared before going out. I thanked Julie silently, as this meant I didn't have to pretend to have an epileptic seizure near sunlight. I had never seen anybody have a seizure, other than what they had shown us on TV a week ago, and I had no hopes my drama performance would earn me any Oscars.

As we walked through the streets I asked a dark-haired, slender girl called Amy who this Duncan was. She told me he was one of the older suckers and leader of a large pack. Due to his military background, he was a good organizer and excellent at providing blood. I noticed she didn't say 'hunter and killer of humans' and wondered why. I was sure that's what she meant.

Could it be that they don't see us as humans anymore, but only as meals on wheels?

As Amy seemed to know quite a lot of who was who, I casually asked if she knew a Caleb, trying not to smile too obviously.

Say, do you perhaps know a sucker called Caleb?

"Oh yes, everybody knows Caleb. He's a hottie," she said. She told me he was the leader of another pack. "His isn't as large as Duncan's. Caleb used to roam with Duncan, but they fell out and now he has his own pack."

I didn't let her know I thought I knew the reason why they fell out, being that Caleb didn't kill children, but I kept my mouth shut. While I was on a roll, I thought I'd find out some more about Caleb's darker half. "What about Sasha? Do you know anything about her?"

Amy's face immediately lost its smile. "Sasha turned Caleb. He would do anything for her." I expected her to tell me more, but that was all she said.

It was strange hearing that remark. My impression had been the complete opposite. But it was clear I wasn't the only one Sasha had a negative effect on. Before I could ask her more, Amy had walked away from me and I kicked myself mentally. I hadn't asked her if Sasha and Caleb were in a proper relationship.

She'd said 'Sasha turned Caleb... He'd do anything for her.' What did that mean? That he was hers forever? That would suck.

Pun not intended.

Monday Evening - Getting Teeth

We stood in the town square while Julie and a few other girls studied the town map at the bus stop, speculating on where the local gym or ballroom could be. Those were the kind of places where Duncan's pack usually stayed. Julie didn't ask me if I knew where it was. Not that it would have helped them one bit as I had never set a foot in any ballroom. Maybe that's why Julie hadn't bothered to ask me, she knew me all too well.

Maxine had been sent to dance lessons when she started high school, but my parents had to drag her there every week for a whole year. So when it was my turn, our parents had told me they weren't making me do it. They said they couldn't go through the whole weekly 'torture of children' tirade like they had received on a weekly basis from my sister Maxine. So, no ballroom experience for Julie and me. And I never went to a gym either. I preferred to jog outside, which was a lot cheaper too.

I looked around the town square while executive decisions were being made. There was the bakery, where I used to get nice, fresh bagels from. Its windows were smashed and there were no bagels or buns displayed anymore. Next door was the fashion shop, where Sue had bought some of her new outfits. Tears welled up in my eyes when I recalled her showing off her latest, brightly colored dress. I forced my eyes to move on to the next shop. The red façade belonged to the family butcher. I had thought nothing of it before, but it was such an inappropriate name now. Its windows were also broken and all produce absent from the shelves. Next door was the one dollar shop, full of Halloween items at the moment. Nobody had touched that store. No surprise there, of course, fangs came included with the virus. Next to the one dollar shop was the hairdresser, where I had my hair dyed red two weeks ago. Sue had convinced me to have it done and afterward I'd admitted that it did look good. She had been so happy that day, showing me off to everyone and complementing me continuously.

Seeing all these shops filled with memories weren't doing me much good and I focused on my shoes to prevent any of the girls seeing my tears.

Like a shot, a thought hit me; the one dollar shop was going to be my salvation.

"I'll be back in a moment," I said to nobody in particular.

I ran to the shop, hoping no one would follow me. I tried to push the front door open, but it wouldn't budge. I had no other option, so I threw my body into the large door window with all my might and it shattered. I never thought I'd ever do anything like this. I hadn't stolen a thing in my life, nor damaged somebody's property with intent. Now I was breaking and entering with the intention to steal. What had I come to?

But at least I'm not killing anybody.

At this moment in time, I didn't care what the other girls thought of me, as long as they didn't come after me to find out what I was doing.

I jumped inside over the shards of glass and tried to be as fast as I could, just in case the girls did get a sudden case of curiosity. The Halloween section had all the Dracula stuff. I remembered I'd seen a little box with fake Dracula fangs. Not the whole-teeth-set, just the fangs that you had to attach on top of your own teeth with some sort of temporary cement. I remembered as I had wondered who would want to put cement on their teeth. If only I could find them again, and a tube of super-glue as I wanted to make sure the teeth were attached more permanently. I found the teeth soon enough, ripped the packaging open and put the two tooth caps in my trouser-pockets. Looking around I saw a small bag of fake blood, which I managed to stuff in one of my back pockets. You never knew when that would come in handy.

I heard a noise and I spun around. It was just a piece of glass falling from the door; nobody seemed to have come in after me. I continued my search. I found a small tube of super-glue. In my pocket with the tooth caps it went. My eyes spotted a rack with lollies near the counter. On cue, my stomach rumbled loudly. Grabbing a multi-pack of chocolate bars, I opened one and stuffed it in my mouth. I always liked chocolate, but this tasted heavenly. Not wasting too much time I tried to put some bars in my pockets, but my skinny jeans didn't entertain the notion of stuffing pockets. I considered which one I needed most and decided the blood had to go. Only three bars fitted my trouser pockets, so I stuffed the other four individually wrapped bars in my bra. I had no doubt they would soon melt into shape.

Before going back I had a funny idea. I decided to take a Dracula cape from a hanger in the dress up section and tied it around my neck. I also grabbed a packet of the fake, plastic fangs, ripped it open, and stuck the fangs in my mouth. After I carefully stepped back out of the shop over the broken shards of glass of the door frame I looked up and saw my sister and everyone else stare in my direction. Blood heated my cheeks.

Here goes all or nothing, Ms. Hunt, I hope your high school drama teaching pays off now...

I took a deep breath and ran into the town square, flapping my cape behind me.

"I am Dracula and I am going to suck your blood!" I shouted as I ran around like a maniac, showing off my fake fangs every time I passed one of the girls.

At first, they were all stunned. I guess they thought I was a raving lunatic. After about a minute my sister started laughing her head off. Thankfully the other girls joined in. It seemed it worked. I had pulled it off. Elated I kept on running and scaring.

When I was out of breath I hunched over, hands on my knees to keep myself upright. My breathing was ragged, borderline asthmatic.

Julie walked over and patted me on the shoulder. "You haven't changed a bit, have you, you weirdo! Good one, Kate."

I nodded in her direction, still focusing on my breathing.

"Don't overdo it, though. You still haven't fed yet," she continued more seriously.

"Okay, I won't," I managed to wheeze.

As I straightened up and gave my lungs more space I contemplated the need to exercise more.

I wonder if I still needed to if I'd been turned...

Monday Evening - Meeting Duncan

Soon after, we were on our way and arrived at the ballroom after about ten minutes. People were coming out of the building and one of them stuck out like a sore thumb. He was tall, with a sportive-built frame and white skin, but his hair was whiter, whatever was left of it. The crew cut shouted military at you. I guessed that he was forty to fifty years old, human age that is, not sucker age of course. I could have been wrong. No matter how old he was, he had Duncan written all over him.

And I was right, as Julie walked straight up to him. She talked to him for a little while and they seemed to exchange the numbers of their 'newborns.' Without warning, she turned around and gestured for me to come closer. Adrenaline flushed through my system. I seriously thought I was going to die from a heart attack one of these days.

I can't handle this continuous stress.

Remembering not to put a big nice-to-meet-you smile on my face I walked up to them. I'd taken my fake Dracula-teeth out when we were still in the town square and I'd no permanent cover-up yet. Instead, I put on my serious face, with pouty lips.

Prune...

Duncan stuck out his hand and when I returned the gesture he nearly crushed my hand. I winced softly as he let go.

"Still very young, as you mentioned," he said as his pale blue eyes darted back to my sister for a moment. "But not to worry, we'll find you some blood in this town soon." His smile didn't reach his eyes.

Saying you're sorry for hurting me would do for now!

I glowered at him as he walked off and began shouting orders to others. Massaging the blood back into my hand I asked Julie, "What will happen now?"

"Now we hunt," she said. She pivoted around to head back to her pack to give them instructions. I made a split second decision and grabbed her by her arm.

"I don't think I can do this, Julie, seriously," I whispered.

She looked shocked, seconds passed. I let go of her arm. After the initial alarm on her face, it turned mellow again.

"Don't worry, I understand, you're still very tired. Why don't you just hang back and you can feed at the gathering after the hunt."

"Um, thanks, sis."

It wasn't exactly what I'd meant, but I'd managed to get out of being found out again, thanks to the kindness of my sister. For now.

Monday Night - Clothes Shopping

It didn't take long before the suckers dispersed in all directions. Some soldier-lookalikes stayed. They were checking out the security of the ballroom building. I decided to go back to the town square. My skinny jeans hid little, so I needed pants with more pockets that could hold more food in them. And, I had to find a mirror to put on my fake fangs.

I don't want to look like a circus attraction, with fangs sticking out at odd angles.

First I went to the fashion shop but found no pants wide enough to contain even the smallest of pockets. With my head hung low, I walked out of the store. When I looked up to seek help from the heavens my eyes fell on the thrift shop on the opposite side of the square. A grin crept on my face and my eyes rolled to the sky before focusing on the shop again. Surely they would have some less-fashionable choices with bigger pockets. Sue had always said that she'd rather be seen dead than go in there... A lump blocked my throat and my grin disappeared. I took a deep breath and focused on the shop.

When I reached the front door my hand hovered over the doorknob. The lock had been forced and the door was ajar. Slowly I pushed it open further.

"Anyone here?" I called out.

No reply. People probably had looted the shop earlier.

Why would suckers want to go in here if they didn't want to come here in their previous life?

I invited luck to stay with me and entered the shop. There was a funny smell, but I couldn't pinpoint what it was. Browsing through a rack with women's pants I found a pair of camo ones, one size too big for me, but they were the only ones suitable I could find. I stripped out of my skinny jeans and hoisted myself into the new ones. My hips weren't wide enough to make them stay up so I took a belt from a mannequin. As I was threading it through the loops I thought I heard something. My whole body stiffened and didn't move.

"Kate!"

There it was again. A whisper, but definitely there.

I turned around in slow-motion. It was against all common sense, but I couldn't help myself. I had to find out where the sound was coming from. My eyes searched the dark of the store. I still didn't dare to move freely.

"Kate, down here." The whisper came from in front of me. I looked down and saw them, a pair of eyes looking straight at me from the inside of the double-story round rack with men's shirts. They scared the hell out of me.

"Smile at me," the 'eyes' commanded.

What an odd question, not something you'd expect in this tense situation...

Then it dawned on me; the voice was Charlie's.

"Charlie! am I glad to see you," and I beamed my biggest smile, showing off my lack of fangs.

The shirts parted and Charlie stepped out. I put my arms out to give him a big hug. I thought of the possibility that he'd been turned, but my gut instinct told me he wouldn't be in hiding if he had been.

"Yeah, glad to see you too," he said, "but you have no idea what I've been through." He grabbed my hands and pushed me away.

"What *you* have been through? What about what *I* have been through?" I asked miffed, lowering my arms again.

"No, Kate, you haven't been through what I've been through..." and he put his hands up in apology to stop me from saying something again. "I've been crawling through the sewers..."

I looked at him stunned. Then the smell hit my nostrils.

"Oh yuck, you stink! *You're* the funny smell in here." I pinched my nose.

"Yeah, don't I know it," he said, hands on his hips.

"And you touched me." I flapped my hands around in disgust.

Charlie's hands went up in an apology again. "Sorry, I tried to warn you. I didn't want to make it any worse."

I wiped my hands on a close by clothing item and nodded. "True. Does it help against them?" To make sure I wiped my nose with another.

"No idea, I didn't hang around long enough to ask," was his typical quick reply. "I came here to get a change of clothes before they could follow the stench trail."

"Good thinking," I said. "I wanted clothing with lots of pockets to stuff food in." I showed off my new pants.

"Yes, I know."

It hit me that he must have seen me getting changed before he called out to me. I wasn't sure how this made me feel. I regarded Charlie and couldn't help but notice his sly smile while he avoided eye contact.

The cheeky bugger!

The angel and devil on my shoulders began a heated argument about what was right and wrong. In the end, I thought it was rather arousing that he had liked watching me undress, but he should have made his presence known earlier. I then dismissed my inner thoughts as there were more pressing matters to attend to.

Ignoring Charlie's remark, I picked up my skinny jeans and transferred all the items from the pockets to my new trousers. While we searched the store for clothing that could fit Charlie, he told me how he had been chased away from me in the schoolyard and how escaping through a storm drain and crawling through the sewers had saved him from his chasers, although they had been very persistent for a long time. Only when he crawled through the smallest of waste drains did they leave him alone.

While Charlie changed into his clean clothes behind the curtain of the changing booth, I took the molten chocolate bars from my bra and put them in my new pants' pockets. I also told Charlie what happened to me as I browsed the shop. I told him about Mr. Ugly Sweater, Sasha, and Caleb... I didn't tell him about my feelings for Caleb but mentioned that he almost turned me. My story ended with me meeting my sister and how I was living like a vampire in her pack now.

"Wow, you've got some guts," I heard him say in awe from behind the curtain.

I know! Not that I had much choice, though.

I kept quiet as I didn't want to seem cocky.

"Did they have more of those fake fangs in the dollar shop?" he asked when he shoved the curtain aside and stepped out of the cubicle in his new, clean outfit.

"I think so. I was in a hurry, but I think there were."

We both looked out the shop window, across the town square. Even though the square was deserted, the thought of crossing it was scary. I had crossed it before, but Charlie wasn't recognized as a sucker yet and being out in the open could be dangerous. When I turned my head towards him my nose automatically crinkled up.

"You still stink, you know. I think it's in your hair."

Charlie looked up from under those heavy brows. "Thanks for letting me know, but there's nothing I can do about it."

"There's a small kitchen at the back. You could try and wash your hair there," I suggested.

Charlie raised an eyebrow and turned to check it out. They even had soap. Charlie stood on a chair while I washed his hair as good as I could under the tap. I found a large flannel shirt to dry his hair with. Automatically I began drying Charlie's hair, even though I knew he could easily do it himself. He didn't seem to mind that did it. When I studied his face, to find out his thoughts about me drying his hair, I noticed his eyes followed my every move, which made me extremely self-conscious. As a smile crept on his face, I'm sure I started blushing. I quickly finished and when I smiled back at him, his smile became even broader. It was a sweet smile. A moment passed.

"Thanks," he said.

I didn't know what to say back, so I threw the towel in the sink. Like the moment, my movement was awkward and the towel didn't make it. Instead, it slid down the cabinet. Charlie and I both reached to grab it and bumped our heads. I laughed as my hand went to my head. Charlie laughed as well as he threw the towel in the sink.

"You okay?" he asked.

"Yeah, I'm fine," I said and turned away.

Charlie joined me standing in front of the shop door, looking across the town square.

"Come on," I said, remembering I was one of 'them' now and shouldn't be afraid. I stepped out into the open.

Monday Night - Town Square

We were halfway down the town square and everything seemed fine when, without warning, my world fell apart. A sucker stepped from behind the war memorial and, lo and behold, of all the suckers on the planet it had to be Mr. Ugly Sweater.

"Well, well, well," he said, swaggering towards us. "Look what coincidence brought back to me..." His eyes shifted to Charlie and back, accompanied by a sneer. "No Caleb here to hold your hand this time, eh?"

The man almost made me puke. Charlie and I looked at each other. I knew we had the same question on our minds.

Does this creep know I hadn't been turned?

Mr. Ugly Sweater stepped inside my personal bubble. With one hand he squeezed my face, nearly lifting me off the ground.

"Time to catch up on that kiss I missed," he said, and his face moved closer to mine. I didn't know if his halitosis was worse than the sewer smell on Charlie or not. So this was what Sasha had meant with 'he won't bother us any more'. They had thrown him out of Caleb's pack and now he ran with Duncan...

Mr. Ugly Sweater's lips were about five centimeters from mine when his face turned from pleasure to pain.

"Let her go or I'll break your hand," I heard Charlie say.

Mr. Ugly Sweater uttered a groan of anger and frustration, but he let go of my face.

Charlie had a slight delay in releasing his hand. "Now piss off before I'll Caleb and Sasha of your little stunt."

I'm sure my grin was from one ear to the other as I watched the offender whimper off, muttering apologies.

"Wow, I can't believe you actually listened to me back there," I said in awe as I savored the sight of Mr. Ugly Sweater disappearing. "What did you do to him?" I asked, still smiling.

Charlie chuckled. "It's one of the perks of being a silversmith, you get really strong hands."

Charlie was new the Arts & Crafts teacher at Bullsbrook high and he had told us about his jewelry making past that first day we met at school. He had explained to Sue and me how he made that woven Celtic ring he wore. It had impressed me.

I'm impressed again!

"No turning back, Smudge, from now on you're a sucker too," I said. "That was so brave."

Charlie's face beamed and I wasn't sure if it was because I'd called him brave or because I'd called him Smudge.

As we continued our walk towards the dollar store we tried to outwit each other verbally on how much braver the other one was.

"You're as brave as a dog biting a bull's balls," I said to Charlie.

"Ah, but you're much braver. You're as brave as a mouse entering a cat convention that just ran out of tinned food," he replied.

"Maybe so, but you're as brave as an Arts & Crafts teacher standing in front of a science class."

"Absolutely not, that is way too scary. I could never do that..."

Monday Night - Preparations

In the store we fitted each other's fangs with the super-glue. The color match was amazing. At first I thought they would be too yellow, but apparently, the average teeth are not sparkling white. I found some scissors and carefully made puncture wounds in Charlie's neck, covering them up immediately with Band-Aids. Charlie also ate his share of lollies and energy bars and filled his pockets with them. As he was doing this I wandered through the store, my mood plummeting.

"What's the matter?" Charlie asked when he found me sitting in a far corner.

I didn't want to worry him, but I decided to share my thoughts anyway.

A shared pain is half the pain after all...

"We have to go back to the gathering now. But I don't think I can do this. I don't think I can go up to a person and scare the living daylights out of them." My eyes brimmed with tears and I looked at every direction but Charlie's.

He sat down next to me. We fell quiet.

Suddenly he punched me on the arm.

"Ouch!" I rubbed my arm and when I frowned at him I saw the spark in his eyes.

"Sorry about that. But we don't have to go to the feeding. We can hide here and wait until they're gone."

I smiled for a second, but my smile soon wore off. "No, we can't."

"Why not?"

"My sister traveled half the country to get here. I don't think she's going to let go of me just like that. She'll come looking for me."

Charlie's smile disappeared too. "Oh, that sucks. Not about your sister caring... I mean, but... you know..."

"Yeah, I know... It sucks."

We sat in silence again. After a few minutes, Charlie said, "What if... what if we said that we've already fed ourselves because we were so hungry?" This was of course true if you included the lollies and energy bars we just ate. I saw the light at the end of this part of the tunnel.

"That's a great idea, let's do that," I said. "They'll have to take our word for it. No, wait. Let's put some fake blood on our shirts. That'll make it more real."

"I don't want to dirty it," Charlie pouted, "I just got this shirt." He always was amazing at lightening the mood. I pretended to hit him on the arm, after which I took a bag with fake blood from the shop and we had a ball splattering each other with blood.

"One more problem," I said, once we were happy with our look of 'just-fed suckers.'

"What's that?"

Looking Charlie in the eye, I sighed. "Julie's group only has girls in it..."

He processed the information, his brows furrowed, and he said, "Oh no, I am not dressing up as a girl. If that's what you are thinking, you are dead wrong. Crawling through human excrement, fine, but I am not dressing up as a girl!" He was clearly upset. He turned around and walked away.

I went after him and put my hand on his shoulder.

"That's not what I meant. I meant that we'll have to take our chances whether she'll let you join her pack..."

He stopped and I let my hand rest on his shoulder but didn't force him to turn around to me.

When he finally did turn around his eyes were teared up. "I...I can't...I don't want...to..." His hand touched my arm and his eyes were pleading this time, trying to tell me something.

"You don't have to dress up, Smudge." I smiled and grabbed his hand. "Like I said, we'll just have to wait and see what she has to say about it."

Charlie took a deep breath. "Oh... okay, that's fine then. I can do that," he said. I hugged him and he also put his arms around me.

My dear friend, you are not alone...

Tuesday Morning, Early - Decisions

We postponed leaving the dollar shop for as long as we could, but we knew we'd had to go back at some stage. Back at the area in front of the ballroom, we found the same eerie sight we'd seen the night Sue had been taken. It was a gathering of humans, like dishes for an evening meal, surrounded by hungry looking suckers. Only this was no smorgasbord, this was a warm buffet...

Charlie and I kept to the edge, trying not to attract any attention. Through the melee I noticed Julie scanning the crowd for me and when she spotted me she came skipping towards us. I mentally braced myself for possibly flunking the teeth test and smiled a wide grin at her when she came near.

"Great! Your fangs have finally dropped," she said. "And who is your buddy?" She turned to Charlie with a big smile on her face.

"Julie, this is my friend Charlie. Charlie, this is my sister Julie."

Julie shook Charlie's hand and I saw her eyes drop down to his grip after which they conveyed their approval in my direction. She cocked her head to one side and I knew she was assuming things, as she always did when it concerned relationships.

"How did you meet Kate?" she asked, her eyes back on Charlie again. I had no time to let her know she was wrong as my breath stocked in my throat, taken aback by the question. Images of Charlie ogling me while I undressed in the thrift shop flashed in front of my eyes. Probably Charlie's eyes too as he didn't reply instantly.

"Um, we used to be colleagues at school," Charlie quickly recovered. "We just bumped into each other in the town square." He was such a good liar.

Julie chatted away and asked Charlie all sorts of questions, like where he came from, what he had taught, and how long it had been since he was turned. I could tell Julie liked him. Charlie put on a good show and answered her questions without blinking. Until she asked whether he liked being in Duncan's pack.

"Eh, I am not in Duncan's pack," Charlie said. "I used to be with Caleb, but I got separated from them after the gathering last night. I'm pack-less at the moment, so to speak," and he elbowed me.

"Ah, yes, can Charlie possibly join your pack?" I twisted the corners of my jacket out of nervousness, rolling my left foot on its side. I felt like a little girl asking the dentist for lollies. Julie's face drained of blood. She blinked at Charlie and then she stared back at me again. Her expression was too tense, disproportionate to the simplicity of the question.

"Can I have a word with you privately?" she said as she pulled me aside.

"Sure," I said. I followed her a few paces, but when I stopped she did a few more away from Charlie. I was ill at ease and looked back at Charlie. His furrowed brow and clenched jaw told me how he was feeling. As Julie didn't step back to me I walked over to where she was.

"I realize you only have girls in your pack..." I started, but she cut me off.

"It's not that, well, not all of it." She scanned our surroundings. If I was ill at ease, she was about to have chemotherapy. I'd never seen her so spooked before. She inspected her feet, glanced at Charlie, who stood there totally lost and then looked me in the eyes. "You are really putting me in a predicament, you know," she said. I thought those eyes were going right through me.

"Why? What is it?" I asked. Goosebumps formed on my skin.

She inhaled a deep breath through her nose and explained.

"Duncan fancies me and has asked me to join his pack. He has helped me a lot with hunts these last few days, so I owe him. But I don't love him, and I certainly don't like the way he runs his pack. Besides, I want to keep my independence. So I refused him, with the excuse that I have a girls-only pack to take care of."

Shit, this screws up our plan big time!

"Shit," was my only reply.

"So you see," she continued, "if I accept Charlie in my pack he will know that I'm bullshitting him. And Duncan doesn't take any bullshit from anybody."

That last sentence was pure terror. Julie's pupils were black holes now. I glanced back at Charlie and he had the same dread in his eyes I'd seen in the pound shop. I was sure he'd heard Julie's words. Seeing him standing there so lost and alone made tears well up in my eyes. I appeared to have more feelings for Charlie than I'd been aware of.

"Look, I can tell you two are really attached to one another, the way he looks at you and you at him... I don't want to stand in the way of your happiness, but you will have to make a choice here."

My eyes shot back at her.

Choice?

I didn't have to word it, the question mark clearly written on my face.

"You either choose to stay with me and dump Charlie or stay with him and join Duncan's pack," she said with no emotion in her voice.

What?!

The screams of the feeding frenzy started in the background, but my shocked brain screamed louder. I couldn't believe what Julie had just said. I thought I'd been dragged through the puddles of hell already, but apparently, I had missed one.

How can she do this to me? She had moved heaven on earth to find me and now she wants to get rid of me? Why?

I turned away from her and she grabbed my arm.

"You do understand my position, Kate?" she pleaded. I yanked my arm free and walked away, trying with all my might to keep it together.

Charlie called my name. The sound of his footsteps coming my way stopped abruptly.

"This is something she has to deal with on her own, Charlie," I heard Julie say.

My mind was a whirlwind of thoughts, I was in Arkansas territory. Julie thought I was in a relationship with Charlie. Charlie probably would like that, but I was in love with Caleb, who was god-knows-where, but not near Duncan. Duncan wanted a relationship with Julie, but Julie didn't want Duncan, nor did she want Charlie in her pack. It was obvious she was terrified of what would happen if Duncan found out she accepted Charlie. I didn't want to lose Charlie, but leaving him with Duncan on his own was the same thing as signing his death warrant. So basically I had no choice.

What had I expected she'd say? I knew she had an all-girls pack.

I stopped walking and wiped the tears that fell when I closed my eyes. I took a deep breath, turned around and regarded Julie and Charlie standing there. Both were anxious to find out what was going on in my mind, both wanting to know whom I'd choose to stay with.

I strode back, their eyes never leaving mine.

"Charlie and I will join Duncan's pack," I said to Julie.

I didn't get to see Charlie's reaction as my sister threw her arms around me and gave me a big hug. "I'm so sorry, sis, I really am," she whispered.

"It's okay, Jules, it's my own choice."

She let go of me and hugged Charlie.

"You take good care of her, you hear. She's special," she said to him.

"I know," Charlie said, "and I will." I could hardly hear him over the screams as he said it.

Julie stepped back and smiled at us, but I could spot tears welling up in her eyes as she briskly turned around and jogged away, joining the feeding frenzy.

Nobody was interested in whether Charlie and I fed or not. As both of us weren't in the mood for mingling with others, we withdrew into the ballroom hall. It surprised me how small it looked on the inside. Behind the entrance with its wardrobe on one side and public conveniences on the other, was the proper ballroom. Horseshoe-shaped booths lined both sides of the dance floor.

Charlie and I looked around and picked a booth that was furthest away from the entrance. The seating was decorated with a red, plush-but-worn material, which gave it all a grand but rather melancholic look. It perfectly suited my mood. We sat down next to each other.

"Thank you," Charlie said.

"Charlie, I don't..., I'm not..." I struggled with my feelings and I couldn't get the words to come out of my mouth.

So this is verbal constipation...

He put his hand over mine and squeezed it. "I know," he said, "Still... thank you," and his expression was the same one I had just seen on Julie's face; his mouth was smiling, but his eyes were sad.

Duncan's pack began filling the ballroom, little groups at a time. Everyone took up a spot to sleep the day away. We had looks and stares from other pack members and I heard whispers here and there, but nobody talked to us. I lay down on one-half of the bench and tried to sleep, suddenly drained of all energy. Charlie sat up for a while longer. I felt his eyes on me and I wondered what he was thinking. Finally, he lay down too. We fell asleep with our feet touching.

Tuesday Evening - The Ballroom

That evening we were woken up early. I knew the sun couldn't have set just yet, but one of the macho-looking 'drones,' as I called Duncan's right-hand men, still woke us up. These guys had a military look and seemed to move on autopilot. Everyone got up and positioned themselves at arm's length on the dance floor, facing the stage. Charlie and I looked at each other in wonder. But we didn't get time to ask questions as we were ushered onto the dance floor as well. One of the drones took center-stage and began performing a series of physical exercises that everybody copied.

Charlie and I followed suit and I happened to look up at the ceiling - it was painted black. This was likely another reason why I'd thought the inside of the building looked smaller than expected. A disco ball hanging in the center of the ceiling caught my eye. It reminded me that they must have music in this place. I scanned the corners of the large room. The ones near the entrance held booths. The left corner next to the stage held the entrance to the bar and the right corner was closed off. There was a door, though. Behind it was most likely where the music installation was. So why didn't they put on some music? I looked up to the ceiling again while stretching and noticed the black lights. An aha-moment made me realize they kept the door to the music installation locked to prevent somebody accidentally flipping on the switch of the UV-lights.

Now why didn't I think of black lights before?

Because the minimal school supply is not equipped with them.

I wondered about this soundless exercise and why everybody was so compliant. But I continued to copy the drone on the stage, just like all the other sheep. When it came to push-ups I was in trouble. I had never been able to do push-ups and had always told everybody I probably couldn't do them even if my life depended on it. My life *was* depending on it now and, if I had been in doubt before, I was now one-hundred-per-cent sure I couldn't do push-ups. There was sniggering behind us, and I felt so bad. Not only because I must have looked ridiculous trying, but I knew that I would have a problem in the long-run. I was supposed to be getting stronger by now, but I would never be able to perform these push-ups.

Give me three months of intensive training and I might...

I wished Julie had informed me more on Duncan's pack habits. I couldn't imagine why she was so scared of Duncan. These exercises weren't so bad. She wasn't scared enough not to go hunting with him. Or maybe that's how scared she was - she normally wasn't afraid to say no to anybody, but she didn't dare to say no to Duncan. This thought was scary, so I focused on doing the exercises as well as I could. I still felt like being the laughing stock for the rest of the hour.

After the gym hour finished everybody went their own way again, getting ready to move out. Charlie and I went back to our booth. I was glad to be inconspicuous again. The relief was of short duration, however, as a drone came up to us and told us we were summoned by Duncan. I didn't know what Charlie was thinking, but I felt like a lamb being brought to the slaughter. As we walked side-by-side I grabbed Charlie's hand. He looked at me in surprise. When he saw my worried look, he squeezed my hand and gave me a short smile.

We were led in front of Duncan, who'd set up headquarters in the bar area. He sat at a table, intently studying a map. It took at least a couple of minutes before he looked up from the map, although I had the idea he knew very well we were standing in front of him. He didn't offer us to sit down, but I noticed the other chairs had been taken away.

What a jerk.

This one word kept going through my mind the whole time he had us waiting, but I dismissed the thought when we finally got his attention and I remembered that this 'jerk' had our lives in his hands. As he looked up he folded his hands and laid them on the table in front of him.

"You're Julie's sister, aren't you?" he asked me, his voice devoid of any human emotion. I had no doubt that this had been the same before he was turned.

"Yes, sir, I'm Kate," I answered in military style.

God, I'm such a sucker!

Using the old connotation of the word that is...

"I remember Julie introducing you to me," he said, "and you must be Charlie." He turned his head to Charlie.

"I am, Duncan," Charlie said, and I nearly fainted.

You will get us killed with that attitude!

Duncan kept looking at him for a bit longer, and then sat back while he moved his hands to the side of the table. "I shall be honest with you guys. I didn't ask for you in my pack and if I had a choice you wouldn't be here. But Julie asked me to take you in and I promised her I would uphold her wishes."

Another silence followed and I thought we had gotten away with it. I was about to thank him and leave.

"There is an issue I have to mention," Duncan continued. Charlie and I exchanged a quick, worried glance. As we waited for Duncan to continue, you could hear a pin drop.

God, this guy loves being in control.

"It was brought to my attention that you can't do any push-ups, Kate. Why is that?" He kept his eyes on me. It was unnerving.

"I...I don't know, sir. I have never been able to do them and I was looking forward to being able to, but somehow I am not getting any stronger."

Sweat was accumulating in my palms, and it wasn't the after-effect of the exercises. I kept looking straight in front of me for I was sure that if I looked at him, those cold eyes would pry the truth out of me.

"Hmm..." he said, "another one..." and he frowned at the drone standing next to him, who just nodded.

'Another one...' What does he mean? Is there another human in the pack? Does he know?

Before I could speculate any further, Duncan gave me the answer.

"You also must have a rare blood disease, so be it. But I can't have you causing any unrest amongst my pack. Ergo from now on you take a spot at the back during the exercises. Dismissed."

And he leaned forward to study the map in front of him again. Charlie and I looked at the drone standing next to Duncan, who indicated with his head for us to clear out.

Tuesday Evening - Meeting Harry

We turned and walked back with a quick step to the booth we had slept in. I couldn't believe my luck. We had survived another firing squad. I wiped my sweaty hands on my trousers and couldn't help smiling. Once we sat down and I was sure nobody was paying us any attention, I whispered to Charlie, "Did you hear what he said? There's another one."

I didn't know if I should have been happy or more afraid. It would be another person to be more ourselves with, but that extra person was also another chance to slip up and get us caught.

"I know," Charlie whispered back, "but how do we find out which one?"

As if on cue a young man sat himself down opposite us. Charlie and I took him in without saying anything. He looked my age, had a blond flattop, wore camouflaged clothing and had a healthy, muscular build. We were sure he was one of Duncan's drones and we were afraid that he was sent to spy on us. His blue eyes were bright, his face bursting with excitement. He gave us a smile and said, "Hi, I'm Harry."

"Hi Harry," Charlie and I replied in sync.

Harry lowered his head towards me and said in a low voice "I understand that you also have a...'rare blood disorder,'" and his expression was full of hope.

No need to look any further...

"Actually, we both have," I replied quietly and Charlie hit me in the shin under the table. It took me great effort not to shout out in pain.

Ouch, Charlie, that classifies as using unnecessary force!

"Mine isn't a rare blood disorder, it's a genetic disorder," Charlie quickly corrected my mistake.

"That's what I thought too. Um, bummer," Harry said as he was lost for words, as most people are when confronted with another person's medical problems. "But you are like me, aren't you?" he said again with a big smile on his face in my direction.

I realized that Harry was a bit of a loose cannon and I chastised myself for almost exposing Charlie to him. Before I answered his question I had to know for sure Harry wasn't a sucker. So I studied his fangs and noticed they were his own, real teeth, not stick-on ones like Charlie's and mine. Blood drained from my head and I felt queasy, thinking he may be a sucker after all.

Harry saw me stare at his teeth and noticed the uncomfortable look on my face. He waved his hands in front of him before quickly putting them flat on the table again. "Don't worry, I was born this way, they have always looked like this," he added.

To make sure he was telling the truth my eyes drifted to his neck where I could clearly see two 'marks', as Julie called them.

"Self-inflicted," Harry softly beamed as he had followed my stare. "I am so glad I'm not the only one with a blood disorder," he said a bit louder with a huge smile on his face.

I sighed with relief as I realized that he was a genuine human. When I turned to Charlie, I found that he didn't appear as relieved as I was. He still eyed Harry with suspicion. Then somebody shouted 'Briefing!' and all heads turned to face Duncan, who had taken to the stage. I was doubly relieved as Harry couldn't get us into trouble for the next few minutes.

Duncan informed us we were leaving Bullsbrook and would move on to the next village. The gathering yesterday apparently didn't give enough of a return as there had been a gathering the night before by Caleb's pack. Duncan didn't mention Caleb's name, but there were whispers amongst the ranks and I knew of course.

What exactly is it between Duncan and Caleb?

Tuesday Night - Marching

When we marched to the next town - and we were literally marching - I took my chance to interrogate Harry. There was so much I wanted to know and Harry seemed eager to please. Charlie had warned me to stay away from Harry as much as possible. He was afraid that Harry would blow our cover. I understood his concern but felt a bit miffed about Charlie not having much faith in me. I too knew the dangers of the life we were living at the moment. Whatever I thought about the matter, I needn't worry. It appeared harder to get rid of Harry than that red wine stain on my favorite white shirt.

Harry was walking in between Charlie and me with a spring in his step. Charlie's grunts and sighs about this somehow circumvented Harry and found their way to me, but I, too, ignored it.

"So who's this Caleb everyone's talking about?" I asked Harry.

"Caleb's a bit of a celebrity amongst us." His face lit up as he spoke of Caleb. "We've all heard the stories of Caleb."

"Oh, what sort of stories?" I asked. I'd never met a celebrity before and was curious about why Caleb was famous.

You already know one reason, girl.

"There are many stories of Caleb; about how strong he is, about how loyal he is to Sasha, about how he saves the children. Not everybody agrees with that one, especially not Duncan. And then there is the one about how he defied Duncan." His voice had dropped to a whisper I could hardly hear.

"How does that story go?" I pushed him. This story seemed to be the most interesting one and I could wait to hear it.

"I'd rather not talk about that one if you don't mind," Harry said.

Oh, I sooo want to know now!

"That's okay, Harry," I said to him, while internally being eaten alive by curiosity. I wasn't going to drop the subject thought.

"Where's Caleb's pack now, you think?" I said.

We both stopped and looked at Charlie as he all of a sudden seemed to have swallowed a bug.

"Are you okay?" Harry asked Charlie.

"I'll be just fine, Harry, don't worry," Charlie said as he quickly recovered. Charlie shot me a quick glance before we began walking again. If looks could kill, I think I might have dropped dead.

What's all that about?

As we continued to walk, I chose to ignore Charlie's objection, repeated my question, and Harry answered after Charlie cleared his throat but didn't seem to choke this time.

"Well, that's the strangest thing, you know. Normally Caleb stays out of Duncan's way. But Caleb's pack accidentally 'cut in,' so to speak, the night before we arrived in that cute little town we were in just now…"

"Bullsbrook you mean. Charlie and I lived there,' I interrupted. I smiled at Charlie, to get in his good books again. I didn't know what I'd done wrong, but I hated conflict. He chose not to look at me and my smile went unanswered.

"Oh, did you? Nice place," said Harry, seemingly unaware of the tension between Charlie and me. "Anyway, everybody expected Caleb to move out as soon as he knew that Duncan was on his way. But during the hunt last night we ran into Caleb's pack, it appeared they hadn't left. They didn't interfere with our hunt, but they kept an eye on us all the same. It was really creepy."

Harry seemed to be deep in thought after this and I let him be. I was thinking about what he said too. Charlie didn't take the silent moment to talk to me. I understood he didn't want me to talk about Caleb, but I couldn't figure out why. So I was left with my own thoughts and questions.

Why hadn't Caleb's pack moved on? What were they still doing in Bullsbrook last night? Why was Caleb hanging around Duncan's pack if they had some sort of feud going on?

Whatever the reason for this strange situation, I wondered if it would be possible to slip out of Duncan's pack and go back to join Caleb's pack.

My thoughts were interrupted when one of Duncan's drones dropped back and fell into step next to me. A bit annoyed with the spatial intrusion I gave him a sideways glance to find out who the intruder was. He presented as another perfect specimen of an army drone; crew cut, wide jaw, muscular build. My attention was drawn to his pronounced chin with a large dimple in the middle.

Ballchinnian...

I suppressed a giggle.

"Hi," he said, looking unsure but still trying to smile, "you must be Kate."

I wondered how he knew my name and what he had heard of my conversation with Harry. I also had no idea what my conversation with him was going to lead to, so I thought it couldn't hurt to be polite.

"Yes, I am. What's your name?"

"My name's Ben," he said, sticking his chest out that little bit further. "Hi Harry," he said to Harry.

"Hi Ben," Harry replied.

Charlie was completely ignored and although I thought he was acting like a teenage schoolboy, I felt a pang of sorrow for him.

"Ben has helped me from the beginning," Harry said to me.

I didn't know if that meant Ben knew Harry was still a human, but I thought better to assume not. Just in case.

"Yes, I took Harry under my wing, so to speak," Ben said. "I stood up for him when Duncan wanted to throw him out of the pack when it became clear Harry wasn't getting any stronger. Such a bummer he's got that rare blood disease. And now you're another one with it, how unlikely is that?"

OMG, I am surrounded by morons...

I thought I'd better go with the flow and said, "Yes, what are the odds of Duncan having two weaklings in his pack, eh?"

Ben put on a grave face. "Don't you worry, Kate, I'll make sure Duncan has nothing to complain about. I'll get you some good blood tonight and you will feel a lot stronger soon. I'll take care of you."

Somebody pinch me, I think I am being courted!

If I had any doubts of Ben courting me or not they were laid to rest when he continued.

"You just stay with me and I will make sure nothing happens to you. I can provide for you," he said.

Charlie got a bug in his throat again. It appeared to be a really big one this time. While Harry and Ben fussed over Charlie, I tapped my foot, arms crossed. This time I knew exactly what was bothering him. Once Harry and Ben were sure Charlie wasn't going to pass out, I thought I'd better make sure he didn't choke again.

"You don't have to worry about me, Ben, Charlie is taking good care of me already," I said to him.

Ben stuck his neck out to look at Charlie. From the expression on his face, I could tell he wasn't convinced.

"Oh, is he? Well, I think I can do better. You can call on me anytime, Kate." He put his hand on my shoulder.

I looked at Ben's hand, not sure what to do with it. I didn't want it there, even though I was positive Charlie couldn't see it. I guess Ben saw me looking at it as he abruptly took it away. I didn't want to hurt Ben's feelings as he, obviously, had nothing but good intentions for me. I had better make things right again.

"Thank you for the offer, Ben, I will keep that in mind," I politely replied. I wondered what book on courting Ben had read.

It surely must have been from the history section in the library...

Tuesday Night - Getting to Know Harry Better

After walking for what I reckoned was three hours, we could see the little village on the horizon. I had asked Harry why we didn't drive there to which he replied that Duncan wanted us to get stronger and get more stamina through the exercise of marching. We walked for another half hour, until we were about five minutes away from the village when we were ordered to sit down and rest. When I asked Harry why he told us we had to get our strength up before 'surprising' the villagers.

Trick or treat!

Just make that 'eat!'

The four of us sat under a tree; Charlie, Harry, Ben and me. I took my shoes off and started to rub my feet. They had been used to standing all day in the classroom, not marching for hours.

"Here, let me do that," Harry said with an authoritative voice. He took my foot in his lap and began a vigorous foot massage. It hurt a bit but felt great at the same time.

Charlie made it his mission to look in any direction but mine. Harry touching my bare foot was apparently uncomfortable to Charlie and I felt bad about it, even though it was only my foot and Harry wasn't touching it in a sensuous way.

Suddenly a bell started ringing in my mind. Was that what was bothering Charlie? Would he be jealous? I reminded myself I'd tried to tell Charlie I didn't love him before we went to sleep and he'd said he knew.

So what's his problem?

When Harry began massaging my other foot, one of the girls from the pack walked up and asked Harry if he could massage her feet too. She had a terrible nasal voice but wasn't bad looking, her bright red lipstick just as notable as her voice. Before he had a chance to reply Ben offered his services to her. There was a flicker of disappointment on her face, but she accepted his offer. Ben excused himself and followed the girl to where she had been sitting.

When it was just the three of us again I whispered to Harry, "Does he know?"

"No, he's too stupid."

I was surprised by the intelligent tone in Harry's voice. Maybe there was more to Harry than I had initially thought. Only time would tell if I was right.

Charlie finally spoke. "So what'll happen when the hunt starts? How have you been dealing with this so far?" He looked at Harry, still not at me.

"Oh, simple," Harry said. "I managed to be allowed to 'hunt and feed' on my own. I guess Duncan only agreed because he keeps hoping I don't survive.

Unfortunately for him, I keep disappointing him." There was a wicked grin on his face.

Charlie and I were impressed with Harry's insight. As Charlie chuckled he accidentally looked at me, but immediately glanced away. It seemed he was still holding a grudge against me. Or was he? I glimpsed the corners of his mouth moving upwards and dimples forming in his cheeks. He was teasing me now.

Oh, in heaven's name, grow up, Charlie!

The words in my head made me giggle. Both Charlie and Harry looked at me with inquiring faces, but I waved them off, keeping my little bit of fun to myself.

Ha, take that, Smudge!

We didn't get much longer to rest and before I knew it everyone was pumped up and ready to go hunting. Apparently, Duncan had a strict routine with little villages as no instructions were given and everybody appeared to know what to do, drifting out to surround the village. Charlie and I stuck with Harry. Ben had again offered to take me under his wing, but I convinced him that together, Charlie and Harry would take good care of me. As we walked into the village, Harry looked at Charlie and asked me quietly, outside of Charlie's earshot, if Charlie needed to go out and feed.

"No, he's like us, Harry," I told him, taking my chances.

"Ah, I wasn't sure after our first conversation. I mean, I figured he knew about you, but he'd said he had achondroplasia, not a blood disorder."

He threw me off balance. I was one-hundred percent sure that Charlie had not used that word in that conversation.

I raised my eyebrows but didn't say anything. Harry must have noticed as he explained his word choice without me asking for it. "I'm a medical student."

Give me a chair and I'll fall off it!

The foot massage! He definitely had paid attention during anatomy lessons...

This explained a lot. Harry was certainly more intelligent than I had originally credited him for. And what's more, he knew how to use it. He clamped onto a moron for cover and pretending to be one too. No wonder he had survived for so long.

Tuesday Night - Hunting in the Village

Harry took us into the village center. It had the same look as Bullsbrook; deserted and rampaged, with no soul in sight. After walking through the main street, passing a primary school, we turned into a side street. Not far from that, he pointed to a house. "We'll take that one."

"Why this house?" Charlie said.

"Children live here," he answered. As we neared the house we saw a bouncy ball and some plastic toys on the front lawn. Charlie and I both looked at Harry with an expression of 'so what?'

"They'll have snack packs for lunch boxes in the refrigerator and, if we're lucky, prepared meals in the freezer," he gloated back at us.

This guy keeps surprising me at every corner.

We followed him around to the back of the house, where he knocked out one of the windows of the kitchen door. The glass shattered on the floor and made a terrible noise. I tensed. Then I reminded myself that we were the top dog now, not the ones that needed to be scared, and let my breath go. Harry opened the provisionally barricaded door. As we entered the kitchen we heard a muffled female scream coming from upstairs; humans were still in the house. Charlie and I stopped in alarm again, exchanging fearful glances, but Harry waved off our concern.

"They won't bother us, they're too scared. As long as we don't go upstairs they won't come down." He said that last sentence a little louder.

Harry was right on all counts, most importantly on the fact that the people didn't come down. There were little packages with cut apples and grapes in the refrigerator that we immediately snacked on. In the freezer, we found a large container with cooked macaroni in tomato sauce that we defrosted in the microwave. While waiting for the meal to heat up, I asked Harry why he had never tried to escape Duncan's pack.

"Don't think the idea hasn't entered my mind," Harry said, "and believe you me, I've tried. But Duncan keeps a tight ship. Whenever we hunt he has suckers placed around the hunting ground to prevent anybody escaping, friend or foe. He doesn't want a second Caleb situation, his ego wouldn't be able to take it. There are guards posted when we sleep during the day, they take turns to stay awake. They're positioned at every entrance and exit, to make sure we aren't attacked by humans he says, but I'm certain he also doesn't want anyone to leave. And it works, which means it makes it impossible to get away, unfortunately." He sighed.

Somebody, please crush this brick in my stomach.

Yeah, and spill the beans about this Duncan-Caleb situation.

We finished dinner on the floor of the dark kitchen and Harry got up first.

"Excuse me for a second," he said and walked into the living room. There he began smashing a chair into the wall, continuing his rampage into the hallway. I didn't know what had come over him. Charlie and I both got up, looking for an explanation I glanced at Charlie, but he looked as perplexed as I felt. We both followed Harry's moves as he punched his fist into a wall, opening up the skin on his knuckles, wiping this blood on the corner of his mouth and then smeared the remaining blood on the walls here and there. Finally, he was done with his rampage and stood content in front of us.

"Gotta make it look real." Harry smiled.

"Oh, okay, good thinking," Charlie said.

In my opinion, he had overdone it a bit, so I thought I'd better keep my mouth shut.

Charlie took a cutting knife from one of the kitchen drawers. He cut the side of his hand and smeared the blood onto the corner of his mouth. He wiped the knife on a tea towel and gave it to me. I took it from him and held it in my right hand and put the point onto the palm of my left hand. I tried to push the blade in, but I couldn't do it. I couldn't make the knife go into my flesh. I exhaled, inhaled, and tried again, but as soon as the metal touched my skin, the hand holding the knife stopped.

"I...I can't do this," I said, and let the knife fall onto the floor. I rubbed the spot where the knife had touched my skin, certain that I was doomed.

Charlie took the knife off the floor and for a second I thought he was going to cut my hand for me. To my relief, he put the knife on the benchtop. He kneeled next to me. I had no idea what he was up to, so I eyed him closely. "Turn your head a bit," he said. I obeyed, but I kept my eyes on him. He squeezed the wound he just made on his own hand until blood was dripping out again, then smeared the blood on my face.

"Thanks."

"You're not done yet, turn your head the other way," he said, and he smeared some more freshly squeezed blood on the other side of my face.

"Can't have Ben thinking I don't feed you enough." His smile was kind.

I smiled back at him, glad his good mood was back again.

We shared the chocolate bars Charlie and I had taken from the dollar shop with Harry. We also drank as much as we could as we were parched. Charlie was disappointed there wasn't any beer in the house, but he didn't linger over it and drank almost a liter of milk. It was nice to know he was not an alcoholic.

Before we left, Harry was rummaging through one of the kitchen drawers.

"What are you looking for?" I asked.

"Pen and paper."

"Why?" Charlie asked. It was the same question I had on my mind.

When Harry had found what he wanted he turned around. "To write a thank you note," he said as if it was the most logical thing in the world.

"Oh, of course," was all I could say.

"Sor-ry for da-ma-ging your home and ea-ting your food," Harry said as he wrote and signed it 'Harry.'

He put the note in the refrigerator. He told us he left it there because no sucker would ever look in there, just in case they entered the house after him. I thought it was so sweet of him to write that note. His parents had done a good job raising him. Thinking of my own parents caused a lump in my throat to swell up and I didn't speak for the next fifteen minutes until it subsided.

Wednesday Morning, Early - Sleeping Arrangements

When we arrived at the town square, the gathering had just finished. Relief washed over me as I realized I didn't have to watch the horror of the feeding. Harry had timed it on the dot. I was so thankful for meeting Harry and my respect for him grew by the hour.

There wasn't a ballroom in the little village and we followed directions to other sleeping arrangements. I was hoping it involved a soft bed this time.

It's amazing how you take simple things for granted.

We walked up to a motel located on the outskirts of the village and as we got nearer, a certain dread began to creep into my mind. Motel rooms usually had double beds. Now I knew that Harry would not suggest sleeping in between Charlie and me, but I wasn't looking forward to sleeping with Charlie in one bed either. We went into the reception area and walked up to a drone who had been tasked with assigning rooms.

"Sorry, Harry, you know the rules, you'll have to sleep in the day care center," the drone said as soon as we walked in.

"Oh, yeah, I forgot," Harry said with this stupid look on his face.

This guy should get an Oscar.

The drone handed Charlie the key to our room, gave Harry directions to the day care center and the three of us walked out again.

"Why can't you sleep here?" Charlie asked Harry.

Harry hunched his shoulders as he put his hands in his pockets.

"Duncan's instructions, I'm afraid, couples only in hotels and motels."

A wave of adrenaline washed through my body again and my mouth went dry.

Why do people keep thinking Charlie and I are a couple? Sure, we're both not the tallest of people, but that doesn't mean we automatically fall for each other.

And that was that, if Duncan had given the order then there was no argument to be made. We said goodnight to Harry and walked to our room. It was a small room, contemporarily decorated in relaxing green tones, with ensuite. As soon as we had entered, Charlie locked the door behind us. I felt like a trapped animal.

Why am I so uptight? I slept in one bed with Sue and she was a good friend. So what's the difference?

Keep kidding yourself, kiddo...

I was standing at the bed end, gazing longingly at it. It had a definite attraction, but the potential price that came with it was keeping me from letting my body do what it wanted.

"I can sleep on the floor if you want," I heard Charlie say.

"Don't be ridiculous," I said as I turned to him, "I don't want you to."

Oh God, please don't take this as an invitation!

"Phew! Thanks," he said, "I must admit I wasn't looking forward to sleeping on the floor with a comfy bed right next to me."

"I know."

And we continued to stand there. Me with my hands in my back pockets staring at the floor, Charlie looking at the bed.

Awkward!

Charlie was the one to break the silence.

"Why don't you go do what you have to do in the bathroom, I'll take second turn."

"Oh, okay, thanks," I said and escaped to the little bathroom. I leaned against the closed door.

Shit, shit, shit. Why can't I just talk to Charlie, say that I have no feelings for him?

How I hated being in situations like these. There had been occasions like this one before, where boys showed their interest in me. All I did was ignore them and try to avoid them from that moment on like the plague. But I couldn't hide from Charlie now, could I?

I couldn't find a way out, so I decided to have a shower in the hope it would relax me, apart from the fact that I was beginning to smell. I made sure I locked the bathroom door before I undressed. I remembered a story from Maxine, how one of her boyfriends had walked in on her while she was getting changed, with more on his mind than using the toilet. She had told us all about it as Julie and I were only just getting interested in boys at the time and wanted to know every little detail.

Sweet memories...

I was half undressed when Charlie yelled from the room. He nearly gave me a heart attack. "What side of the bed do you want to be on?"

Does it matter?

When I slept with Sue in the double bed we just took a side. We hadn't argued over who took which side. I didn't know if there were any perks of sleeping on one side or the other.

"Um, I don't care...you pick where you want to sleep," I said.

"Okay, I will, thanks," came the reply, but he didn't say which side he chose.

The shower was sooo great. I couldn't remember when I had my last one and I had to force myself to get out of it again when my fingers started to get wrinkly. As I was drying my hair this image of a naked Charlie lying on the bed, waiting for me, popped up in my mind.

Oh no, he wouldn't, would he?

My stomach tried a Celtic knot. I used the hair dryer, brushed my teeth, cleaned my nails and dressed again. Looking in the mirror I couldn't think of anything else to keep me in the bathroom for longer.

Pretend he's Sue, Kate...

My sight started to tear up.

Maybe not...

I opened the bathroom door slightly.

"Ah, you're finally done. God, you take a long time to freshen up. I hope you left some warm water for me," Charlie said as he jumped off the bed and waited for me to exit the bathroom. To my relief, he was still completely dressed and the knot in my stomach untied itself a fraction.

From the wrinkles in the blanket, I could tell Charlie had chosen the side of the bed closest to the exit, which I thought was a nice, protective gesture. Anybody storming into the room would get to him first. Not that I thought they could as the door was locked, but still, it was a nice gesture. I walked over to the window on my side of the bed. Charlie had already closed the curtains, but I adjusted them again to make sure no light would come in during the day. I wasn't a sucker, but I still liked it dark when I tried to sleep. I shuffled towards the pillow end of the bed between the little space of the bed and the wall and then decided it was better to get undressed at the bed end, where there was more space. So I side-stepped back again and put my clothes on the back of the desk chair.

Why do they always put desks in bedrooms? They are too small and wouldn't it be better to have a place to put a suitcase on?

By the time Charlie emerged from the bathroom I was already lying under the sheets and had my back turned to him. My eyes and ears were on full alert.

I heard Charlie put his clothes on the seat of the chair. My mind refused to think of what could happen next. To my surprise, Charlie got into bed, but between the blanket and the top sheet, so the sheet was a barrier between his body and mine.

Thank you, Charlie, thank you!

I closed my eyes, now knowing that I was going to be safe with Charlie.

"Goodnight, Kate," Charlie said as he turned the light off.

"'Night," I said and we didn't talk anymore.

The snoring started in no time and I wished I could fall asleep so easily. Instead, my whole body yearned to be with Caleb. I kept seeing his eyes in front of me, those dark, deep eyes I had drowned in. I wanted so badly to look into those eyes again, to feel his body close to mine, his breath on my neck. My love for him was so intense, it was an ache that was almost unbearable. It was torturing me slowly, consuming every cell of my body. I had no sense of time, but it seemed like an eternity before I finally fell asleep.

Wednesday - Memories

When I woke up I was in the same position as I had fallen asleep in, but the blankets had dropped to my waist. I may have kicked them down, maybe Charlie did it, I don't know. It wasn't cold, so I didn't feel the need to pull them up again. To my annoyance, rays of sunshine were still getting through the sides of the curtain, despite my adjustments earlier. I didn't like it and moved my head slightly to avoid the rays on my eyelids. This time the darkness brought back memories I treasured, like saying goodbye to my parents on the day I left for Bullsbrook.

Mom and Dad had stood on their porch to wave me off in my over-packed hatchback. I thought I didn't own much and was amazed at how much effort it had taken to stuff my humble belongings in my little car.

Mom had promised me earlier they'd come and visit me as soon as I had settled. I thought she was very brave to let me, the last one, leave the parental nest. It would be so empty without any of their daughters living at home. I had thought of asking for a job in Portland and living at home to keep Mom and Dad company. However, when this position in Bullsbrook came up it was an offer I just couldn't refuse. Mom cried when I had told her the news and Dad had hugged her, kissing her hair and telling her everything was going to be alright. At that moment I had felt like the 'Daughter of Doom,' but when Dad looked at me, his eyes told me Mom would be okay. Dad was a cool guy and didn't talk much, but I knew he loved Mom very much and that they were happy together.

Dad had his arm around Mom's waist as they stood on their porch. I stuffed my last item, my childhood teddy bear, in my car.

"Please drive carefully, darling," Mom said.

"Nope, I'm going to hit every lamp post on the way I think!" I joked as I walked back to them.

"Oh, you know what I mean, silly," and she put her arms around me and gave me a big hug. "Make sure to give us a call when you arrive. I'll be worried sick if I don't know you've arrived safely."

"I will, Mom, I will," I soothed her as I kissed her goodbye. Then I gave Dad a hug and a kiss.

"Don't do anything I wouldn't do, kid," Dad said with a smile on his face. He never called me Kate, I was always his 'kid.'

"Well, that basically means I can do anything I want." I smiled.

Mom poked Dad in the ribs with her elbow and gave him her angry stare.

"Ouch!" Dad pretended to be hurt. He replaced his arm around her waist and they both waved as I reversed off their driveway. I missed them as soon as I drove away.

The realization I probably would never see my parents again brought out emotions I had stored deep down these last days. I missed my parents, I missed Sue. I would never have dinner with them again, talking about the little things we thought mattered in our lives. Never would I hug them, tease them, quarrel or laugh with them again. The realization left a hole in my heart that ate its way through it like acid. Emotions hit me full on, my mouth contorted in an effort not to cry out loud and wake Charlie. I bit on my hand to prevent sounds escaping from my mouth. Tears from my left eye were streaming over the bridge of my nose, underneath my right eye and merging with the tears from my right eye before wetting the fabric of the pillow cover. Watery snot created another patch of wetness. My body started to shake with every sob I tried to suppress and I thought of how Mrs. Sloan's body had shaken with her sobs. How I wished I could let it all out, cry out loud, scream even, but couldn't. I felt like I was drowning in a pool of tears, completely surrounded by my sadness and misery.

Wednesday Afternoon - Revelations

I felt a touch on my arm.

It was a soft, gentle touch and it was soothing, stroking me from my shoulder to my elbow. I turned my head and saw Charlie lying on his side, looking at me. He didn't say anything. Turning around completely, not ashamed to show him my red-rimmed eyes and snotty nose. I could be myself with Charlie. His touch had calmed me and I had stopped sobbing. Somehow he always made me feel better.

We didn't talk, we just looked at each other, like we did in the cabin. Since then we'd gone through so much together, shared so many horrible things and survived. If it wasn't for Charlie I probably wouldn't be here right now. I studied his face, his bushy brows, his cute, little nose, the overgrown stubble covering his jaw. His eyes weren't as dark and deep as Caleb's, but they were kind and caring, with that extra something I couldn't place.

After a while he lifted his hand and stroked my arm again.

No, no, no, this is going the wrong way.

I rolled onto my back.

"Please don't, Charlie," I whispered. I didn't dare to look him in the eye and see his hurt as I rejected him. To make sure I didn't make eye contact I closed my eyes.

"I love you, Kate," he said. Not in a husky voice, or anything like that. Not a whisper either. More like a statement. But there was an emotion behind it I couldn't describe in words as if it cost him a great deal of effort to say it.

NO! Please don't spoil what we have.

Thoughts went into hyper-drive in my mind again.

How can he say he loves me? Yes, we are close, very close, but we're just good friends. He always called Sue 'My Lady', which made me think he was interested in her.

He says he loves me, not that he's 'in love' with me. That means that this is not some whim, but rather something that has been going on for longer.

Nevertheless, he has never made any passes at me, not even last night, when there were plenty of opportunities. Oh for crying out loud, he told me yesterday he knew I didn't love him.

"I thought you loved Sue," I said, trying to keep my voice as neutral as possible.

"True, I liked Sue," he said, "but making jokes with Sue was just a distraction...to hide my insecurity. I fell in love with you the moment I laid eyes on you."

I was frowning, trying to figure out his words. I kept my eyes shut knowing that if I opened them I would have to face him and I wasn't sure if I could handle that.

"I just had no idea how to let you know. I've tried so many times..." Charlie continued. "I didn't know if you felt something for me. These last few days you gave me hope and, considering the situation, I thought I'd better find out. You know, on the off chance that we could drop one of the lies. I realize I'm not the dream prince most girls are looking for, but I can't hold in my feelings for you any longer. Being so close to you and not knowing is unbearable..."

The silence that followed was unbearable as well. I didn't want him to go on, torturing himself over me, the girl who didn't love him.

I do love you, Charlie, but not in that way. Why can't you see that? What am I to do now? I don't want to hurt you...

I had to take him out of his misery. I had to be cruel to be kind, which was making me even more miserable. Opening my eyes, I swung my legs over the edge of the bed and sat up. My knees almost touched the wall and my face was right in front of the curtain, the green color of it not having the relaxing effect for which it was chosen. I took a deep breath.

"I don't love you, Charlie, I love Caleb."

There, I said it, now he knows...

"Caleb," Charlie spat, and I heard him turn onto his back. "What do you know about Caleb?"

Goosebumps appeared on my flesh. The temperature in the room seemed to have dropped a considerable amount of degrees. To my surprise, my mind switched sides to Charlie's.

Yeah, what do you know about Caleb?

"I...I can't explain, Charlie. I just know I love him and that he loves me."

"You don't know he loves you, Kate," Charlie said a tad bit too fast for my liking and with a tone that reminded me too much of the one my mother had used on occasions.

I didn't know what to say. I was struggling, trying to find the right words to express my feelings. Yes, I had feelings for Charlie. Dare I say I loved him? Yes, just not in that way. My feelings for Caleb were so much stronger, so much more intense. Yet my body winced at the thought of hurting Charlie, who had always been so good to me, always had such a positive effect on me. He was right that I didn't know much about Caleb, but every cell of my body yearned to find out. How could I let Charlie know how I felt about Caleb without hurting him at the same time?

I didn't need to worry for long about how to dispute his words as I heard Charlie get up, grab his clothes and slam the door of the bathroom behind him. His emotions of love, hurt and anger were swirling through the room like a whirlwind. They pulled out more sorrow I didn't know I had from deep within me and I dropped my head so my hands could catch my tears. I'd forgotten how close I was to the window and smacked my forehead on the windowsill concealed by the curtain.

Fuck!

"Fuck!" escaped from my lips. It was a true sign I was really upset as I hardly ever swore. I was annoyed for letting myself go like that and even more so by the fact that Charlie didn't come out of the bathroom to find out if I was okay. "Fine," I said under my breath, rubbing the bump that was coming up on my forehead. I quickly got dressed, grabbed my jacket and stepped out the room.

Wednesday Afternoon - Ponderings

Outside the sun was still shining. Standing in the shadows of the verandah, I blinked heavily and I hesitated to move.

I can't do this anymore...

I wanted to go away so badly, get in a car and leave the misery behind me. I wanted to feel the warmth of the sun on my face and just drive, I didn't care where to. True, I wanted to find Caleb, but it was more than that. I wanted normality, the boredom of going to work every day, laughing children around me. And I wanted to visit my parents and my sisters.

"Please don't go," I heard a quiet voice say behind me. It took me back to reality. I turned around and saw Charlie had come out of the bathroom. "You'll expose us all..."

Again, he looked so helpless standing there, his fate depending on my decision. The stupidity of what I had just contemplated hit me. I let my jacket fall to the floor. Guilt mixed with despair overtook me and I dropped to the floor. I cried. Charlie hurried over. He kneeled down and put his arms around me. I returned the embrace, put my head on his shoulder, and continued to cry and cry. Charlie let me and was silent all the while. When there were no more tears coming he unlocked our arms and wiped the remaining tears from my face.

"Look, if you are so sure about Caleb, I will help you find him."

They were the sweetest words I had ever heard.

"Would you do that for me, Smudge?" I asked as I held his hands.

"Of course, Kate, I would do anything for you. I thought you knew that by now."

You're the best, Charlie!

I smiled at him. Even though I had been so upset with him a few moments ago, I was so glad to have Charlie in my life. He was the rock I could cling to, while the turbulent torrent of chaos that surrounded me was trying to grab me, trying to drown me.

He noticed the bump on my forehead and gently touched it. "You want some ice on that?" he asked.

"No, it's okay," I said, and I couldn't suppress a yawn.

"Let's go inside again," Charlie said. I nodded.

We lay on the bed and I put my head on his shoulder, my arm around him. Charlie hesitated for a moment, but then probably decided that I would be okay if he put his arms around me. With one hand he stroked my hair and we lay like this for a while. Being so close to Charlie was soothing and I was feeling safe enough to fall into a deep sleep. When I woke up again the sun had gone down.

Wednesday Evening - Mysteries

This time the exercise class had to wait until the sun's rays left the sky as we had to do it in the open space of the square in the center of the village.

"How was your rest?" Harry asked with a big grin on his face while we were stretching our calf muscles.

"None of your business," Charlie replied before I could think of an appropriate answer.

I glanced at Charlie, but he continued with the exercises as if nothing had happened. I didn't want Harry to feel bad about the question, so I returned it.

"How was yours?"

"Probably not as good as yours," he said with a wink, "but not too bad either. I may sleep in a hotel as well one of these days." His smile was from ear to ear. I noticed a blush on his cheeks.

"Oooh, who's the lucky girl, Harry?" I asked him as we switched to stretching the other leg.

I saw Charlie shook his head, but he didn't say anything.

"It's Rhona over there. Remember her? Ben massaged her feet yesterday." He tipped his head in the girl's direction. I surveyed the crowd and recognized the girl. She was the one with the nasal voice. A petite thing with dainty features, I guessed of Italian blood. Her hair was short and curly, brown with a hint of auburn. She had big, dark eyes, with long lashes, a pixy-like nose, and full lips, covered in red lipstick. She was chewing gum with her mouth open, which I thought never suited anybody. It made me think of cows.

"Does she know about your, eh, rare blood disease?" I asked worriedly.

"Well, not how 'serious' it really is," Harry said, and his smile disappeared. "I haven't figured out how to deal with that yet, so I've been taking it real slow."

"Good thinking," Charlie said dryly.

I guessed Harry didn't hear him as he didn't react to Charlie's words. I couldn't help pick up the hint that Charlie regretted not taking the advice himself.

At the briefing, we were told we'd move on to the next town. This little village hadn't given enough blood to feed all of us and we needed to move on.

During the march, we didn't have to worry about Ben as he got the message of Charlie and I being an item after he heard from Harry we'd shared a room at the hotel. When everyone else around us appeared to be in conversations of their own, Charlie beat me to it and quietly asked Harry if he could help us get to Caleb's pack.

"Why do you want to?" was Harry first reaction.

Charlie glanced at me before answering. "We have our reasons, let's keep it at that. Would you be able to help us?"

You could see the cogs working in Harry's head. "It's going to be tricky, for reasons you already know. I've got to find out where Caleb's pack is first," he said. "But leave that to me." He smiled and increased his pace to join Rhona and her girlfriends.

I observed him chatting up the girls. They were laughing at every remark he made and Rhona was eyeing him all the time, full of adoration.

Yes, I think you'll be sleeping in a hotel room soon too, Harry...

From the corner of my eye, I saw Charlie look at me. When I turned my head to him, he gave me a quick smile and faced forward again. It occurred to me I should thank him for actually helping me, not just saying the words. I took his hand and squeezed it.

"Thanks," I said.

Without looking at me, he squeezed my hand back and kept holding it. I.t should have felt uncomfortable, but I wasn't. He let go when Harry returned.

"And?" I asked, doing a little skip.

"Good news and bad news," Harry said.

"What is it?" I was hanging off Harry's lips now.

"The good news is that I know where Caleb's pack is," Harry said.

"What's the bad news," Charlie asked. I held my breath.

"That Caleb's no longer with the pack."

What? Why?

The skip in my step disappeared instantaneously. Fear and dread coursed through my veins and I contemplated being sick or fainting. To keep myself going I wrapped my arms tightly around me, hugging my stomach and squeezing the blood in them towards my brain. My breathing became a conscious effort.

Could Caleb have died?

"The word is that he instructed his pack to continue," Harry said. "They're traveling parallel to us. But Caleb and Sasha have left the pack."

"Why?" Charlie asked, giving me a meaningful look. I was feeling slightly better, knowing that Caleb wasn't dead, although I still wasn't happy. It meant I had no idea where to look for him.

Harry shrugged his shoulders. "Nobody seems to know."

We walked on in silence for a while.

Where could Caleb be? How am I ever going to find him now?

"So what do you guys want to do?" Harry asked all of a sudden. "Get to the pack or to Caleb?"

"I need to get to Caleb," I replied instantly. I tried not to put too much emotion in my voice, but Harry picked up the vibe.

"Why? Are you...? You and Caleb...?" He looked at Charlie and then back at me. Neither of us said anything. "So you two are not...?" and he pointed his finger from Charlie to me and back to Charlie again. I could tell he had a million questions.

Charlie remained silent.

"No, we are not," I said with downcast eyes.

"Wow," Harry said, eyebrows raised, "you could have fooled me."

Charlie and I both tried to avoid eye contact with anyone at that point.

"Okay," Harry continued, "let me think on it and we'll talk about this when we have a bit more privacy."

We walked in silence for the rest of the march. My mind went round in circles trying to find a reason why Caleb had left his pack and where he could be right now. But I couldn't come up with anything solid.

Wednesday Night - Disagreement

That night, when we were sitting on another kitchen floor, eating a reheated batch of lasagna, Harry told us of the plan he thought up and a hefty discussion broke out between Charlie and himself. Charlie didn't like it that Harry wanted to involve Rhona.

"But it's only to save everybody's neck," Harry explained. "If she also testifies that she saw you two getting killed by humans then we have a greater chance they will not get suspicious."

"But can you trust her?" Charlie muttered, rather agitated.

Harry sighed. "I already told you, I don't know until I ask her."

It was obvious Charlie had set his mind on dismissing the plan. As we didn't have another plan I had to convince him.

"Charlie," I said as calmly as I could, "we don't have to tell her we're normal. All she has to know is that we want to leave Duncan's pack. Everybody knows Duncan doesn't want us in his pack, so everyone will be happy when we're gone."

Charlie looked at me, shadows making his face look ominous. "I don't like putting more lives at risk." He slid his finished plate onto the floor.

His words made me feel so selfish. Involving Rhona would make her an accomplice and put her risk the wrath of Duncan, whatever that was, should things go wrong. "Okay, let's think of another plan."

"No," Harry said resolutely. He pointed his finger to Charlie. "This is the only way. Duncan will never let you leave, and he will certainly never let you go over to Caleb's pack. We must set it up as if you've died. It's the only way to get you two to leave."

"I know..." Charlie said. His words sounded like coming from a corpse.

Why is Charlie so negative? Harry's got a good point...

"I tell you what, Charlie," I said, "let me talk to Rhona tomorrow night. If I can persuade her to help us out of her own free will, we'll go ahead with it. If she shows any sign of objection, we won't do it."

Harry and I had to persuade Charlie a bit more but in the end, he agreed with the plan, pending on Rhona's reaction. It meant I would be another day away and possibly further from Caleb, but it was the only way.

After the feeding that night, Harry invited Rhona to come hunting with us the next night. She was over the moon with the fact he was taking a step towards a relationship. She was obviously madly in love with Harry and it provided me with the angle for my upcoming talk with her.

We slept in a large bar at the edge of town this time. It was one of those truckers' stops and even had a dance floor. After the gathering, Duncan called out the names of the suckers who hadn't survived the last few days' hunts. They were too many, but a small number compared to the humans who hadn't survived the sucker attacks. Instead of everyone being down, the whole pack went into a state of ecstasy, apparently very happy to be alive. They threw a party to celebrate the new additions to the pack, the fact that everybody had fed enough, and their survival. And according to intel, I realized Duncan had his trained drones for this, there was no enemy movement in the area and the remaining citizens posed no threat. They felt safe enough to throw a party. The music was loud and the crowd was heaving with sweaty bodies.

I too wanted to dance. Knowing I could soon leave Duncan's pack and finally get back to Caleb made me feel happier than I'd been in a long time. Unfortunately, Charlie told me to keep a low profile.

"The less of them noticing us the better, as the less of them will miss us and get suspicious,' he said.

I knew he was right of course. But my soul ached to dance. So I watched the heaving mob from the sidelines and imagined myself dancing with Caleb.

Thursday Night - Involving Rhona

We were told we'd begin the next night in the same town before moving on. It appeared Duncan didn't want to leave anyone behind unturned or dead. At hunting time, we set out with Rhona in our group. She was as giddy as a teenager in love, which she was of course if I guessed her age right. I could relate to her. I just hoped I could get her to relate to me as well.

She was walking next to Harry, chatting away with him when I linked my arm with hers and asked if I could have a private word with her.

"Oh, okay," she said, disappointed on her face as she looked at Harry.

"It's okay," Harry said, "I won't go away."

I held her back but continued walking with her a few paces behind Harry and Charlie. "You love him?" I asked her.

"Hell yeah, I do." Her whole face lit up as she said it. "He's so cute!"

"How long have you known him," I asked her, sincerely curious.

"Only a few days," she said, "but it was love at first sight. The other girls think he's cute too, but they aren't interested in him as he's got this blood disease and isn't strong at all. I don't care about that. I'm not as shallow as the other girls. They only think he's a nice piece of ass. But I saw how he took you and Charlie under his wing when you arrived and I how he cared and all for you two and I knew he was a keeper." She went on and while she talked, I watched the bubblegum going through her mouth.

She must have an endless supply of the stuff.

I had to suppress the teacher in me who wanted to make her spit out the gum. I realized she was drifting off the track I had tried to steer our conversation along. I had to stop her chatting.

"So you love him very much?" I cut in while she was taking a breath before continuing her gossip on the other girls of the pack.

"Yeah, yeah, I do. I just told you," she said.

"There's someone I love very much too," I said. I put in a smile for good measure.

"Yeah, I know. Charlie seems to be a really nice guy," she said, without blinking an eye.

Ouch!

"It's not Charlie, Rhona."

She stopped and looked at me. I thought her lower jaw was going to hit her knees.

"It's not Charlie?"

"No, it's not," and I pulled her along to keep her walking. I continued before she could ask who it was.

"Charlie is very dear to me, but I love someone else and Charlie is helping me to get to him." Rhona listened full of curiosity. "In order find the person I love, we need to leave Duncan's pack and we are wondering if you would be willing to help us with that." This time it was me who stopped walking and I looked her straight in the eye.

"Oh, okay, eh, I'm not sure what I can do," she said. As she moved her weight from one leg to the other, her hand rubbing her neck, I realized that she was uncomfortable.

This isn't going as well as I had hoped...

Fortunately, Harry came to the rescue.

"You don't have to do much, Sweet Pea," he said as he and Charlie had turned around and were walking back towards us. They obviously had been following our conversation.

Harry put his arm around Rhona's shoulders.

"All you have to do is agree with what I tell Duncan when we get back to the pack."

Rhona didn't need a long time to think.

"Oh, is that it?" she asked and with a big smile on her face she said, "I can do that."

"Great!" Harry said.

"Yeah, you're a real life saver, Rhona," I said. I put my hand on her arm to emphasize my words.

And with that, the matter was settled. A heavy weight lifted itself from my shoulders. Charlie didn't say anything, but I could read his face like an open book.

Although... I can see you're not happy. But are you moping about the setup or is it because of what I said to Rhona?

Thursday Night - The Escape

We had decided the night before that if Rhona decided to help us out, Charlie and I would steal a get-away-car and try to escape immediately. Suckers would go over the whole town to make sure they didn't skip anyone, so going into hiding would still be dangerous, I argued. My main reason was that I didn't want to waste precious time, but I didn't tell them that.

Soon after Rhona agreed to help us, Charlie and I said our goodbyes to Harry and Rhona. I gave Harry a big hug, thanked him for all his help and wished him good luck, winking in Rhona's direction. I hugged Rhona as well and told her to take good care of Harry. She giggled and wished me luck finding my man. Charlie and Harry shook hands but didn't say anything. Charlie only nodded to Rhona, but she gave him a hug anyway. As we walked away, I wondered if we would ever see them again. It was beginning to be a normal question nowadays.

Charlie and I went to the part of town closest to the Bullsbrook exit, in order to make the escape as straightforward and complication-free as possible. We picked out a huge 4WD standing on a driveway. It looked like it was fast and sturdy enough to withstand some damage, should we encounter any resistance. We were lucky to find it as there weren't many vehicles left in the streets.

The moon cast shadows and we used them to hide our movement. When we thought there was nobody around we casually walked to the side of the car and I lifted the handle. It was locked. I looked at Charlie, but he shrugged his shoulders. "I would lock it too," he whispered.

I scanned the ground around us, but couldn't find a rock or anything to throw through the window.

Why is there never one when I need one?

I tried breaking a side window with my elbow, as you saw them do in the movies and as I had done with the thrift shop door-window, but all it resulted in was me silently doing a bent-over rain dance, holding my elbow. Charlie clapped his hand over his mouth and tried not to laugh out loud.

Thanks for the compassion, Smudge!

I stopped dancing and gave him my evil stare.

"Sorry, it just looked too funny," he whispered. "Are you okay?"

"Yes, I'll live..."

"Come on then," and he pulled me by my jacket to the back of the house the driveway belonged to. When we got to the back door Charlie broke one of the windows without a problem and we went into the house. It was a mess, with upturned furniture throughout. There would be no humans here anymore.

"Let's look for the car keys," Charlie said.

"Great idea."

We looked in the usual places; kitchen drawers, pockets of jackets, and key rack. After a few minutes we found them in a dish on the hallway cupboard, the logo on the keyring matched the one on the car. We sneaked around the back again and as we walked, crouching along the side of the house to the front, I tapped Charlie, who was walking in front of me, on the shoulder.

"What?" he asked but didn't stop moving.

"We're stupid."

He stopped now.

"Why? I thought we were very clever finding the car keys," he said as he turned his head to me.

"Yes that was clever, but we probably could have left through the front door."

Charlie shrunk with a giggle and I had to suppress laughing myself.

"Never mind, we're almost here now," he said and walked on.

We crept into the shade of the left side of the car and Charlie pressed the button on the key fob. 'Bleep,' the car said and the four blinkers flashed simultaneously. We waited, but nobody turned up to have a look. Charlie opened the door and motioned for me to get in first. Once inside, I moved over to make space for him and he closed the door as quietly as he could. We sat in the car with our heads low, waiting until we were sure nobody would jump out at us from the shadows. Nothing happened.

"Drive," I said to Charlie, anxiously keeping a lookout for anything suspicious.

"I can't drive this car," he said, with a tone suggesting I was an idiot. I looked at his face and then at the movement of his legs.

How can I be so stupid?

"We've got to change seats," Charlie whispered.

"Okay, you shove this way and I'll climb over you," I said.

We both began moving and as I lifted my body Charlie grabbed me by my hips and helped me lift myself over his without touching him. I thought it was thoughtful of him to do so as there wasn't a lot of space for the maneuver and it could have put us in an awkward situation. When we had swapped seats he giggled.

"What?" I asked him, as I adjusted the seat and the rear view mirror.

"Don't worry, just drive," he said, waving his hand, but still grinning.

"No, tell me," I insisted.

"You really don't want to know," he replied again. Apparently, it was extremely funny as he couldn't get the smile off his face.

"Yes I do, and I won't drive until you tell me," I whispered, taking my hands off the steering wheel and demonstratively laying them on my thighs.

"You asked for it," and he suppressed another giggle. "I just couldn't help noticing that this was the second time this week you were on top of me." He was looking straight ahead, trying to suppress his laughter.

The cheeky bugger!

I couldn't believe my ears. Here we were, fearing for our lives, trying to get me to the love of my life, and Charlie was thinking dirty thoughts about me. Again!

But it was funny.

"Smudge!" was all I could think of saying and slapped him playfully on the arm. Charlie laughed out loud. I couldn't help but smile, hearing him laugh again was good, and I turned the ignition key.

The car made a hell of a noise, which we could have expected from the size of it. It was facing the house, so I had to reverse into the street. The car was almost parallel with the street when I saw them stepping onto the road about thirty meters in front of us. Two suckers blocked our way.

"Hit it!" Charlie shouted.

I changed gear and floored the gas pedal. One of the suckers pulled out a gun and began shooting at us.

"Holy shit! They've got guns!" Charlie yelled ducking down.

We'd heard gunshots during the hunts, but somehow I'd always assumed they were used by humans in defense, not suckers attacking. I thought suckers would want to prevent to spill their food. Unfortunately, these suckers were of the opinion that if they couldn't have our blood, neither could we.

"Get down!" Charlie shouted, pulling my jacket, but I was pumped with adrenaline. Nobody was going to keep me away any longer from finding Caleb. While I kept my head low, I decided to play chicken. I kept going straight for the guy with the gun. A shot was fired and the windshield shattered, blocking my view for a second. Glass fell everywhere, but fortunately it was safety glass. I noticed the shooter's aim was getting better as the next shot whizzed past my head, whirling my hair. Just before I was about to hit him, I recognized him. It was Mr. Ugly Sweater. In a flash, I went back to the town square in Bullsbrook and saw his ugly face close in front of me, smelled his horrible breath. I willed the car to go even faster, but the other sucker pulled Mr. Ugly Sweater out of the way just in time.

Such a pity...

It didn't take him long before he was on his feet again, shooting at our backlights. I started to drive erratically from left to right, throwing Charlie from side to side in the car, desperately trying to avoid being hit. Both of us had forgotten to put on our seatbelts and I nearly lost control of the steering wheel. I hit a parked car and heard a bullet hit metal, but nothing happened. We got away unscathed.

Friday Morning, Early - The Village

When we were at a safe distance from the town and sure we weren't being followed by suckers in cars, I told Charlie I had recognized Mr. Ugly Sweater as the shooter. He didn't get my point immediately, so I had to spell it out.

"If I recognized him, do you think he could've recognized me?" I said. I was back to biting the skin next to my nails again.

"Oh shit..." Charlie said as he realized the implications. "Do you think Harry is in trouble?" I threw a glance at him and noticed he was looking pale.

"I don't know, Charlie. Harry does have Rhona as a backup for his story. It's their word against his. I just hope Harry can pull it off and they believe him..."

My mind drifted off into possible scenarios, but I didn't dare to utter them out loud, just in case I would jinx them. The brick in my stomach tried out an Irish dance.

We drove on in silence along the highway. Clouds appeared and blocked out the moonlight. The road ahead was dark, like my mind was now. I wanted to talk to Charlie, but I didn't know what to say to him. I felt so stupid and irresponsible. I had put so many lives in danger because of my love for Caleb. It was my problem, not theirs. Yet Charlie, Harry, and Rhona had risked their lives for my happiness. I could've hit my head on the road surface again and again. And I would have if it wasn't for the fact I'd have to stop the car first and it wouldn't make any difference to the situation.

I found Charlie's silence upsetting.

He's silent because he was against the whole plan in the first place. We didn't foresee this complication.

And because he's fighting his own demons for letting me go ahead with it, taking me further away from him, emotionally speaking.

I glanced at him and I saw his furrowed brow. Now and again he rubbed his face, as if trying to get rid of a thought. I decided not to start a conversation. There was nothing positive I could think of that Charlie would like to talk about.

The little village where we had spent the night at the motel came into sight. We were to drive past it and go straight to Bullsbrook, but the car began to slow down.

"Why are you slowing down?" Charlie asked.

"I'm not." I didn't understand what was happening.

Before long the engine stopped and we came to a complete halt. I tried to start the car again, but it refused to move an inch further. It took me a while, but I finally realized we were out of gas. I didn't know if we were just out of gas or whether the fact that the car had been hit by a bullet had anything to do with it. Whatever the reason, the fact remained that the fuel gauge was at zero and the car wasn't going anywhere.

"Well, that's it. We can't walk to Bullsbrook tonight," I said, my heart growing heavier with every word. I felt the pain of Caleb getting further and further away from me, despair strangling me like a boa constrictor, squeezing the life out of me.

"No, we can't," Charlie said. "But if we walk fast we could get another car in the village and still make it to Bullsbrook tonight."

His words cheered me up big time. I looked at him with a great grin on my face and said, "Awesome thinking, Charlie."

We set a fast pace towards the village.

The last few nights had been clear, but tonight clouds had kept gathering and as we hurried to the village it began to rain. We held our jackets over our heads and ran. Expecting the village to be deserted, we made no effort to hide our presence. As before, it still looked dreadful, the rain adding to the misery. Puddles were forming in the streets and we had to jump over them here and there. As we slowed down, we noticed movement. Slowly, a group of people came out from the shadows. They didn't look friendly. In no time we were surrounded by these angry-looking people. We hadn't anticipated this situation at all. We thought everyone in the village had fled, been killed, or turned and moved on. The number of survivors wasn't great, but they were there and I felt proud that humans could be so successful in hiding from a deadly enemy.

Go humans!

Unfortunately, these good people were not as happy with us as I was with them and, quite frankly, they were scaring the life out of me. They didn't know Charlie and I were unturned, but they weren't taking any chances. They had taken some effort to look like a lynch mob, carrying guns and stakes and all sorts of other pointy implements. Slowly, we put our hands up. As they got closer and surrounded us, Charlie and I put our backs together. I looked around, hoping to find a person in charge but couldn't see one. What I saw was a mix of people; old, young, male, female. And they had one thing in common; they all had hate written across their faces. Suddenly someone yelled out 'They're suckers. Kill them!' This roused the whole group into shouting as they moved in.

"Hang on," Charlie tried to make himself heard over the top of them. "We're human! We're like you!"

But the people were shouting things like 'Look at their fangs!', 'Filthy suckers!', and 'Murderers!' They didn't listen. They didn't *want* to listen. As we showed no sign of resistance they grabbed us and dragged us to a blind wall. Charlie kept on trying to convince them, begging them to listen to him.

The whole situation was terrifying and I too began shouting.

"We're human! We're in disguise, please, listen to us!"

It was hopeless. These people were angry. Their families, friends, and neighbors had been taken from them and they wanted revenge. They pushed us against the wall and as one they backed off.

"Charlie?" I hoped he would come up with a miracle rescue. But he too couldn't think of something.

As two guys with rifles stood opposite us and lifted their weapons to aim, the people went quiet. Charlie turned towards me and said, "I'm so sorry, Kate," and he took my hands and turned me towards him, preventing me from directly looking at the death squad.

I put a hand on his face, a gentle and caring touch. As I closed my eyes, a tear escaped and images of my life flashed in front of me. I always thought people made this stuff up, but it really happened. I heard the two guys cocking their guns.

My eyes flew open and I yelled out.

"Harry!" I took my hand from Charlie's face, looked around at the crowd and again yelled, "Harry. We were with Harry!"

Somebody must have found the note in the refrigerator.

People were looking strangely at me, tipping their heads and turning to each other with confused expressions.

"Wait!" a woman shouted. She stepped forward and put her hand on one of the rifles aimed at us, pushing it down. Both the gun men looked at her quizzically. The woman's hair was disheveled, her dress ruffled. Her appearance was one of somebody who didn't care anymore. She peered at me and tucked a string of hair behind her ear as if all of a sudden she did care. "What do you mean by 'we were with Harry'?"

My mouth went into overdrive. "We didn't kill anybody. We had to pretend to be suckers to survive. At night we went into houses and ate the food from the refrigerator and freezer to survive. We didn't kill anybody. We left notes in the refrigerator signed 'Harry,' to thank the people for their hospitality and apologize for the mess we made... We didn't kill anybody. We... didn't kill anybody." I was out of breath and fell silent, hoping the woman understood my waterfall of words. For a second it was quiet.

Then the woman gasped. "That was our house. You left the note in our house." Her eyes nearly fell out of their sockets as she turned around and yelled at everybody. "They left the note in our house!"

"Eh, yeah, we left the note in their house," I said to the people.

The woman took her turn to be a waterfall of words, explaining to all how they had survived the sucker attack. I bit my lip and put one hand in my back pocket. Charlie was still holding my other hand and squeezed it. We exchanged hopeful glances.

The woman turned to us and gasped again. "Oh, my God, and we nearly killed you." She ran towards me and hugged me, held my head in her hands, patting my hair, crying, and thanking me a thousand times. With one arm she pulled Charlie into the hug. The angry mob turned into a confused bunch of humans.

The whole situation wasn't over yet as most of them still didn't accept our innocence. They looked at our necks and pointed at our marks. We explained we'd made them ourselves to avoid being discovered. They aimed bright torchlights into our eyes, one of them being a black light. As much as I tried, I couldn't look into it. Charlie had no problem with it and he gave the villagers the explanation I couldn't because we'd spent most of our time in darkness these last few days and my eyes, being blue, were more sensitive. The villagers believed him, but as he shot me a quick glance I knew Charlie wasn't so convinced himself.

We let them inspect our fake fangs as if we were horses on a market. Only when we ripped our fake fangs off, with much trouble, did they believe us.

Memo to myself: remember the brand of glue.

There were a hundred and one questions for us, but I didn't want to deal with them. I desperately wanted to get to Bullsbrook to begin looking for Caleb. I came up with the story that I needed to save my sister and asked them if anybody had a vehicle we could borrow to get to her. The husband of the woman who saved us didn't hesitate and gave us his car keys.

"Thanks, man," Charlie said to him, "we owe you."

But the man shook his head. "No, it is us who owe you." He turned around to pick up his son and embrace his wife.

Charlie and I said our goodbyes and soon went on our way in our newly acquired vehicle.

Friday Morning, Early - Back to Bullsbrook Again

At last, we were on our way to find Caleb again, which made Charlie's mood worsen. I could only imagine what he felt right now, getting closer to losing me.

In contrast, I felt elated. How lucky were we, to not have been turned, able to escape from Duncan's pack, surviving a lynching party, and finally on our way to find Caleb. There was a huge grin on my face. Every time I looked at Charlie he smiled back at me, but it was the smile of someone who'd just had a root canal treatment. I didn't want to hurt him unnecessarily, so I stopped looking and didn't start a conversation. He didn't either.

It was still night-time when we arrived in Bullsbrook. I stopped in the middle of the road and let the car run stationary before we reached the first house. My knuckles turned white on the steering wheel. I hated not being in control, not knowing what was going to happen.

"Charlie, I don't know what to do now."

He thought for a while and said, "You want to find Caleb."

"Yeah, but I don't know where to look. He may not be here anymore." I sighed.

"We'll find him, Kate. Let's begin where you saw him last. That's usually the first thing to do."

My eyes glazed over as I let my memory wander. Caleb had me pressed into a corner, his fangs caressing my flesh... I took a deep breath. "The school it is then," and I put the gear into drive.

I drove slowly to avoid the obstacles in the streets such as upturned trolleys, garbage bins, and the likes. Nothing had changed since we left. I didn't drive too slow either as I didn't want to be surprised by people trying to attack us.

We entered the school grounds and parked the car in the staff parking lot. After killing the engine we scanned our surroundings. When we didn't see anyone, we got out of the car and together we hurried towards one of the auxiliary buildings. We hugged the wall as we moved on. I took a peek around the corner towards the main schoolyard. My heart skipped a beat as I couldn't believe my luck. There stood Caleb! Excited, I turned to Charlie and whispered to him, "Caleb's here!"

Charlie wasn't mirroring my enthusiasm, quite the contrast actually. His face showed a mix of disappointment, sadness, and fear, but I refused to see it.

I turned around again to go to Caleb, but Charlie grabbed my arm. Annoyed, I looked at him.

"Kate," he whispered, "are you sure you want to do this? What if…"

"Charlie," I interrupted him and grabbed both his hands. "We talked about this before. Yes, I really want to do this. And no, there is no way on earth you can stop me now."

I can't believe he is even trying.

"I don't know, Kate, I have a bad feeling about this." Charlie's expression was of somebody in pain. His shoulders were hunched and he had a grimace on his face. His hands were squeezing mine so hard it almost hurt.

He was staring at me now. It was obvious he expected me to say something. When I didn't, he took a deep breath and let his body relax, letting go of his grip of my hands.

"But if you're one-hundred percent sure, I'll let you go. I'll be in the staff room if you need me."

Again, he waited for me to say something. Eventually, he gave one hand a little squeeze. Without another word he turned around and walked away from me.

Rubbing my hands I watched Charlie go. As he walked away, it was as if a part of me was walking away. I always felt so at ease with Charlie, he made me laugh and soothed my pains. He made me whole. He was my dearest friend and I loved him so much. But I wasn't in love with him, I was sure I wasn't. Yet I had feelings for him I couldn't explain. It confused the hell out of me. I'd hurt Charlie by rejecting him and it was painful to see him hurt. How I wished there was something I could do to ease his pain, but what he needed was something I couldn't give.

Would be a nice book title; 'The girl who didn't love him.'

Life can be such a bitch...

When I returned from my thoughts to the here and now I realized Charlie was gone. Had he looked back at me? Had he hesitated and waited for me to come running for him at the last moment? I didn't know. I didn't want to know.

I turned around, closed my eyes, and breathed deeply a few times. I wasn't sure what I was going to say to Caleb, I was too excited all of a sudden to have any coherent thoughts. So I turned the corner and walked in the direction where I had seen him a minute before.

Friday Morning -Reunited with Caleb

As I walked onto the schoolyard my mind registered the scene. The sky was overcast, the ground still wet from rain that had fallen here earlier, and the moonless night colored everything in different shades of gray. The school buildings loomed a near black as the rainwater had darkened the brickwork. The schoolyard was empty but for Caleb and the dead bodies from the feeding. The bodies were piled up in two distinct heaps and stank a horrible smell of death. Water dripped from lampposts, like huge teardrops mourning the loss of all those innocent lives, their drips a monotonous sound of sadness. The whole scene could very well have been taken from some gruesome Second World War movie.

The downpour in the village had soaked me and I was chilled to the bone, but I wasn't sure if the wet clothing clinging to my body was the cause of my chills. All my senses were screaming at me to get away.

I resigned to be more focused on Caleb, who stood in between the two heaps of bodies. He was going through the pockets of a dead person he was holding. I shivered and wrapped my arms around me. As I walked on, I saw that the body Caleb was holding was in an unnatural position, as if it was being held up by somebody else. Walking closer, my view swept around the pile of bodies.

Sasha...

When I had first seen Caleb I had thought him to be alone. What a disappointment the sight of Sasha was. Her presence brought an acid taste to my mouth. It appeared Sasha and Caleb were searching the dead bodies from top to toe, together. When they finished searching the body, they added it to one heap and picked up another one from the other heap. I heard them talk now. I got the feeling they were very agitated, arguing, their communication tense. The closer I came, the louder my senses screamed at me.

Get out! Get away now you still can!

Sasha saw me first, she let go of the body.

"Well, well, well. Look what the cat dragged in," she said to Caleb in that accent of hers. I realized I wasn't looking my best after the recent downpour and lynching party.

At least my hair is real, bitch!

Caleb looked up from the body he was searching, followed Sasha's stare, and threw me a quick glance.

Did I see a smile?

"Who's that?" he said with a frown that seemed a bit over the top, as he turned back to Sasha.

If I had been too dumb to listen to my senses, Caleb's words were like a slap in my face. I couldn't believe my ears. I hesitated, taken aback for a moment. I walked on, rebelling against the frantic screams of my common sense which couldn't get any louder. Surely I had been too far away yet for Caleb to recognize me.

"Don't you remember, darling?" Sasha said. "She's the one you left behind."

My common sense rested its case.

She calls him 'darling,' he is her 'darling.'

But there's something off about it.

"Ah, now I remember," Caleb said as he fully turned towards me and looked me straight in the eye.

Immediately I was lost in those deep, brown eyes like I had before and our souls were one. We were floating together in eternity until, within an instant, my stare was thrown out of the deep and hit a shallowness that belonged to a cold-blooded killer. My body halted; footsteps, heartbeat, and breath. I struggled with the flood of feelings thundering through me. Confusion, disbelief, betrayal, hurt. One moment I had found my soul mate, the next I was eye to eye with a murderer. Yet there was something, or at least there had been for a split second. I made up my mind. I hadn't come all this way for nothing. I had to know for sure.

I'm not a quitter!

"What are you doing?" I asked, changing the tense air into that of common chitchat.

He laughed the laugh I once thought was cute. It sounded so hollow now.

"If you must know, Sasha here lost her heirloom necklace in the hunt a couple of days ago and we're still looking for it, can you believe it?" He half-pushed, half-dropped the body he was holding and threw an angry stare at Sasha, blaming her for the predicament he was in. He was clearly not happy with her. She crossed her arms in reply.

"So you weren't looking for me?" I asked before I could stop myself.

"Oh my god, Caleb!" Sasha screamed while throwing her hands in the air. "I am really getting so tired of this bimbo fan club of yours."

Caleb sighed as he half turned to Sasha. He hung his head, turned it slightly to me, and lifted an eyebrow.

I frowned. He was sending out such mixed signals.

He inhaled deeply before he said to her in icy tones, "*Darling*, you've got to let me have these little pleasures. At least I don't cheat on my partner like you did with Duncan." His mouth may have smiled, but his eyes were as cold as an arctic winter's day.

"You don't tell me what to do, Caleb. I am not one of your cutesy toys," Sasha screamed, pushing her finger into Caleb's chest.

I couldn't believe they were having a fight right in front of me as if I wasn't there. My parents had never exchanged angry words in our presence. I had assumed it was 'not done' and nobody had ever proven me wrong. I shivered from the emotions racing through the atmosphere, mine and theirs, and I put my hands in my trouser pockets to try and stop myself from shaking.

"You chose to be mine, Sasha, and I told you I wouldn't share you with anyone else." Caleb's face was turning red, the veins in his temples stood out. He was really upset.

As I dug my hands deeper into my pockets, I found the packet with the little strip of magnesium. Without thinking, I tore open the little bag, letting the oil seep out. Automatically my thumb started to scratch the surface of the strip of magnesium. My other hand gripped the lighter in my other pocket.

"Well, look who's calling the kettle black! You're throwing yourself at every floozy you see!" Sasha threw her arm out in my direction.

So that's what I am to you, a floozy...

"And I am not yours. I belong to nobody," she continued, still pushing her finger into Caleb's chest. "You are the one who is mine, *I* made *you*, remember. And I am sick and tired of you treating me like one of your little sluts." They were standing very close now, their noses almost touching, her face color matching the crimson of Caleb's.

"Go back to your Duncan then, if you want him so badly," Caleb shouted to Sasha.

You don't have to shout, you know, you're standing right in front of each other...

"I could, you know, Duncan still loves me," Sasha shouted back.

"No, he doesn't," I said. The words slipped out of my mouth before I could stop them.

They both slowly turned their heads to me. Before I could think of a way of making time go backward, Sasha had raced forward and held me by my throat with one hand, my feet dangling. I flung my arms out for balance.

"What do you mean?" she screeched at me. I couldn't say anything with her hand tightly around my throat, making the blood pressure in my head rise. I suppose my head turning the same color of hers made her realize I couldn't answer this way, so she let me down enough for my toes to touch the ground and she could lessen her grip. "Say it!"

I balanced on my tippy toes like a ballerina and managed to take a deep breath. "Duncan doesn't love you, he loves my sister Julie," I said through the pain of her still pinching claws.

I saw Caleb grab Sasha's free arm, but she yanked it loose and lashed out at him with such force that he fell. I thought Sasha was going to explode as her face was turning a deeper shade of red now. I had to act fast, being sure I was only seconds away from my demise by Sasha's hand. Now that I was touching the ground, I managed to get my hands behind my back and tried to ignite the magnesium strip with the lighter.

"You're lying, bitch. You're lying. Tell me you're lying!" Sasha screamed, again and again, shaking me to and fro on the rhythm of her words. It was almost impossible to get the flame near the strip of magnesium in my other hand, but then I heard a sudden whoosh as it ignited. With no idea how long it would burn, I wasted no time and swung my arm forward, throwing the flimsy piece of metal, engulfed in a bright, white light, straight at Sasha's face. The next moment went into slow motion.

I saw the ball of light bounce off her skin and her whole body shook as if she were electrified. The light burnt on my retinas as well and I went into a state opposing complete darkness. Engulfed in light and, paradoxically, completely blinded, I felt Sasha let go of my throat. Stumbling forward I struggled to keep my balance. There was a dull thud as Sasha fell to the ground. When I tried to look at her, I could see only the outline of her convulsing body.

Another outline raced towards me and Caleb grabbed my arms.

"What have you done?" he yelled. There was a guttural rasp of despair in his voice. "This time I won't let you get away." And he moved for my neck.

Forcing myself backwards, I fought to get away from his face, but he threw his arm around me, preventing my escape. It was as if he held me in some perverse imitation of a loving embrace.

How different this was from our first encounter. That first time I'd felt only exhilaration when he was close, his breath on my neck and his lips on my skin sending ecstatic shivers through my body. Dreaming of the touch of his lips on my skin again, reliving that moment of lust and longing, was all I'd thought about.

Now it was actually happening, I was paralyzed with mortal fear. His body was a shimmer, but his closeness was ever more present and threatening. I'd never been this scared my whole life.

Without another word, he sank his teeth into me, his fangs piercing my skin and jugular in one go. The pain was excruciating and I knew he was going to drain my blood in revenge for what I had done to his beloved Sasha. As he sucked at my neck, drinking my life's juices, I knew there was nothing I could do to stop him. The world around me was turned upside down, my insides were being sucked out, and in a haze of pure light I slid into darkness.

Friday Morning - Bitten

When I regained consciousness, I was lying on the ground. Slowly rolling onto my side, I sat up and looked around me. My vision still wasn't okay, with everything being a few grades lighter than normal. My mind was dazed and for the life of me I couldn't remember a thing. I saw two figures run off in the distance. I turned towards a noise coming from the opposite side and saw a large vehicle with a huge, bright beam of light on top entering the schoolyard. The light frightened me and I scrambled up to get away. Stumbling to the side of a building, I hid in the shadows, leaning against the wall. From the safety of the darkness, I could make out a shape hurrying towards me.

"Kate," the shape yelled. I recognized the voice as Charlie's.

Man, am I glad to see you!

I began walking towards him. As Charlie came running I felt the earth drop from under me. He caught me before I hit the ground and my head flopped backwards, exposing my neck.

"Oh god, no!" I heard him say, just before I passed out again.

When I came to for the second time, my hearing returned first. I heard someone crying "No, please no! Please, god, no!"

What's the drama?

Then I became aware of the sensation of movement, as if I were on a boat.

Strange.

I opened my eyes and reality returned. Charlie was holding me. He was rocking my body back and forth in his embrace.

"Charlie," I said.

He stopped rocking me. When he looked at me I saw his red eyes and tears streaming over his cheeks.

"Charlie," I said again, smiling, and lifted my hand to his face, his long stubble wooly underneath my fingertips.

Charlie took my hand and kissed it. "I'm so sorry, Kate," he kept saying. More tears rolled over his face.

His presence was so soothing and it made me happy. His crying confused me though.

Why is he crying? Why is he sorry?

I blinked a few times, trying to get my brain into gear, then moved to get up.

"Are you okay to walk?" Charlie said.

"I don't know. I think so." He helped me up. I needed a few seconds to get stable.

"Let's get you out of here fast," he said, "the army has arrived."

We started moving further into the shadows, instinctively knowing Charlie was taking me home. All of a sudden my brain processed what Charlie had just said and I stopped.

"Shouldn't we go to the army then?" I asked him.

Charlie looked at me as if I'd asked him why the sky was green. I didn't understand his reaction.

"Let's get you to your place for now," he said.

I accepted his decision and I didn't think more of it. I let him guide me to wherever he wanted me to go.

As Charlie directed me through town, I realized he also hadn't taken me to our newly acquired car. At first I wondered why, but then figured I was in no state to drive. I still had no clue as to what was going on, so instead concentrated on moving forward step by step. We must have been walking for about five minutes when I heard a car drive up behind us. Charlie had heard it too and tried to pull me into the shadow of a house. The car stopped where we were and the door swung open.

"Charlie, Kate, get in," a voice said.

I couldn't believe it, it was Harry! Charlie turned me around and walked me to the car. I was so tired, I could hardly keep myself upright. Harry opened the hatchback and helped me get in. I thought it was a station wagon, but there were no seats. I didn't mind. I lay down on the floor, desperate to get some sleep. The windows appeared to be heavily tinted, so I knew they weren't going to cause a problem. I became aware of the presence of someone else in the back of the car. Charlie talked to this other person as he climbed in beside me and gave directions to Harry on how to get to my house. It wasn't far and before I could drift off, we arrived there. The back door opened again and Harry pulled me out. I tried to hang on to the inside of the car in vain. I was annoyed they didn't let me have a nap. Lifting me in his arms, Harry carried me inside. I liked being in his strong arms, it felt so much more comfortable than the car. His body was warm and soft, his arms strong. I put my arms around his neck.

When we got inside, however, he laid me on my bed and left me.

Finally, they are letting me sleep...

I heard them close the curtains and not long after I heard a woman's voice. I recognized it as Rhona's - she had such a typical nasal voice. She must have been the other person in the car. I drifted off, happy the band was back together.

Friday Morning - Realization

I must have drifted off for only a second as I didn't feel rested when I woke up. Somebody was touching my neck. It scared the hell out of me and I flung myself to the other side of the bed against the wall, unable to go any further. I heard Charlie say my name and try to calm me. I took a deep breath and took in my surroundings. I saw a strange scene.

Harry was sitting on the edge of my bed with gauze pads in one hand and a brown bottle in the other. It looked as if he was about to drug me with chloroform. He was watching me, concerned.

To his right was Rhona. She stood in the doorway, her red lips a beacon to my eyes. I couldn't read her expression.

Moving my head along, I saw Charlie. He was on the bed on his hands and knees, one hand had moved onto my knee. Part of my brain wanted to smile, but the other part was too frightened to let me. All eyes were focused on me.

"It's okay, Kate," Charlie said, "We're trying to help you."

I frowned.

Why would I need help?

"You've been bitten, Kate, by Caleb. We need to tend to your marks," Charlie said. He watched every move I made, his body tense and ready to move away from me.

Then the images came flooding back. My meeting with Caleb and Sasha, their arguing, my big mouth, Sasha grabbing me, the bright, white light, ... and Caleb biting me.

My hand went to my neck. It was sticky and my neck felt sore. Moving my hand into my view, I saw the blood. As my fingers touched my thumb, one at a time, I could smell the blood.

Holy shit, this is real. This isn't just a bad dream!

I kept looking at the blood on my hand. It stopped me from getting my mind to work.

"Kate, Harry needs to have a look at your neck," Charlie said again.

"Oh, okay," I said, and moved back towards Harry. Still not appreciating the situation fully, I understood I had to let him do what he needed to. I trusted Charlie. I trusted Harry.

Harry tended to my wounds and finished by sticking Band-Aids on my marks. "They're looking good, no tears," he said to Charlie.

Rhona gave a packet to Harry, who took out two pills and handed them to me. Rhona passed a glass of water and Harry told me to take the pills. I looked at the little white tablets in my hand.

"They're pain killers, for the pain of your fangs dropping," he said.

Crap...

I finally realized what was happening. It felt like I was sinking into a pit of tar, no way out but down. It was like the core of my being was being pulled into hell.

Do I still need to breathe?

Without another word, Harry packed up his stuff and left the room, taking Rhona with him. He closed the door behind him.

After I took the pills, I sat up against the bed head and looked at Charlie. He still sat on the bed, watching me.

"I'm so sorry, Kate," he said. There was a sadness in his eyes that was indescribable.

Why does he keep repeating himself?

I knew I was the cause of his sadness and I didn't know how to say sorry to him for making him feel this way. He didn't need to. I was the one that was stupid and dumb and immature. I was the only one to blame for the mess I was in.

"Why? This isn't your fault."

"Yes it is, I should have stayed with you," and he cast his eyes down.

"Look," I said, "I started this mess. I'm the one who's sorry for dragging you along with me." I leaned forward to put my hand on his shoulder, our faces now very close.

He looked up at me again with those sad eyes. They were baring the guilt of my soul. I couldn't keep my thoughts inside me anymore. I threw my body back against the bed head.

"Oh, how could I have been so stupid to think Caleb loved me?" I cried out.

My hands went to my head and I wanted to pull my hair out. I wanted to cry, but there was nothing there. It was as if Caleb had sucked the essence out of me and all that was left was an empty shell, a hollow person. I curled up in a ball and tried to hide behind my arms. I didn't want to face Charlie with my shame.

Charlie moved to sit next to me and put an arm around me.

"We all have our silly moments," he said.

I put my arm around him, laid my head on his shoulder, and we sat like that until we fell asleep together.

Friday Morning, Late - Hunger

I must have had a nightmare, because when I woke up I was upset. My mind had had some time to mull the whole situation over and I felt sad, angry and frustrated. I'd spent the last few days living towards a climax. I had expected to find love and be loved.

Instead, Caleb had treated me like a nobody, a floozy. All the love I saved up for him had gone unanswered, but the love was still there. I had so much love to give it was almost like it was spilling over from my body.

I turned my head and saw Charlie sleeping beside me. Charlie, who had been there for me from day one of this hellish nightmare. The jester, who had shown me in so many little ways that he loved me. And all I did was reject him. Still he had risked his own life for me to find Caleb. Why would he do that for me? Was I really so stupid to have missed what was right there in front of me, all along? Was I really such a cliché?

I had always liked Charlie. He was funny, sincere, and reliable. His presence made me happy. I couldn't say why, it just did. And lately there had been a tension of a sexual nature between us, I couldn't deny it. Definitely in the cabin, and that time when I found out he had been watching me get undressed in the shop, and when I had washed his hair. What about the way my feelings for him had flooded through me when my sister made me chose between Charlie and her. Not to mention the feeling I had for him when I was about to confront Caleb. I'd refused to believe it was love at the time, but now I realized the truth.

Charlie had feelings for me as well. He'd spelled it out for me in the motel room, he couldn't have been any clearer. I hadn't wanted to choose between him and Caleb then, but even after I had chosen Caleb, Charlie still stood by my side. I hadn't seen who he really was, what he really meant to me.

All of a sudden, a rush of love for Charlie washed over me and I kissed him softly on the cheek. He opened his eyes, looking pleasantly surprised. His reaction made me smile and impulsively I kissed him again, this time on the lips. I moved back and hesitated to open my eyes. When I did, he was smiling at me.

He moved up on his elbow. He brushed some hair out of my face, put his hand under my chin, and moved closer to kiss me more intensely. His kiss made me so happy and I put my arms around him. I'd finally found my fairy-tale prince to give all my love to.

The kisses were soft and sweet. He put his hand through my hair and it fueled my passion. Blood flooded into private places and it aroused me. It was as if I was getting drunk with love, my senses all going haywire. My kisses became harder and more urgent.

"Kate," Charlie said, in between his kisses, trying to get my attention. "Kate..."

I didn't reply. I kept kissing his face, my hands going through his hair, over his back, moving to the front...

"Kate, no," Charlie said again, and he stopped kissing me back.

Tears began to flow over my cheeks. I wanted to make love to Charlie so much.

Why are you saying no? I want you, Charlie. Isn't that what you want too?

I kept kissing him.

Charlie grabbed both my arms and pushed me away from him. "Kate, I can't do this," he said, "not like this."

In an instant, the passion that was flowing out of every single pore of my being turned into anger, from top to toe. It was like somebody had pulled a switch. I yanked myself loose, grabbed his arms and flung him from the bed. I had no idea where the strength came from and I didn't care. Looking down on him I could smell his fear. And it made me feel amazing. My eyes went to his neck and I could hear his jugular calling out for me. Drink me, drink me...

I saw Charlie's pupils go large and a split second later he scrambled up and ran out the door. Instantly I was up and on his heels, chasing him into the living room. I craved his blood more than anything in my whole life.

Rhona had been lying in Harry's embrace on the couch. They both sprang up when we dashed into the room. Harry was still taking in the situation as Charlie grabbed a chair and held it between him and me. Rhona, however, knew exactly what was going on and threw herself in front of me.

"No, Kate!" she yelled. "Not Charlie!" She pushed me away from him, throwing me against the wall.

I felt my pulse thumping in my head as my anger redirected itself from Charlie to Rhona. I scrambled back up, lunged forward, and pushed Rhona. She fell backward against the window, clutching the curtain in an attempt to stay upright. It tore from the rod and light flooded the living room. As sun rays fell on Rhona's skin she went into a seizure. The sight was horrible and yanked me brutally out of my rage. I just stood there, watching her, blinking against the light, feeling stupid and helpless.

Harry pushed back the chair and moved Rhona away from the window. He then tried to put the curtain back up again. Seeing him struggle, I got out of my shock and moved to help. Charlie grabbed a cushion from the couch and put it under Rhona's head to stop her from injuring herself. To my relief, Rhona's seizure ended as soon as the light was blocked from the room. Harry lifted her up and laid her on the couch.

"I'm sorry, I'm so sorry," I cried, standing in the middle of the room. Charlie had gotten up from the floor, but stayed clear of me, watching me like a hawk. I felt more alone than I had ever felt before.

Running into the bedroom, I threw the door shut behind me and flung myself on my bed. I wrapped my arms around my knees, rocking myself to and fro. Tears were flowing again.

I was a walking disaster, causing pain to everyone around me. I couldn't stop biting my knee. My teeth hurt and it was sort of soothing to bite on something, anything, even if it was my own body. I turned my head for a moment. I heard their voices in the living room, but couldn't make out what they were saying. All of a sudden one sentence stood out.

"She needs to feed."

It was Rhona who'd said it. The voices went quiet.

Friday Morning, Late - Offerings

Later, the bedroom door opened. Charlie stood in the doorway. He held a mug in one hand, the other hand held onto the door handle.

"Can I come in without you attacking me?" he asked.

"Yes, of course," I replied as I wiped the tears from my face.

Charlie let go of the door handle, but I noticed he left the door open, just in case.

I don't blame him.

He sat on the edge of the bed and offered me the mug.

"Here, drink this."

"What is it?"

"Blood, you need to feed."

"Where did you get it from?"

"Don't you worry about that, just drink it before it congeals."

He put the mug in my hands. As he did, I noticed his wrist was bandaged.

OMG, he is giving me his own blood!

A shiver went through my spine. I looked into the mug and noticed it was only half full.

"Smudges don't give a lot of blood, do they," I said, immediately regretting my words and hoping I hadn't offended him.

Charlie smiled.

"Well, no, they don't. Just drink it, will you?"

I lifted the mug to my mouth. The rim touched my lips. The idea of drinking blood from a mug was not appealing to me at all somehow. It looked like black slurry. I held the mug in front of my mouth.

"It's not blue either," I said, hiding my grin behind the mug. I didn't know if he remembered that time in the cabin when I'd almost compared him to a fictional blue character.

"Just drink it," Charlie urged me. With a broad smile he pushed the mug back to my mouth. I closed my eyes and took a deep breath. It took me some courage to actually tip the mug up enough to make the lukewarm liquid run into my mouth.

To my surprise, it tasted great. With a few large gulps, I finished the drink and licked my lips. I held the mug upside down above my mouth to catch the last drops. I even tried to lick it clean.

"You like it that much, eh?" Charlie said with worry in his tone.

I nodded to Charlie and gave him back the mug.

"Well, I'm afraid there's not much more where that came from," he said and sighed.

"Is Rhona okay?" I whispered to him after I wiped my lips and licked my hand for good measure.

"Yes, she's fine. But please don't do anything like that again."

How can I promise this? I don't know if I can control my thirst in the future.

"I'll do my best," was all I could say.

I expected Charlie to leave, but he stayed sitting on the edge of the bed. I looked at him expectantly.

"Kate..." he started. He seemed uneasy. "Kate, when the curtain fell...you just stood there..."

I kept looking at him, expression turning blank.

Are you really trying to rub in how wrong I was?

There was an awkward silence before I realized what he was saying.

OMG! Rhona had gone into a seizure and I hadn't.

As I was sucking in air, Charlie said my thoughts out loud.

"You didn't have a seizure," and his brows furrowed, eyes intent on me.

I felt like a student who had to give the teacher the answer to his question, but I didn't have one.

"I know," I said slowly, trying to buy time. "What are you trying to say?"

"I'm not saying anything," he said, quickly looking away, trying to straighten a small part of my bedding. "I just noticed you're different," and his eyes locked on mine again.

I smiled, punched him carefully on the arm and said, "But you knew that already."

Charlie's face became mellow.

"You try to sleep now, you need to rest."

He got up, kissed my forehead and left, closing the door behind him.

I undressed this time and slid in between the sheets. I was so tired. Before I drifted into a restful sleep I heard those words in my head again, the words that Charlie had said.

'You're different...'

Friday Evening - Harry and Rhona's Story

Late that evening, Charlie woke me. I supposed he'd let me sleep as long as possible but wanted to wake me before I woke up hungry. He sat on my bedside again and handed me another mug. This one had a substantially smaller amount of blood in it than the one he'd given me earlier. I must have looked disappointed.

"Sorry, but Harry told me I couldn't give you any more or I'll get into trouble."

I realized Charlie's sacrifice but didn't know how to express my gratitude.

What do you say to somebody who offers you their blood, literally?

"I... um... You shouldn't have ..."

Oh god, what to say?

I looked this way and that, avoiding his gaze. I had put him through so much and yet he was offering me his blood. Again. I couldn't handle such a sacrifice.

Charlie saw me struggle and said, "I'm okay, just drink it."

I emptied the mug as I did the first time. As he took it from me, he kissed my forehead and left the room. I couldn't help but like his kisses. They made me feel loved, maybe even more so than him giving me his blood.

That could just be self-preservation...

I got dressed and walked into the living room. Harry and Rhona were sitting on the couch. The first thing that came into my mind was that I needed to apologize to Rhona.

"I'm so sorry, Rhona, for what I did, for pushing you..."

"It's okay, Kate, I'm fine," she said. "I understand what you went through. Been there, done that." She smiled.

It was a load of my mind that she didn't hold a grudge.

"Yes, but still... I shouldn't have done it," I said as my right hand grabbed my left arm. I felt silly standing like that and let my right arm swing back down.

I didn't know what else to say, so I let myself fall into one of the chairs. I heard Charlie doing dishes in the kitchen.

"Is it okay for Charlie to be doing this?" I asked Harry, and I pointed at my wrist.

"Yes, but not for long and it won't be enough to feed you," he said. He threw a glance at Rhona, who nodded.

I turned to look at Charlie and sighed. Automatically my hand went to my mouth and I began biting the skin next to my nails. Being a sucker didn't take away any nasty habits.

"You're not the only one with a supply problem," Rhona said, mistaking my biting for hunger. "I didn't feed last night and I'm starving too."

All of a sudden it hit me that I'd no idea how Harry and Rhona had come to be here with us.

"What happened?" I blurted out at the both of them, ignoring Rhona's remark. "How did you guys get here?"

They looked at each other and Rhona prodded Harry in the ribs.

"You tell her," she said.

Harry kissed her and began to tell their story.

"We'd done as we'd agreed and went back to Duncan to tell him you two had been killed by a couple of humans," Harry said.

I didn't want to interrupt, but I couldn't contain my curiosity.

"What did Duncan say?"

"He didn't say much, actually," Harry said. "He took in the information and dismissed us."

Jerk...

I frowned. "So why are you here? Something must have happened?"

"Just hear them out, Ms. Impatient," Charlie said as he walked into the room.

Flashes of Sasha shot through my mind.

"Please don't call me that," I whispered.

Charlie walked up to me, sat on the armrest of my chair and put his arm around me, hugging me gently. "Okay, I won't," he said.

Harry continued his story.

"I didn't know if Duncan would believe us, so before we joined the gathering I prepared a get-away car," and he nudged his head in the direction of the car in my driveway. "We came across a funeral center and I hot-wired a hearse, ready for take-off."

I laughed at that.

"OMG, how in heaven's name did you know how to hot-wire a car?" I asked.

Harry chuckled. "My brother taught me. Our father is a military man and very strict with his rules. Tom's more of a rebel than I am and hangs out with a different crowd than my father likes. He learned a set of skills Dad doesn't approve of. Fortunately, Tom taught them to me, as a good brother should."

Would Harry have another brother called Richard?

All the time Rhona was looking at Harry with adoration, her arm hooked into his, chewing gum to death in her mouth.

"Anyway, we thought we had gotten away with it and that you were safe, but then this guy stormed in and told Duncan two suckers had escaped in a car. Before Duncan could put one and one together we ran for the hearse and drove off." He looked at Rhona and put his hand over hers. "I was so happy Rhona actually wanted to come with me. I can't imagine what Duncan would have done to her if she hadn't." He smiled.

"I'd go anywhere with you, honey," Rhona beamed back at him and they kissed.

I looked up at Charlie and he kissed my head, again.

"So would I, Kate," he said.

I couldn't help the huge grin appearing on my face.

Number three.

OMG, I'm counting his kisses now!

Charlie smiled back at me but with a single-eyed frown. I kept my thoughts to myself and turned my attention back to Harry.

"Did you have any problem getting out? Did you stop in the little village?" I asked, dreading how the story would go on.

"Nope. No problems whatsoever. We told the guys on the perimeter that you escaped and that we were ordered to get you back. They let us go without a hick up. Charlie told us about your crisis in the village. Good thinking, Kate."

"We should thank you," I said. "It was you who saved our lives there, again."

"That may be true," Charlie said, "but it was you who thought of saying Harry's name." And this time he was beaming at me with adoring eyes instead of kissing me.

Bummer.

I looked at Harry again. "So how did you know where to find us? I can't remember telling you where we were going."

"That was just pure luck. We drove to Bullsbrook as it was the place Caleb was last seen with his pack and I assumed you would start your search here. Seeing you in the street was such a coincidence."

You have no idea.

I looked at Rhona. "When did he tell you... you know, that he...that we...all... weren't suckers?"

Rhona smiled a wicked smile and put her gum to the side.

"As you entered the hearse it was clear you were bitten, with the blood dripping from your neck and all. I didn't understand at first why anyone would want to bite another sucker, you know. I thought what the fuck?! But as I looked at Charlie for an explanation he told me you were unbitten. And then he told me he was still unbitten too."

I turned my head to Charlie in alarm. "Weren't you afraid she was going to bite you?"

"Don't worry," Rhona said before Charlie could answer, "there was too much urgency to get you to safety and tend to your marks."

Charlie chuckled. "You did offer to bite me."

Harry looked at Rhona in surprise. "You did?"

"Well, you know..." she said slightly embarrassed, "if Kate was one of us now, maybe Charlie wanted to be too...and I was hungry!"

Charlie rescued her from Harry's accusing stare and said, "I did consider it and I thought you were very kind to offer, Rhona."

I kissed Charlie's hand as I thought it was kind of him to make the awkward situation pass. Apart from the fact that I wanted to keep the kisses going.

"But what about Harry? AT that time you thought that Harry was bitten too. When did you find out about him being unbitten?" I asked Rhona.

"After we cared for your marks and we lay down to sleep I realized this 'rare blood disorder' had been a cover-up," she said. "I asked Harry if he was still unbitten too and I only had to look into his eyes to know the truth." She looked into Harry's eyes again, reliving the moment.

"Weren't you afraid she would turn you?" I asked Harry.

"I was," he said, only having eyes for Rhona, "but she didn't, she just kissed me."

Rhona was drowning in Harry's eyes, "I love you just the way you are, honey," and she kissed him to make her point.

Love is a strange thing...

Yeah, why does he get kissed on the mouth?

I wished I could have given them some alone time. I would have liked some with Charlie too.

Friday Evening - Deductions

Charlie broke the moment.

"We still have the mystery of Kate not being affected by sunlight."

"Yeah, how did you manage that?" Rhona asked wide-eyed.

"Do you have any special medical conditions, Kate?" Harry asked.

"No, not that I'm aware of. I'm not allergic to anything that I know of and haven't got any disease," I said.

"Okay, tell me everything that's happened to you since your first encounter with a sucker. It must be something that's happened to you in the last few days."

I told him everything. How Caleb had pierced my skin but not my jugular. How I had an aversion from light from then on, but didn't have seizures. How the magnesium had sent me into this white place. My aversion to the light beam from the tank after I was truly bitten. I ended with my exposure to sunlight with no ill effects, which he of course already knew about.

"Hmmm, I think I understand."

We were all hanging off his lips as Harry explained his theory.

"When you were first bitten by Caleb, his saliva must have entered your bloodstream, but it wasn't enough to infect you, turn you. It must have done something to your immune system though, preparing to prevent your body going into a full response to light after a proper infection."

"Like a vaccine?" I said.

"Yes, exactly, like a vaccine," he said. "But the vaccination only affected your light sensitivity, not your need for blood." He looked at Charlie with a knowing smile.

"No need to tell me," Charlie huffed. "But then how do you explain about Kate's white light experience from the magnesium? And her not liking the light beam of light from the tank after she was bitten by Caleb?"

"Yes, that..." Harry nodded, and the cogs in his head were working overtime again. "The magnesium light exposure happened before she was bitten and probably was so intense and close-up it must have caused the effect. Not being like a normal seizure, but an overall reduction of being able to move, and, for some reason, not being able to see colors."

"But what about my aversion to the tank light?" I said. "I'd been bitten when that happened."

"Yes, but it happened very shortly after Caleb's bite, so your system hadn't had time to adapt yet," he said as if it were as clear as day.

"Wow." I sat back, deep in my own thoughts.

No-one spoke. Charlie had been right. I was different. I was a sucker that could walk in daylight, a day walker.

And I even haven't got real red hair...

Holy shit, this is scary...

The possibilities and implications hit me.

What if there are more like me? No human would ever be safe.

At the same time, I was hoping nobody would ever find out about this medical glitch of mine. If anyone found out, they would be able to create a day walking sucker army. Duncan for one would love that. I bet there are more and worse like him as well.

"Could I get vaccinated so I can walk in sunlight?" Rhona said all of a sudden.

The three of us stared at her.

Oh no, here we go...

Harry's face turned into delight. "Oh Rhona, if it worked we could live in daylight together!"

I could understand his point of view. For Harry to live with Rhona as she currently was would mean to live in eternal darkness. I could understand they wanted to have a normal life like we all used to have, before the outbreak. I knew, however, that Rhona was still feeding on humans. I could see the future horror of gatherings in daylight. Suckers roaming free, attacking anybody, anywhere, anytime.

Would they cause their own extinction at some point?

"Would you be willing to try, Kate?" Harry asked me.

Hearing my name brought me back from my time warp.

"Sorry, Harry. What would I be willing?"

"Well, biting Rhona like Caleb bit you the first time," he said.

"But wouldn't that be too little, too late?"

"Not necessarily. Chickenpox vaccinations given after exposure work. It's worth a try..."

Both Rhona and Harry were staring at me full of hope, sitting on the edge of their seat. How could I refuse them their happiness?

Suddenly I felt drained of all energy, unable to struggle anymore.

"Alright," I said.

Besides, it may not work at all...

Friday Night - Vaccination

My fangs dropped that night. It hurt like hell, much more than when I had braces. I'd thought that had hurt, but this was the super-sized version of it.

After showering, I admired my new slicers in the mirror. They looked so much better than the fake ones, so much more deadly. For a moment, I even pretended to bite into a neck with them but stopped when the images of dead bodies floated back into my mind. My mouth closed with a snap. I felt disgusted as I looked upon myself in the mirror. I quickly finished brushing my teeth and got out of the bathroom.

The others took their turn to freshen up after me. When everyone was ready, Rhona stood in the middle of the room, ready to be vaccinated.

"Let's do this," she said.

"I'm not biting you in your neck if you don't mind, Rhona," I said when she presented her jugular to me. "I'd hate to accidentally bleed you to death."

"Oh, okay, where do you want to bite me then?" She let go of her collar.

"How about her triceps," Harry said, "there's muscle enough to sink your teeth in without slicing a vein or artery."

Rhona rolled up her sleeve as high as she could and offered me her arm.

"Her glutes are the safest location though," Harry suggested.

Both Rhona and I stared at Harry for a second, both realizing he had just implied I should bite Rhona in her butt. We decided to ignore his last remark.

"Just a thought," Harry said.

Not in a million years, Harry...

"Okay, here we go," I said and held Rhona's arm in front of my mouth. "Let me know if I hurt you."

She didn't say anything. I guessed she was as nervous as I was. Her arm was tiny but relatively muscular. Like Harry had said, I wouldn't have a problem biting into it without causing fatal damage. As I was staring at her arm I felt awkward as I'd never bitten a human before in my life.

Let alone somebody ask me to bite them.

"Here goes," I warned her again, maybe more for my sake than hers, and I sank my teeth into her flesh.

As I tried to make my bite as big as possible, getting as much flesh in between, I caught my lip in my bite. The sharp pain made me make a little noise. At the same time I heard Rhona's sharp intake of breath and felt her muscles tense as her blood spread into my mouth. She hadn't noticed my cry, but I saw Charlie's frown.

"Are you okay?" he asked, more worried about me than about Rhona. Harry was worrying over her already, holding her free hand.

I nodded minutely as I didn't want to cause any more discomfort to Rhona than necessary. I kept my bite and Rhona's blood tasted delicious. It made my mouth water. The fact that Charlie had fed me a little more of his blood not long before had convinced me I wasn't going to get carried away and I had indeed no problem withdrawing my fangs from her flesh a little to let my saliva get into the two wounds. After about ten seconds, I let go of her arm.

Harry began bandaging the two marks immediately. I wiped my mouth clean, but the blood kept coming.

"Let me have a look," Charlie said.

"I think I bit my own lip," I said before he pressed a tissue on the corner of my mouth. When he pulled it away there was blood on it and I felt new blood well up from the little wound.

"Don't worry," I said, "I'll live."

"I'll grab an ice cube anyway," Charlie said and went to the kitchen. I kept licking the blood until he returned.

I don't taste too bad either, if I may say so myself.

I asked Rhona if she was okay, to which she nodded.

Is she still in too much pain to talk?

I watched on as Harry did what he was trained for.

I hope those scars will be nicer looking than a pox vaccination.

"How long until it works?" Rhona asked Harry.

Can't be that painful then.

"I don't know," he said, taping the bandage, "but we better make sure we don't expose you to sunlight for as long as possible, just to be on the safe side."

Saturday Morning, Early - Out for Blood

Harry and Charlie prepared a meal from the meager food supply I still had in my kitchen. I became hungrier seeing them eat. Now that there was no urgent matter to attend to, or any emotions welling up, my need for a feed was making itself heard. My stomach grumbled terribly and all eyes focused on me.

"I'm sorry, I'm still hungry," I said, looking apologetically at Charlie, who couldn't possibly give me any more of his blood. I glanced at Rhona, who must have been starving as well. We both needed blood, but where to get it?

We all tried to think where we might find human blood without killing anybody. I suggested trying to get some last drops from the people that were already dead, but Harry said this wasn't a healthy option. It took some time before Charlie came up with the answer.

"Bullsbrook Medical Center. They should have a supply of blood in case of emergencies, shouldn't they?"

We all thought this was very likely. It was a temporary measure, but it would have to do for now.

"Great idea," Rhona said. "I classify the situation as an emergency. Where is it?" She looked at Charlie and me for the answer.

I looked at Charlie and he raised his eyebrows at me.

"Don't look at me," he said, "I've no idea where to find it."

"Neither do I, I haven't been sick either. My hand went to my back pocket but found no cell. I had put it in my bag in the cabin when the batteries had died. "Anybody got a cell, so we can look it up?"

"No network, remember," Charlie said, pulling a grimace.

"Oh yeah, duh, I forgot." I rolled my eyes at my own stupidity. Since buying my first cell, I'd become addicted to it and used it to look up everything I wanted to know. I missed it so much.

"We'll just have to drive around until we find one," Harry said and stood up to get going. The others followed suit. I was the only one who didn't move.

"Eh, is that a good idea?" I said, looking up to them.

"How else are we going to find it?" Harry said, turning his head slightly.

"No, I mean, driving around in a hearse. It would look suspicious, wouldn't it? You said the army was in town. They'd be sure to suspect suckers in a darkened car." My attention turned to nobody in particular. "As a matter of fact, driving around in any car would be suspicious. There's nobody else but the army here. They'd certainly stop and interrogate us," I said.

I thought it was a miracle the army hadn't been knocking on my door about the hearse being in the driveway yet, but I didn't mention this.

They all sat back down. Nobody said anything, as there was no point, they all knew I was right.

"We'll just have to walk then and try to keep out of sight," Harry said, getting up again. He seemed determined to provide Rhona with blood, no matter what.

By the time we went outside, the night was almost over. We probably only had an hour of darkness left. We discussed where to look for the medical center and thought it best to start in the center of town. Walking in single-file, we stuck close to the houses. We didn't know what the army would do with Rhona and me if they picked us up. We didn't want to find out either.

The town looked eerie, as if all the color had drained out of it.

I don't think I can ever be happy living in a world without color.

There were no signs of residents, but there were plenty of army cars driving through the streets and we had to hide several times. It took forever to get to the town center with us constantly ducking and hiding into shadows, even though it wasn't that far from my place. Once we got there, it was busier than we expected. We hid in the shadow of the bakery building. We saw army vehicles arriving and bringing civilians. They were being loaded onto a bus. When it left the bus stop, the soldiers returned from wherever they had come from.

When all was quiet again we looked for some sign of a medical practice. I didn't dare study the map at the bus stop like Julie had done days before. Memories of that night came floating up. I was too hungry to linger on them and willed them back to the depths they came from.

We couldn't find anything remotely looking like a general practice, apart from a plaque next to a door stating the person inside offered pedicures, so we agreed to move on. Not too much ducking and hiding from army vehicles now, but no medical practice either.

I almost suggested we head back, when we found it on the outskirts of town in a nice street with lots of trees. The practice was a stand-alone, one-story building, surrounded by manicured lawns and bushes. There was no moon, but the streetlights cast black shadows across the gray grass. We moved from the shade of one tree to the next and finally made it to the back of the building.

Harry was preparing to smash a window when Charlie stopped him by pulling his sleeve.

"Wait!" he whispered.

"What is it?" Harry hissed.

"There may be an alarm," Charlie said.

"Didn't Tom teach you to open locks?" I asked Harry, pointing at the door.

"He did, but I'm not that good at it. Even if I could manage, I don't know how to undo an alarm." He rubbed his chin.

"Motherfucking shit pile," Rhona said. "Now what?"

My ears turned red hearing those words coming from Rhona's mouth. Everybody turned around to her. I saw no sign of shame on her face whatsoever, just extreme annoyance, and guessed it wasn't the first time she'd uttered these words. I could only imagine how hungry she was by now. It couldn't be much worse than what I was experiencing myself, but my vocabulary wasn't as good as hers in expressing it, apparently. Only the prospect of finding blood in the center kept me from going for Charlie's throat. I looked at the stars for help.

"What about the roof?" I said, pointing upward. "Do you think we could get in unnoticed through there?"

They all looked up.

"I can't get up there," Charlie said.

"Yes, you can," Rhona said. She looked at me, at Charlie, then at the rooftop with a bit of an arc and at me again. I got her drift and together we giggled.

"Okay, I suppose I *can* get up there then..." Charlie said, but Rhona and I didn't tell him what we thought of doing.

We told Harry to get up there already. He had no problem climbing up the drainpipe. I followed him like a monkey scooting up a tree.

Not bad for a person who not so long ago couldn't do push-ups if her life depended on it.

Rhona stayed below. When I was up and indicated to her I was ready, she took Charlie by surprise as she grabbed him under his arms and threw him high in the air. As soon as he cleared the roofline I caught his hands and pulled him towards me. It was an awkward move and we both fell. Charlie landed on top of me.

"Rhona's pretty good at dwarf throwing, don't you think?" I grinned at Charlie, his face close to mine.

"Yeah, it's a pity you're not so good at dwarf catching," he said as he rolled off me and got up. I felt a bit bad about that until I noticed his wicked grin as he offered me his hand to help me up. "Not that I'm complaining," he said and he made an effort to wipe the dirt off my bum while standing very close in front of me. I laughed.

As soon as Rhona was on the roof she created an opening with her hands in the roof as if it was butter. We were all extremely impressed. One after the other we dropped down into the building.

Saturday Morning - An Unfortunate Meeting

The signage in the medical center was pretty good and in the nurses' station we found the refrigerator with the so-desired blood bags. It was like finding a bar in the desert.

There weren't a lot of bags, five in total, but it would have to do for the night. For a split second, I thought about blood types and wondered if it mattered which one I drank. My hunger, however, didn't care about this. It urged me to open a bag and drink it.

Rhona and I each gulped down the blood like two alcoholics in a drinking contest. It tasted so good. We sat down and after we'd had two bags each, we were quenched. There was only one bag left and I told Rhona to have it.

"No, you take the last one. You need it more than I do." She shoved it back in my direction.

"You better take it with you, we need to get back asap," Charlie said, standing at the window, peeking through the blinds. "The sun's about to rise."

At that moment, we heard two thuds in the hall. Somebody had entered the building the same way we had. Rhona and I got up and we all were about to leave the room when the door flew open. Caleb and Sasha stood in the doorway.

"You," Sasha said under her breath as she saw me. The hatred in her eyes and voice was unmistakable. I hoped to find a friendlier vibe in Caleb's eyes, but he was scanning the room, taking in the situation. I noticed his lingering glances on the refrigerator and the empty blood bags on the floor.

They too must have been in hiding without an opportunity to feed...

"Charlie, Harry, stay behind us," I said.

Sasha spotted the blood bag I had in my hand. She made a dive for it. In a reflex, I turned and flung the bag upwards. Sasha crashed into me and the shock made me let go of the bag. It flew into the air in a wide arc. We fell hard onto the floor. Caleb leaped to catch the blood bag, but Rhona threw her body against his, knocking him off course. He and Rhona also crashed to the floor.

Charlie caught the bag.

"Get out!" Rhona screamed at Charlie and Harry, knowing they were no match for Caleb and Sasha.

The way out for them was through the door, which was blocked by us four suckers clambering around on the floor to get up. Their only available exit was the floor-to-ceiling window behind them. Harry hurled himself full force into the window and fell through it as it shattered, setting off the building's alarm. Charlie ran out after him. Harry got up and shook off the glass. They both turned and yelled for us to get out too.

Rhona and I tried to get up and out, but Caleb and Sasha were grabbing us. They were older suckers and much stronger. Charlie didn't blink an eye and threw the bag of blood into the room. Sasha and Caleb let go of us and dove for the bag before it could explode on the floor of the nurses' station. Once free, Rhona and I scrambled up and ran outside into Harry and Charlie's arms.

We turned around to check if we were being followed. The four of us looked at Caleb and Sasha and... they were looking back at us. They'd caught the bag but weren't drinking. I didn't understand why they were just standing there, staring.

"How is this possible...?" Sasha said.

Then it dawned on me. Rhona and I were standing in the dappled daylight that shone through the trees and we didn't even blink, let alone have a seizure. I stepped into the full sunlight and Rhona, hesitant at first, followed me. Nothing happened. We couldn't believe our eyes. I looked at Rhona and she went into a victory crouch.

"It worked, your idea worked!" she yelled. She lifted me from the ground in a hug, spinning me round.

The building's alarm kept ringing. Harry and Charlie pulled at us, reminding us we had to get out before the army came to investigate. Charlie took my hand and we ran as fast as we could through the sun-filled streets. I glanced back before we turned the corner and saw Caleb and Sasha running off into the street, using their coats and the shade from the trees to avoid being hit by the sun's rays.

Once back at my place, we collapsed exhausted on the chairs and couch. We laughed. We were so excited that the 'vaccination' bite had worked and that Rhona could now go out in daylight as well.

"Oh, the possibilities!" Harry kept saying and Rhona kept hugging him again and again.

"How is it possible it worked so fast?" I said to Harry. "Vaccines normally take time to work, don't they?"

"The only reason I can think of," he replied, "is that you passed on some of your antibodies with your blood when you bit your lip while you were biting Rhona. That would work pretty fast."

"OMG, you're right. Now that was a blessing in disguise."

Rhona kept hugging and kissing Harry. Watching them I struggled with feelings of embarrassment and jealousy. I tried to look away, but every time my eyes drifted to Charlie and I began blushing, forced to look away again.

"We have a future!" Rhona kept repeating.

Saturday Morning - Agreement

The more often I thought of Caleb and Sasha's faces at the moment of our escape, the quieter my mood became. I didn't say anything to the others as I didn't want to spoil their happy time. It seemed that Harry and Rhona were already planning their entire life together. To prevent being a party pooper I went into the back garden.

I stood there with my eyes closed, my face absorbing the warmth of the sunshine. It had been too long since I'd felt how good it was. Opening my eyes, I took in the blue sky, the green pines, and the multi-colored leaves on the deciduous trees. Their colors were so beautiful this time of year. I loved the different shades of yellows, oranges, and browns. I'd really missed this kaleidoscope of colors during my nightlife this past week.

When I heard the kitchen door open and close, I knew it was Charlie. He stood on the porch for a while before he spoke.

"You okay?" he asked.

I turned around. As always, I was so happy to see him. Since this whole drama began there'd been a dark veil of sadness over me, but seeing Charlie was like a glimmer of light. It was as if he lifted that veil, bringing me to higher spirits. And I liked it, it was almost an addiction.

"Yes and no," I said. I walked towards him and we sat down on the steps of the back porch. "I am happy for Rhona and Harry, I truly am," I said after some thought.

"But...?"

"But it's wrong." I kept my gaze in front of me. I needed Charlie to see the bigger picture. I needed him to realize the possible danger caused by Caleb and Sasha knowing our secret and in order to say it right I needed to focus.

"Suckers should not be able to walk in daylight. Nobody would ever be safe anymore from the likes of Caleb, Sasha, and Duncan."

"And Julie..." Charlie said quietly.

"And Julie..."

Where would she be now?

I hadn't thought about Julie that much lately. My fear for suckers mainly focused on the other three. I tried to suppress the knowledge that Julie was the same, that she also killed. How else was I to deal with this? Julie was my sister. She was to me, but not to others. They would all see her for the only relevant thing she was to them; a sucker. And I had no doubt she would kill in daylight too if she had the chance.

"Sasha and Caleb will soon figure out how we did it and then all hell will break loose."

I made up my mind there and then.

"I have to warn the army." I turned around as I expected a reaction from Charlie. I wanted to know if he thought I had made a stupid decision or not.

Charlie didn't say anything, his expression blank. He just gazed at the garden and nodded. I suppose he agreed, but I figured he probably also realized the army wouldn't let me go after I walked into their arms. I would be too much of a threat to let go. I didn't want to think of what they would do to me, but there was no other option. Too many lives were at risk.

"Charlie..." I said and waited until he looked at me. It took a long time. When he finally turned his head, his eyes were red and rimmed with tears. His pupils were so big I could almost reach into his soul and touch his sorrow.

I was touched by his display of emotion on the thought of losing me, impressed by his calmness considering the situation. He had done so much to be with me and now he agreed to let me go, for the common good. The pain this caused him echoed my pain. I didn't want to lose him either. A lump formed in my throat and tears welled up in my eyes too.

Charlie didn't say anything.

I already knew what his feelings were for me, but I found it necessary to speak mine out loud. I swallowed, trying to get rid of that lump. I took a breath with my mouth open, forcing air into my lungs.

"I do love you, Charlie," I finally managed to say.

As I blinked, a tear escaped, rolling over my cheek. Charlie wiped it away with his thumb and hugged me.

"You do pick your moments," he whispered.

He made me laugh and cry at the same time.

Saturday Morning - Goodbyes

"No!" Rhona yelled.

Charlie and I had just told her and Harry our intentions, that we planned to warn the army. Charlie had been adamant in coming with me.

"You can't do this, they'll kill you. Are you insane?" Rhona kept on shouting, pacing around the room.

"Are you sure you want to do this?" Harry asked both of us, without taking his eyes off Rhona.

"Yes, I have no choice," I said. For a change, I didn't have the urge to bite the skin next to my nails.

"What do you want us to do?" he asked, ignoring Rhona's continuing tirade for a moment.

"We want you to get out, get as far away as possible, as soon as possible," I said. "Now Rhona can move in daylight it'll be easier to mask her condition. As a medical student, I'm sure you'll find a way to get her the blood she needs in the future."

Harry nodded. "Thank you."

I smiled at him. "I'm glad I can do something for you for a change."

We helped Rhona and Harry pack. I gave them the food that was left over, toilet paper, towels and the likes. I put it all in one of my suitcases. We agreed the hearse was still too conspicuous and they didn't need the blackout windows anymore.

Looking at the hearse I saw Mrs. Babcock's window from the corner of my eye. The thought occurred to me that Mrs. Babcock could still be there, that she somehow, miraculously, survived the attack.

When we went to her house, we found her front door forced open and her beautiful home trashed. I had to assume she hadn't survived and wouldn't need transport anymore, so I told Harry to hot-wire the old lady's car.

We didn't want to upset Rhona more than necessary so kept our goodbyes short. Rhona refused to wave to us as they drove off. Charlie and I did wave and I really hoped they could have a relatively normal future. A mobilized army suggested there was still hope for the human race.

Fingers crossed...

After their car disappeared around the corner, the fact that we'd been up all night kicked in. I couldn't suppress a big yawn. I suggested we have a rest before leaving as it was likely we'd be kept up for a long time once we faced the army. Charlie agreed and we went inside and lay on my bed.

I think it was about noon when I felt Charlie stroke my arm, like the time he had done in the motel. I turned around to face him. He stroked my arm again.

This time I didn't turn away. I moved closer and kissed him. His lips responded in sync. Happy that we were finally together, with mutual consent, I made a trail of kisses over this nose, his eye, his cheek. Charlie kept caressing my arm in the meantime. It gave me goosebumps.

When my kissing trail arrived back at his lips we began kissing each other again. His lips were so soft and his tongue twisted with mine. Without a word, I began unbuttoning his shirt.

I was about halfway down when Charlie put his hand on mine, stopping me from going any further. I opened my eyes.

Not again?

"Is this what you really want?" Charlie whispered.

"What do you mean...?" I frowned. "Yes, of course it is."

"I mean, you're not doing this because I'm second best, or because you feel sorry for me..." Charlie lowered his eyes.

I felt for him. There hadn't been much time to express my true feelings for him, to talk about it. I wanted him to know I had always loved him, and exactly the way he was. I wanted him to know that his physical appearance was part of the package I had fallen in love with.

"No, of course not, silly. Don't you get it? I've always loved you. I just didn't know it then." I let my hand slide under his shirt, onto his back, and pulled myself close as I kissed him.

Charlie backed away again. "I know I'm not prince charming..."

I couldn't take it anymore.

Enough with being gentle.

"Oh, shut up and kiss me, you idiot." I grabbed his wrist, rolled him onto his back, and straddled him. After a long kiss, I sat up and unbuttoned the rest of his shirt. This time he didn't stop me.

I lifted his T-shirt and let my hands go over this hairy chest. I never had a boyfriend with a hairy chest before. Charlie's hands rubbed my thighs, this thumbs putting pressure on the insides. When they moved up, it made me wish he could go a little bit further. I was getting an itch that needed to be scratched.

I took my top off and unhooked my bra. I threw it in the corner of the room and leaned forward to kiss Charlie again. Kissing and having my breast fondled at the same time was certainly something worthy of repeating in the future.

I rolled off Charlie and slowly we took the remaining clothes off each other. I was pleasantly surprised not all his extremities were short.

Nothing small in that department.

His hands on my bare skin sent shivers down my spine. Emotions that had been built up were finally unleashed and every touch, every sensation was experienced exponentially.

If I had worried I would hurt Charlie in our lovemaking, as my strength had increased dramatically since my last feed, it was for nothing. Being with Charlie came so natural. Every move was anticipated and reacted upon. We caressed each other's bodies until we were so aroused we could hardly stop ourselves.

Charlie looked at me and there were no words needed to know we both wanted to go all the way. He entered me and it took my breath away. I thought I would drown in my happiness. He was gentle at first, taking it slow. Not soon after I urged him to move faster and we climaxed together. Every single nerve in my body exploded, tears ran from my eyes, my emotions so raw I screamed. I clutched at his body, making sure he didn't move away while the feeling lasted.

Afterward, we lay together for what seemed like an eternity as neither of us wanted the experience to end. As we cuddled, I took in his closeness, his smell, his warmth. I didn't want to let go of this moment, ever. But I knew I had to, so I finally took a deep breath.

"Let's go," I said.

Saturday Afternoon - Show and Tell

Soon we went on our way. We decided a direct approach was probably the best and went to the school, as this appeared where the biggest concentration of army vehicles seemed to go. Charlie held my hand as we walked up to a soldier standing on guard duty. My heart started beating noticeably in my chest.

"Halt," the guard shouted, aiming his gun at us. A flashlight was strapped to the barrel, but the light wasn't on. We stopped walking about three meters away from him.

"State your name and business," he said.

"We would like to speak to your superior officer," I said. "We have important information."

The soldier lowered his gun and operated his walkie-talkie. When he finished he said, "We have no time for civilians, you need to leave this area as soon as possible. Buses are taking civilians to Portland, they leave from the town square." He pointed in the square's direction.

I decided to give him a nice smile and proudly showed off my fangs.

"Holy shit!" he yelled and picked up his gun again. He fumbled to flip the switch on the flashlight.

Charlie and I stood and waited until he was done. When he finally flicked the light's switch on, it emitted a faint purplish-blue light. He aimed the light at us and looked puzzled when he noticed nothing was happening.

I pointed to the sun.

He realized the black light had been superfluous.

I liked the way his cheeks turned red, imagining how sweet the blood in them would taste.

"We mean you no harm, but we have important information to share with your superior officer," I said again.

The soldier stepped back a few paces and did some more frantic talking into his walkie-talkie, not lowering his gun this time. "Wait here," he said when he'd finished his conversation. Four soldiers came running, all armed with guns and switched-on black lights. They obviously weren't taking any chances.

Charlie and I were escorted into the main school building. I was glad to see they had disposed of the pile of bodies that had been lying in the schoolyard before.

The army had set up headquarters in the teachers' staffroom. They had rearranged the whole room. It now looked like a busy office, with people sitting behind desks piled with paperwork. There was a long row of old-fashioned radios on desks against one of the walls, each with their own operator.

Where there is a will, there is a way...

The man in control had set up his office in Mr. Finkle's room. He looked very much like a typical soldier, with the same hairstyle and build as Duncan, Harry, and Ben. The distinctive difference was his big mustache. He was the first soldier with facial hair I had ever met. Not that I'd met many soldiers before, but it still seemed unusual. I didn't particularly like mustaches, but somehow I instantly liked this man. I gave the credit to his blue eyes. They were happy eyes.

The sign on his desk stated he was Major Moore and he took a moment to study us with interest. His eyes glittered in the beam of sunlight that shone through the window, which had been mended. The whole room had improved, in my opinion, now Mr. Finkle wasn't the occupant anymore.

The four soldiers who'd accompanied us were not dismissed. Finally the Major spoke.

"I've been told you're suckers who can walk in daylight. Is this true?" he asked. His voice was low, with a pleasant timbre.

"Only me, sir, my name is Kate. This is Charlie, he's unbitten," I said. The Major didn't respond, so we both showed him our teeth.

"I'm not sure I can believe you. Having fangs doesn't mean anything," he said. This was a blow to my plan. I had to find a way to prove that I was truly a sucker before this man would believe anything I had to say. My eyes darted all over the place, looking for a solution. I guessed that going for the jugular of one of the soldiers was not a good move, nor would throwing Charlie through the window be.

Not sure if they would appreciate to have to repair it again.

Apart from Charlie's objection to the action of course.

I decided to grab the edge of the heavy, wooden desk with one hand and lifted its side as easy as if it was made of cardboard. The paperwork and lamp began sliding off the desk. All four soldiers at once cocked their guns. I dropped the desk and stepped back.

"Stand down," Major Moore commanded the soldiers, and after rearranging the lamp and paperwork directed his attention back to me. "Can you tell me how this is possible?"

"It's why we're here, sir. We only discovered this ourselves last night and we fear that other suckers, who we accidentally met, now know about it too and will use it to attack humans in daylight."

Major Moore's eyes glinted and his cheeks rose ever so slightly. "You still haven't answered my question," he said.

So I told him what had happened to me. I did my best not to mention Harry and Rhona as I didn't want to involve them in this.

"Hmm..." He looked at Charlie. "Why are *you* here?"

"I love Kate, sir," Charlie said.

Aww...

I had to bite the inside of my lip to suppress a smile. Charlie's answer had sounded so funny. I had just told the Major, risking my own life in the process, that I was a day walking sucker and was here to warn the army of an impending attack of day walking suckers. And Charlie said he was here because he loved me.

To Major Moore, we may have seemed like an unlikely couple who were acting like two silly teenagers in love. To me, however, Charlie's confession of his love for me in this situation meant more than any kiss he could have given me. I glanced at him, trying to convey my love through my eyes. I took his hand to prove to Major Moore that the feeling of love was mutual.

Against my expectations, Major Moore didn't laugh at Charlie's answer.

"What about the blood sucking?" The Major directed the question at me again. "Is that any less?"

"No, unfortunately not," I replied.

"Did you kill anybody?" he said, a more serious tone in this voice.

I couldn't blame him for asking, he was only doing his job.

"I drank Charlie's blood which he offered me in a cup voluntarily. And some blood from the medical practice."

"Ah, that was you," he said with a smile behind the mustache.

And Rhona, and Sasha, and Caleb...

"Look, sir, as soon as those suckers I told you about know how to turn into daylight suckers they'll be able to attack at any time of day. You need to find them before more lives are lost."

I was getting a bit impatient with all the questions. We needed action, not discussion. Caleb and Sasha had to be found.

How I wish Charlie and I hadn't wasted precious time by laying together before coming here.

Really?

"We will do our job, don't you worry about that," and with that he signaled to the soldiers. "Take them away."

I was one step away from the door when I turned around. "Please, sir..."

Major Moore looked up from his paperwork.

"Could I ask you to find out if my sister's okay? She's married to a naval officer."

Major Moore said he could try and I gave him their names and last known location. I hoped he would keep his promise. It was the least he could do for me after what I had done for him.

The soldiers took us out of Mr. Finkle's office and escorted us down the hallway.

Saturday Afternoon - Torn Apart

I don't know what I had expected to happen next. I suppose I thought we might be let free, having done our duty, but that was wishful thinking. Instead, two of the soldiers pushed me up the stairs and the other two continued to escort Charlie out the door.

"No, no, no, Charlie is staying with me," I said, struggling to hold on to his hand.

"You are going upstairs, Ma'am," one of the soldiers said.

I had no idea when they had decided this, whether the Major had given the orders before we talked to him or whether this was standard procedure with all suckers they had caught. The other two soldiers continued to push Charlie out the door.

"Kate!" Charlie yelled as they kept pushing us further apart. Our hands separated and I lost control. A surge of power went through my body that needed release. I grabbed one of the soldiers pushing me and threw him through the air. He landed at least five meters away and slid for a couple more over the slippery, yellow tiles.

Without hesitation, the other three let go of us but cocked their weapons. Two guns were instantly pointed at my head. How I hated these weapons. I lifted my upper lip and showed off my fangs. I could smell the soldiers' perspiration and the fear in it.

"Kate," I heard Charlie say.

I whipped my head around and saw that the third gun was aimed at Charlie's head.

"Kate, it's okay. I'll be okay. Just do what they want for now."

Charlie was an ocean of calmness in my world of turmoil. An instant headache accompanied the frustration of feeling helpless. I was so strong and yet so powerless. But Charlie was right. I knew he'd be okay, that they wouldn't hurt him, as he was still one of 'them.' I took a deep breath, collected myself, and nodded.

"Okay, okay, I can do that." The surge of power was gone and with it my will to fight.

Charlie, seeing that I had calmed down, nodded to me once. I returned the nod.

The fallen soldier returned and joined the one who had his gun aimed at Charlie. Together they guided him towards the doors.

"You hurt him and I'll hurt you!" I shouted after them. The other two soldiers pushed me up the stairs, their guns still at the ready. I looked around once more and saw them take my Charlie away from me. The veil of darkness fell over me again.

Upstairs they put me in one of the classrooms. Unfortunately, it wasn't mine. My guards remained outside the door. I guessed they didn't expect me to jump through the window. I walked over to it and spotted Charlie being escorted into one of the auxiliary buildings. They'd probably interrogate him further before sending him on his way. In contrast, I had no idea what they were going to do with me.

I didn't have to wait too long for the answer. I soon heard steps coming up the hallway. They sounded like eager steps. The person entering the classroom wore a white lab coat. He was an old man with black rimmed glasses, a nose like a hawk, and a skinny neck. If I'd met him on the street I'd have taken him for a prison camp survivor.

Maybe he is a prison camp survivor.

"I'm Doctor Haley and I'm going to take a couple of blood samples from you," he said.

No 'how are you feeling today,' or the other usual chit-chat doctors always had while you knew there were at least another five patients in the waiting room anxiously looking at their watches as their appointment times had come and gone. This guy's communication was short and to the point. He told me to sit down and roll up my sleeve.

He had brought a tray with him. On it was a rack with different sizes of glass tubes, each having a different colored stopper. I found the number of tubes frightening. Instead of injecting me as many times as there were tubes, however, he attached one needle to half a syringe and stuck it in my arm, connecting the tubes to the other end of the syringe, one after the other. Apart from the initial jab, I felt no pain. It was obvious he'd done this before.

I tried to read the text on the tubes. The only one I could make out said IgG/IgM. I knew from my studies that this had something to do with immunity.

While the doctor was changing out another tube, I couldn't help but look at the veins standing out in his skinny, long neck. They were so inviting and my mouth started to water. I swallowed as I was appalled by myself for even contemplating putting my lips on this old man's neck.

"Don't even think about it," Dr. Hayley said without looking up.

My stare went from his veins to his eyes.

Says he who is draining me of my blood.

"Can I get a replacement for that?" With my free hand, I pointed at the tubes on the tray that were already filled with blood. I hadn't told Major Moore that suckers get stronger when they drank more blood as newborns, so I thought it was worth trying to ask for some. Dr. Haley looked at me briefly but didn't answer my question.

When he was done, he stuck a bit of cotton with a Band-Aid on my arm. He told me to fold my arm to keep the pressure on it and to open my mouth. With a long cotton swab he swiped the inside of my cheek. The swab also disappeared into a tube with a stopper.

The doctor picked up his tray and left without a word. The guard who had come in with him shut the door and joined the other guard on duty outside.

I walked back to the window and looked at the schoolyard. It was a lot busier than it had been before. For a second it appeared like a normal school day at lunchtime. However, instead of children, there were now soldiers running around. Something was afoot. I hoped they were working very hard on finding Caleb and Sasha. My worries would be over when they were found.

I sat down and resigned myself with the thought that what I had done was the right thing and I would soon be reunited with Charlie. I didn't care what they did to me afterward, as long as they let me be with Charlie one more time. I needed a proper goodbye.

As I was watching the scene in the schoolyard I realized the army was doing more than making war. Yes, they had soldiers, tanks and weapons, but I also noticed they were bringing civilians in from the surrounding villages, taking them to safe places. I saw trucks loaded with water, food supplies, and blankets. They were being pointed into various directions. The army was doing its best to make life possible for survivors.

I had been sitting in the classroom for several hours when I noted a movement in the corner of my eye. Most of the action outside was muted yet purposeful. This movement at the parking lot, however, was chaotic.

I saw two people being escorted from a truck by soldiers. One was tall, of muscular build, and dressed in khaki; a soldier. The other, smaller one was fighting, resisting the transport. This female had two guards with guns aimed at her head, being pushed forward and she was obviously not entirely agreeing with her transport. There were profanities coming out of her mouth that I had never heard before, but it somehow sounded familiar. I recognized that voice.

I did a double take and couldn't believe my eyes. They were Harry and Rhona.

WTF!

Saturday Afternoon, Late - Clarifications

Adrenaline rushed through my blood. Why the hell were they here? I got up and placed my hands on the window, multiple thoughts running through my head. I began banging on the window, trying to get Rhona's attention, hoping to warn her, to make her get out of here.

This will be a bit tricky of course, with guns pointed at her head...

Rhona was too busy insulting the soldiers with all she had, but Harry did notice me. I stopped hitting the window when Harry looked up. I didn't understand what I saw. When I read his face...it was cold. There was no smile and his eyes seemed as hard and dark as lava stones. He looked so unlike the kind, helpful Harry that I knew. They disappeared into the building. I sat down hard on one of the wooden chairs. My mind was racing. What had Harry done?

Would he have done a 1-80?

Why would he do that? He loves Rhona, I am one-hundred percent sure of that.

Or am I so stupid to have misunderstood him all along? He does wear army clothing.

I didn't understand it. I couldn't make any sense of it all. For at least ten minutes, I was racking my brain about what I had just seen when I heard Rhona coming up the stairs.

"Get your fucking hands of me, you cluster fucking pile of shit!" she was shouting, and much more. I imagined steam coming out of her ears. If I thought I had been cursing too much lately I knew I could learn a lot more from Rhona.

Who would think that such a sweet little thing is able to utter such unpleasantness?

The door was flung open and Rhona was thrown in.

"You fucking ass wipes!" she yelled back at the soldiers before they shut the door.

"Rhona," I called and made my way over to her.

She turned around as she heard my voice. I don't think she had realized I was there when they had thrown her in. Her eyes were bloodshot and her face flushed from all the yelling she had been doing.

"Oh Kate!" she said as we hugged each other and her body shook with sobs. Her anger made way for other emotions as she realized she didn't need to look strong anymore. Now, she was balling her eyes out. I let her cry for a while, but after a few minutes I tried to calm her down. Wiping the tears from her mascara-streaked cheeks I told her to take deep breaths.

"Come, sit down. What is happening? Why are you and Harry here?"

"They've taken Harry away," she cried, tears still streaming down her face.

"What do you mean, 'taken away'?"

My mind went into overdrive again.

Had she decided to come to the army like me and now Harry is being questioned like Charlie?

No, that is highly unlikely. It was obvious Rhona did not come here out of her own free will.

Why would they want to split Harry and Rhona up? How did they know she was bitten?

"What do you mean, Rhona? Please tell me what is going on," I urged her.

She calmed down a bit and in between sobs told me they had come upon an army roadblock when they wanted to cross US Highway 2. They'd thought they would get through without a problem as it was daylight but had been pulled over. The soldiers got them out of the car and drove them back to Bullsbrook.

"Why would they do that? Did they think you were suckers?" I didn't understand how this could be possible as we had discussed earlier that they would try not to talk to anybody and to hide their fangs. I knew Harry was a very good actor and had thought he'd be able to pull it off easily.

"No, it's much worse," she said with hatred in her voice and her chest heaved in little bits as she exhaled. Her eyes turned cold, like Harry's eyes earlier.

"What, Rhona? What?" I was holding my breath and almost died with her not telling me.

"Harry's father put an APB out for him. They were looking for him." And she doubled up crying again.

I got up and walked to the window. The pieces of the puzzle were falling together. Harry's father had put out an APB for Harry. Harry had told us before that his father was military. Suddenly, in my mind, I saw the eyes of Harry change into those of Major Moore's. Major Moore was Harry's father!

Fuck!

I cursed under my breath, knowing full well that Rhona wouldn't have minded if I'd said it out loud. Now I realized why Moore's eyes made me feel so at ease with him. And why he'd said having fangs didn't mean I was a sucker. Moore must have suspected Harry was in serious trouble because of his natural fangs and probably wanted to get him off the street and into the safety of army protection. He hadn't anticipated Harry getting a sucker girlfriend in the meantime of course, especially not one who could walk in daylight.

"That's not all," Rhona continued, trying very hard to stop her sobs. "There's more you need to know."

I turned around to face her as she didn't continue.

"We were told they hadn't been able to find Caleb and Sasha and are going to get all the suckers in this area tonight, to make sure none of us will ever walk in daylight."

She had stopped sobbing and sat with her hands folded in her lap, her face emotionless, staring in front of her.

I sort of fell on the chair next to the window. Rhona was implying that all daylight walking suckers weren't allowed to live, which included her and me.

Oh no, no, no, this isn't happening!

My hand went to my mouth and my thoughts were racing. I remembered the tubes of blood from Dr. Haley.

But they're working on a vaccine.

And they'll probably find one. They always do in the end.

Harry had said so himself that being a day walker had something to do with my immunity. If they found a vaccine they would be able to cure suckers in the future, only not these packs of suckers. Not Caleb, Sasha, Duncan, or Julie and all her girls. These suckers weren't given any time to wait for the cure as I had just signed their death warrant. The army would never let them get away. They'd never let the secret get out.

And all because of me.

I clenched my teeth. The thought of my sister being wiped out while a cure was on its way was something I couldn't live with. She was my sister and I loved her. I had to stop this, I had to save her. So I made up my mind.

"Rhona, I'm getting out of here, I've got to warn my sister."

Saturday Afternoon, Late - Getting Out

Rhona didn't have a chance to react to my statement as the door opened and Dr. Haley came in, holding another tray with empty tubes. Rhona looked at me as if to say 'what now?'

My mind was racing. I needed more time to come up with a plan. I slowly blinked and dipped my head, which made Rhona stay seated. Dr. Haley introduced himself to her and continued his preparation to take her blood. In the meantime, I circled as inconspicuously as I could towards the soldier who'd followed Dr. Haley into the classroom. He had his gun aimed at Rhona.

Since my arrival in the classroom, I had been no trouble to the soldiers. I had come here of my own free will and had given them no reason to think I wanted to get out. Hence the second soldier was still keeping watch outside.

Big mistake, boys!

As I neared the soldier guarding Rhona, he threw an uneasy glance at me. I was getting close, but I wasn't close enough yet. So as I walked on, I tried my cutest smile on him, tilted my head which exposed my neck, and seductively let my fingers trail a desk. I completely forgot I had fangs now. The soldier was quick-witted and realized the mistake he and his colleague had made.

He called out to his comrade, but I was close enough now. I lunged and a moment later he was unconscious on the floor. The other soldier came into the room with his gun at the ready. I was still on top of his colleague and too far away to do anything. Getting to my feet, I thought it had all had been for nothing.

The soldier unexpectedly raised his hands as I heard Rhona say, "Drop it, or the doc gets it!"

I turned around and there she was; this tiny, fragile little thing, so innocent looking, holding Dr. Haley with one hand by his wrinkly neck and with her other hand holding a needle to his jugular. She had her thumb on the back of the syringe, threatening to pump Dr. Haley's vein full of air.

Way to go, Rhona!

The soldier was well trained. He put his gun on the floor, kicked it in my direction and stuck his hands back in the air. I picked up his gun as fast as I could. I'd never held one before and was surprised how light it was, but that was probably because I was stronger now than I'd ever been. I cocked the gun, aimed it at his head, and told him to move away from the door. Rhona pushed the doctor towards the soldier and came to stand beside me.

"What do we do now?" she asked.

I licked my dry lips, I was nervous as hell. My heart was pounding in my chest. I had never held a gun, never threatened anybody with their life, and, to be honest, I was a bit surprised we got this far.

"We'll have to lock them up so they won't sound the alarm," I said.

"No, we have to take one with us as a hostage. Otherwise, we'll never be able to get out of here alive." Rhona sounded like she'd done this so many times before and knew exactly what would come next.

So why did she ask me what to do?

I threw a quick frown in her direction.

"You don't watch a lot of movies, do you?" Rhona said.

She had no idea how true that was.

And you don't know how little spare time teachers have.

I made a split second decision. "Okay, grab the doctor. He seems less expendable than the soldiers."

Rhona grabbed the little man by his skinny neck again and I told the soldier to drag his still unconscious comrade with him and walk in front of us into the hallway. As we followed him, I studied the still unconscious soldier. I had expected him to come round by now.

I hope I didn't give him any permanent brain damage when I hit him.

We took them to my classroom and I told Rhona to get some plastic tightening straps from one of the shelves in the storeroom. She tied the soldiers' hands behind their backs. While she attached them to the work benches, to make sure they couldn't leave, the unconscious soldier came to.

Phew! Weight of my shoulder.

We proceeded down the stairs with the doctor in front of us. I had uncocked the gun as I was terrified of accidentally shooting the man through the head. Halfway down the lower staircase, we were spotted by two soldiers on guard at the exit. They reached for their weapons but I warned them with as much conviction as I could muster not to do anything foolish.

"One move and the doctor gets it," I yelled, copying Rhona's phrase from upstairs.

Charlie would be so proud of me if he could see me right now.

One of the soldiers continued to reach for his weapon and I cocked the gun. That stopped him in his tracks.

Ha, I'm not a stupid little girl, you know.

I told that soldier to go and get Moore. I didn't need any heroes close by. It didn't take long before Moore appeared as Finkle's office was only a little way down the corridor.

"You can't go anywhere, you know," was the first thing Moore said. I knew he was trying to bluff me.

"Yes, I can. And I will. You'll do as I say or the doctor gets it."

To prove my point I pushed the gun to Dr. Haley's temple. I was so glad the man didn't struggle as I had no intention of hurting him. I pursed my lips to make convince Moore I was determined enough.

"You will take Rhona and reunite her with Harry," I then commanded Moore.

"No!" Rhona shouted before I could continue. She had not seen this one coming. "Kate, I'm coming with you." She was pulling my sleeve as she said it, not making me any more comfortable holding the cocked gun to Dr. Haley's head.

"No, Rhona, you'll be safer here, with Harry," I said, keeping my eyes on Moore. To him I said, "You'll keep her safe until this is all over and give her the vaccine you're working on."

Moore's expression became puzzled. I guessed he wondered how I knew. He nodded.

"What do you want?"

"I want a car and safe transport out of Bullsbrook."

"I can't let you go."

I pushed the gun again into Dr. Haley's temple, pushing his head to the side this time.

Moore put his hands up.

"Where will you be going?"

"To the others."

He knew exactly who I meant.

"I can't let you do this," he said again.

I liked the man, but he was getting on my nerves with his repeated statements that I couldn't have my way.

"Yes, you can. You have my blood, my saliva. You don't need me anymore. You've had all afternoon to prepare for the attack. My warning won't give them much advantage. And if I can't make them surrender, I'll be just another one of the day walkers you want to kill so badly. So, in all honesty, I don't think you give a fuck whether I go or not."

Shit, swearing feels good, I should do this more often!

I hadn't taken my eyes off Moore and nothing seemed to have changed. Nevertheless, I got the idea that all of a sudden there was more depth in his eyes than there had been before. It was almost as if he admired me. He didn't think about it for long.

"Fine, you get your wish. But the doctor stays."

You wish!

"Oh no! He's coming with me until I'm well out of Bullsbrook, as insurance that you'll keep your word. I'll let him get out unharmed on the highway and you can pick him up after I've gone."

"How do I know you will keep your word?" Moore asked, still as calm as if we were making an appointment for a coffee later on.

"Because you have Charlie."

Saturday Afternoon, Late - Questions

I was given the keys to a 4WD and I made the doctor get in the driver's seat first. I kept my gun on him while I walked round the front to the passenger's seat. As I faced the auxiliary building I saw Charlie in one of the classroom windows and my heart sank. He was slamming his hands on the window and I could hear his muted voice calling out my name.

I didn't know if he knew what was going on, but I it didn't matter. I wanted him safe, which meant I had to leave him behind. I saw the fear on his face. In an instant, I relived the climax of our union whilst the pain of leaving him ripped through my body. The result felt like a combination of butterflies and razor blades dancing in my stomach. Leaving him now was like throwing myself willingly into the deepest pit of hell, but there was no other option.

The things we do for love.

Moore was following my every move. I tried to keep it together. Rhona had been taken outside too, to be reunited with Harry. I assumed he was in another one of the auxiliary buildings. With one foot in the car, I told Rhona to tell Charlie I loved him and asked her to take care of him for me when I was gone. Tears welled up in my eyes and my voice went funny on the last sentence. I didn't want to cry in front of Moore, so I quickly got into the car and told the doctor to get going.

Once we were well out of Bullsbrook, I asked the doctor politely to get out. He had been a good hostage and hadn't tried to escape or attack me. I moved into the driver's seat, but hesitated to drive away. This fear of being incredibly stupid took a hold of me. I needed to know if I wasn't going on this escapade for nothing, so I lowered the window.

"Doc, please tell me, how far from making the vaccine are you?"

He smiled, took a step towards the car again and leaned forward. He sounded genuinely happy when he replied.

"We were getting closer, but not very fast. Your blood is the key we need to speed things up."

"Keep at it, doc," I smiled back at him and drove off.

I continued driving to the little village where Charlie and I nearly got lynched. As with everything I'd done in these past few days, I had no idea what to expect and hadn't really thought through what I was going to do.

What if Julie is long gone and safe somewhere far away? What if she doesn't want to get vaccinated? What if they never find a vaccination?

So many fucking ifs again!

For now, I had to focus on finding Julie.

While driving through the countryside with its beautiful colors, I saw Charlie's face before me. The face of that funny guy who'd made me laugh so much in the last few months. That guy I'd hurt so often during these last few days. That guy who now meant everything to me, the one I wanted to wake up next to every day.

I had no idea if there was going to be another day for me and the thought constricted my throat. My eyes filled up with tears and I could hardly see the road ahead. I didn't need to talk to anyone, nor did I have to be ashamed to let the tears flow freely, but I was still trying to keep it together.

For Charlie.

Saturday Evening - Finding Julie

As I got to the village, the sun had already set and the world was that of suckers again. Gray and gloomy. When I arrived at the square I had to stop the car. In front of me was a huge crowd of suckers, there were more than I had ever seen together before.

Where did they all come from?

I assumed Caleb and Sasha had used motorized transport to make it to Duncan's pack and gather the other packs so quickly here.

What the hell was I thinking?

I recognized several of them. Most were from Duncan's pack, some had to be from Caleb's pack, but I also saw girls from Julie's pack. 'Julie must be here,' I thought elated at first. I then acknowledged that this meant it would be harder to get her out of here.

Before I got out of the car I tucked the army gun into the back of my pants. 'For safety measures,' I told myself. Some of the suckers had noticed me arrive and had moved away from the car. I wondered why they were doing this; I wasn't a threat to them.

I walked towards the center of the square and the crowd parted ahead of me. At the other side of the square, I saw Duncan, Julie, Caleb, and Sasha. My hands instantaneously became sweaty. Despite my fear, I forced myself to walk towards them until I was close enough to communicate, but at a safe distance. From the look on their faces, it was clear Caleb and Sasha had told Duncan their news and possibly knew about the army's plan to annihilate them.

Caleb's problem with Duncan doesn't seem to be big enough to stop him from forming an alliance with Duncan, and vice versa.

Duncan called out.

"Are you joining us again?"

I couldn't tell if he was happy about that prospect or not.

"No, I am not. I am here to warn you the army is preparing a major attack and I ask you all to surrender so no lives will be lost."

A wave of laughter went through the crowd, including Duncan, Caleb, and Sasha. I noticed Julie wasn't laughing.

She's probably wondering what the hell I am doing.

"You must me joking," Duncan said. "Why would we surrender? We are the superior species. We are gathered here to crush the last resistance to a new era!"

The crowd cheered.

OMG, this guy is a raving lunatic. No wonder Julie didn't want to join his pack. So what's she doing here right now?

I looked at Julie again. She looked shifty, seeming none too happy with the whole situation at all. It was almost as if she didn't want to be here.

A shiver ran through my spine. Duncan's hand wasn't holding Julie's hand, he was holding Julie's wrist.

Shit, shit, shit! How could I have been so stupid?

I realized they had known I would come and look for her.

They still don't know how to become a day walker and they need me. She's the bait, I'm the prize. And I walked straight into their trap.

There was no way I could get out now. My only chance was to try and make the others see this man was insane. They didn't stand a chance against the army, especially as they weren't day walkers yet and I knew the army was coming with huge UV-lights mounted on their trucks. It would be a massacre.

Sasha addressed the crowd this time. She pointed at me and shouted.

"She's the key, she can walk in daylight! When we get the secret out of her we can all walk in daylight."

Another cheer went through the crowd.

For heaven's sake, is there a sale on idiocy?

"Listen, we don't have time for this," I shouted to the people. "The army is coming and they have lights, lots of UV-lights. They're going to wipe you out before the night is over."

I looked around me and didn't see a single rational-thinking being. What I saw instead was a crazy mob. And I knew what they looked like, I had some previous experience. At the exact same spot, come to think of it.

Looks like I'm having déjà vu...

These suckers weren't single individuals anymore; they were a mob, with mob mentality. They weren't an aggressive mob yet, but they could easily become one and Duncan knew it.

"You will tell us your secret," Duncan commanded. The tone of his voice suggested he thought he already had me under his control.

"No, I will not. When I do I'll seal your fate and you'll all die." I was still hoping I could convince them to give up. "Everybody, listen, please. They're working on a vaccine and will be able to turn you back into normal humans again. You can have your old lives back!"

The crowd roared with laughter. I knew it had been a long shot of course. I didn't know what the army would do with these people who had killed over and over again. And what made me think they'd want to return to their previous feeble selves? The crowd kept on screaming, growing angrier.

All of a sudden Duncan let go of Julie's wrist. He grabbed her by her neck and with his other hand held a gun to her head. Julie yelped and this fueled the mob even more.

"You *will* give us your secret!" he shouted over the top of the crowd.

In an instant I had my gun out and aimed at Duncan. It didn't scare him as he knew I wouldn't shoot as long as he held the gun to Julie's head. Caleb must have been thinking the same thing as without an order he came jogging towards me. I knew it was now or never. If he reached me he would take the gun from me. That would be the end. I had to pull the trigger, I had to stop him. Caleb slowed down halfway and continued walking towards me. He had a smile on his face. It was a victory smile as he knew they'd won. He knew I couldn't pull the trigger.

He's still a human being. If I kill him, I'll be as bad as they are. I, myself, will be the reason why I hate guns.

I dropped my arms, defeat written all over my face. Caleb's smile became a smirk. Seeing this smirk on his face fueled a simmering fire in me and a sudden, hot anger welled up. This guy had caused me so much pain, so much misery. To hurt Sasha he had pretended to love me and, as a result, I had hurt Charlie again and again. I had put so many lives at risk. I had no idea how much I really hated Caleb, but in that instant I knew. I raised my arms again and shot him.

I feel so much better now...

Caleb went down on one knee. I could see the blood seeping from the wound in his right shoulder. I heard Sasha screech with rage. I began walking in

Julie's direction with my arms outstretched, holding the gun aimed at Duncan.

I've got a gun and I'm not afraid to use it!

I was about to pass Caleb and I thought I had warned him enough to let me be. But the guy was as tough as he was portrayed in the stories about him. He dove at me, grabbing my upper arms. We flew in an arc through the air. When we hit the ground, the sudden impact caused the gun to go off.

Caleb looked into my eyes as his body pinned me to the ground. There was love, surprise, and fear in them. These were the eyes I'd instantly fallen so deeply in love with. The eyes I'd come to hate. And now, in this last moment, I couldn't help but love them again. It was as if this wave of eternal love washed around us, engulfed us, connecting us for evermore. Then the light in his eyes faded as he collapsed on top of me.

Saturday Evening - War

At that exact moment, a bright flare dropped in the middle of the village square. The suckers closest to it fell to the ground, unable to control their seizing muscle movements. The rest of the mob scattered in all directions.

I pushed Caleb's body off me. As I got up I saw the suckers donning all sorts of hoods and masks and sunglasses as they fled. Obviously, they had prepared their attack and anticipated the army fighting with light. Duncan may have been a lunatic, but he knew warfare. I scanned the crowd. I spotted Duncan dragging Julie away from me.

Oh no, you don't!

I sprinted after them. They disappeared into the supermarket. From all sides the army surrounded the square with 4WDs and tanks. They had enormous black lights alternated with normal lights mounted on them, shining in all directions.

The suckers didn't seem to have a chance, but they didn't seem afraid either. As one they fell upon the soldiers. Instantaneously it was a proper battle scene as hell broke loose with flashes, shots, explosions, and screams everywhere. Some screams from suckers being hit, others from soldiers being bitten. The lights cast horrible moving shadows on the walls, making it all look even worse.

I made it halfway to the supermarket when I heard my name shouted. I turned around and immediately saw Charlie. My heart stopped and I felt the blood drain from my head.

No! Not here, not now!

Charlie was standing in an open jeep with Moore. Chaos was all around and I saw Moore's car being attacked by suckers. Fearing for Charlie's life I sprinted back as fast as I could and threw two of the suckers off the car. Charlie was thrown on the floor, being protected by the soldiers and Moore, who were fighting off masked suckers in close combat. I grabbed two more suckers by the scruff of their necks and bashed their heads together. I grabbed Charlie's hand and pulled him out of the car. With Charlie out of immediate danger, I turned back and yanked the remaining suckers off the car, hitting them unconscious. One of the soldiers was being bitten. I jumped on the sucker, yanked his head back and knocked him unconscious. I threw a glance at Charlie, to check if he was okay, before grabbing Moore by his jacket.

"Why did you bring him here?" I shouted, pointing at Charlie. I strained to be heard over the screams, helicopters, and gunfire.

"I thought I could use him as leverage," he said. He sighed and I took it as an acknowledgment that he'd misunderstood me.

You're an idiot! I wanted Charlie safe!

I had to control my anger and not hurt Moore for being so stupid as I had no time for it. Instead, I told him the suckers could and should be saved. I glanced at the carnage happening all around us, then turned back to Moore.

"They don't know how, Moore, they are not day walkers. They have no idea how to do it," I yelled. I didn't spend any more of my precious time explaining. My words were clear and I hoped Moore would use the information to save as many lives as possible. I turned around to leave, but Moore grabbed me.

"I've got to go save my sister, Moore. I'll be back after that," and pulled myself loose.

I turned back to Charlie and grabbed him by the arm. Together we ran to the supermarket.

Saturday Evening - Saving Julie

Charlie and I ran into the supermarket, into what seemed like an oasis of calm compared to the village square. I motioned for Charlie to keep low as we positioned ourselves behind a checkout.

"Julie!" I shouted out.

"Kate!" she yelled back and I heard Duncan smack her face.

I am so going to hurt that bastard!

"Duncan, let her go. She's of no use to you."

"Oh yes she is, Kate, and you know it. You give me the secret or I'll blow her head off."

My nostrils flared and I clenched my fists. Charlie indicated he was moving to the other checkout. I didn't want him to, but he was out of my reach before I could stop him. And I couldn't say anything as I didn't want to give away he was here as well. I had no choice but to keep Duncan focused on me.

"Okay, I'm coming out, don't shoot!" I yelled. I emerged from behind the checkout. Walking into the middle aisle I saw Charlie duck into the third aisle.

Part of the shelves' content had been thrown on the floor by looters and I had to take care where I put my feet. As I took my time to walk the length of the aisle, hands held at shoulder height, I studied the layout of the store. It appeared to be a typical one. I had heard Julie's and Duncan's voices come from the end of the first aisle. This meant they were in the aisle with food items. I was in the one with detergents and personal care stuff, so Charlie had to be in the aisle with the pet food, wine, and camping accessories. I tried to keep Duncan talking to me while I wrecked my brain to come up with a plan.

"Promise me you will let Julie go as soon as you have me."

"We'll cross that bridge when we get there, shall we?"

The bastard's not going to playing fair.

Suddenly I heard a snicker. My eyes squinted and the hairs on the back of my neck stood up.

Sasha!

Although I hadn't seen Sasha enter the shop, it was obvious she must have followed Duncan and Julie. I glanced toward end of the aisle and thought I could see her black, fake-leather boot sticking out. She was right at the end of the shelves between the first and second aisle. My eyes spotted the items on the shelves at the end of the aisle and I smiled. After another two steps, I grabbed a lighter from one of the cardboards hanging from the shelf posts.

"Okay, almost there ..." I said as I walked on slowly.

"Stop!" Duncan shouted suddenly.

My heart stopped, as if on command. I thought he had seen through me and that it was all going to end now.

"Throw your gun on the floor in front of you."

Phew!

He hadn't read my mind, so I did as he said, sliding the gun in front of me. It bounced off the skirting board at the deli counter and stopped in the middle of the back aisle.

"Now step forward with your hands up."

"Okay, don't shoot, I'm unarmed now."

Just before I turned the corner I grabbed a can of hairspray from the shelf with one hand and flicked the lid off with my thumb. Bringing the lighter in front of the can, I pressed the button of the spray can and flicked on the lighter. A huge flame shot out, hitting Sasha full in the face. She screamed out in pain and anger, her fake hair alight within seconds. She fell backward, hitting her head on the hard, concrete floor, and she was out immediately.

In slow motion, I saw Duncan swing his arm holding the gun to Julie's head towards me. At the same moment, Charlie threw a bottle of camping gas in my direction. I caught it and used it as a club to knock the gun out of Duncan's hand. Duncan had fired at me and missed me by millimeters. I shoved the bottle with all my power into his face. Duncan fell back against shelves with canned vegetables, which collapsed, the cans falling around and on top of him. Unfortunately, he didn't feel anything as he was already unconscious from my blow.

Don't you worry, sir. You will have an extra big headache in the morning.

The moment she was freed, Julie flung herself into my arms and I rushed her away from Duncan and Sasha before they could come to. I wanted her out of here and quick. We were halfway down the aisle when I heard movement at the back. I turned around to see if Charlie was safe. My body stiffened when I saw him pick up the gun and aim it at Duncan.

"Charlie, no!" I screamed.

The gun went off twice. I was shocked, stunned. How could he have done this? I let go of Julie and slowly made my way back to Charlie, who stood there with the gun at his side. Standing beside him, I saw that he had shot both Duncan and Sasha, both in the right shoulder. Sasha looked horrible with her burned skull. I was perplexed and stood there, blinking, not knowing what to say.

"I can do what you can do," Charlie said and smiled at me.

"You saw that?"

"Sure did, my love. You made me proud." He put his hand on my butt and we kissed.

I looked at Duncan and Sasha again, saw they weren't going anywhere soon.

"Feels good, doesn't it?" I said with a wicked grin.

"It sure does!" Charlie chuckled.

When the three of us walked out of the supermarket, the battle between the suckers and the army was as good as over, with the army having the winning hand. The square still looked like a war zone. Fires were burning, lights flashed, and sirens wailed. Bodies lay on the ground everywhere. Helicopters and ambulances were taking the dead and wounded.

As I saw them put Caleb's body on a trolley I felt the energy drain out of me. I thought of all these lives lost. When we passed one of the bodies, I saw a tranquilizer dart sticking out of its neck. It appeared that Moore had organized that the suckers were shot with tranquilizers, not bullets, and they were now being loaded into trucks to be securely confined. One of the corners of my mouth curled up. I had underestimated Major Moore.

Julie, Charlie and I walked up to the Major, who had obviously survived the assault and was giving instructions to his soldiers.

"Can we hitch a ride?" I asked.

He turned around to us and smiled behind his mustache.

"You sure can, hop in."

Aftermath

On the way back to Bullsbrook, Julie asked me what had happened since we parted and what this thing about being a day walker was. I told her how I had been 'vaccinated' by Caleb, how I 'vaccinated' Rhona and how we both were immune to daylight now. Major Moore wasn't happy that I'd told Julie about it and back at the school he quickly drafted a statement for me to sign in which I agreed I wouldn't tell anybody else about this anymore. I had no objection signing it as I didn't want to have any more day walkers on my hands.

All the suckers, including Rhona, Julie and myself, were kept in close confinement for a few weeks. It was now the army's problem to feed us. Charlie and Harry were allowed to see us as often as they liked, which they did of course. Julie chose to be confined with her girl pack instead of the solitary, more comfortable confinements they had for Rhona and me.

Moore was able to inform me that Maxine and her husband were okay. However, as I had dreaded I found out that my parents were not among the survivors. Maxine arranged their funeral and Julie and I were allowed to attend it, under heavy military escort.

There was a major investigation into the origin of the virus and, after the necessary forceful interrogations, it appeared that it was the military that had created it. They had taken a man-made medical virus, built to stop a muscle wasting disease, and turned it into a treatment to build better, stronger soldiers.

Unfortunately, the virus appeared to have unwanted side-effects, that of the blood craving and UV-sensitivity. There was an accident in the laboratory and infected SEAL soldiers escaped. Trained to survive, they eluded the search and destroy teams sent after them and the rest is history. Ever since, the army had been working round the clock to create a vaccination, fearing what was about to happen, but had no luck until they met me.

From my blood, having been vaccinated before being infected, they found that the solution didn't lie in the standard antibodies IgA, IgG and IgM, but in the more mysterious and often ignored IgD. Two weeks after the final battle the treatment was ready, mass produced, and given to every single person; bitten and unbitten, willing or unwilling, young and old. Due to the fact that the virus was still active in the body weeks after infection, the treatment still worked.

The worldwide vaccination became the greatest medical feat ever. It took a fortnight of daily monoclonal antibody treatments, but every sucker on the planet returned to being a normal human again.

A special hunt force was created to hunt down those that tried to remain suckers. Many were caught, but the threat lingered as there was no way of telling how many were still out there.

Obviously, heads of military leaders in charge of the medical experiment rolled, so to speak. It wasn't over just like that though. People still wanted to see others hang for the murders committed. In the International Court of Justice in The Hague, The Netherlands, mitigating circumstances concerning the majority of ex-suckers were accepted due to the fact that it was proven the succedaneum virus had changed their 'needs.' They simply had had no other choice than to behave the way they had.

However, some of the suckers had shown extreme violence and/or cruelty during their turn. They were put on trial and found guilty, Duncan and Sasha included. Long-term sentences were unavoidable and some would never walk outside again.

A lot of ex-suckers who were acquitted chose to live in closed communities. Most of them were ashamed of their actions and didn't want to confront family and friends with their presence. Some lived there to avoid continued harassment from humans who couldn't forgive or forget or both.

Julie chose to live in a closed community farm with her girls not far from Bullsbrook. I don't know if she lived there for her own good or to help the girls. Maybe it was a bit of both for her too.

Harry and Rhona moved into a flat in Portland, where Harry continued his medical studies. He refused to have his fangs put in a normal position. This was a free service offered by the government and taken up by nearly everybody. Nobody wanted to be reminded of what they had started calling 'Black October.'

As soon as my treatment started, my strength dwindled back to normal. I had my fangs surgically put back into their original position and by the time I was released I was able to put more variety in my diet. Life slowly started to be normal again.

There was a monument erected for those fallen during Black October. My parents' names were on it, so was Sue's, and so was Caleb's. Whenever I brought flowers to remember them, I always made sure there was an added rose, for Caleb.

Charlie and I decided to continue to teach in Bullsbrook. From inheritance money, Charlie's aunt also wasn't among the survivors, we bought a bigger place as it appeared I was pregnant and due to give birth to a baby girl nine months after our ordeal.

We were over the moon with her upcoming arrival and she was very special to us. We decided to name her Sue, in honor of the dear friend we lost. I bought the most colorful baby outfits I could find for her. Other than that, I was so glad I'd be able to give her a normal, quiet, boring, family life.

No holidays in caravan parks though.

The End

First Feed

Halfway through lunch, Sue began to cry. We all looked up and I was already half out of my seat when Charlie told me to stay put.

"You relax and finish your lunch, love, and I'll give Sue her bottle." He got up to prepare the formula milk. We had decided together for me not to breastfeed. We both wanted to keep teaching, so we had booked Sue into daycare from fourteen days after her birth.

Both Maxine and Julie stared at me with perplexed faces.

"Hellooo, where did you get *him* from?" Maxine said after she finished her mouthful. "Are there any more like him left over? I may swap one for John!"

"Unfortunately, ladies," Charlie beamed at them, "there is only one Adonis and I'm already head-over-heels with your sister." He threw me a hand-kiss while he was waiting for the milk to warm up. I pretended to catch the kiss and threw him one back. I had no problem with showing my love for Charlie anywhere, anytime. Not anyhow, though.

I have y limits on what can be shown in public.

Both Maxine and Julie pretended to throw up at the overt display of love between Charlie and myself.

"Don't you worry, honey," I said to Charlie, "it's not your food, they're just extremely jealous they can't have you."

"That's what you think. You don't know what I've put in the quiche..." Charlie left us with that information as he went into the living room to give Sue her milk bottle. He had a huge grin on his face.

Both Maxine and Julie immediately scanned the food on their plates and I giggled when I saw their faces.

My sisters and I finished lunch and began doing the dishes. I excused myself for a moment to check up on Charlie and Sue. Charlie was holding Sue on his lap on the couch and my heart warmed at the sight of my loved ones. When I sat down next to them I saw that the bottle was still as good as full.

"Honey, you must be doing something wrong, she's not drinking," I said irritated and tried to take Sue from Charlie. He didn't let me take her from him and I frowned at him.

Surely, a mother knows best.

Charlie nodded his head in Sue's direction.

"Kate, she *is* drinking," he whispered. "Look!"

I studied Sue again and saw that she was sucking.

How odd...

What I hadn't seen before was that she didn't have her mouth on the teat of the bottle, but on Charlie's thumb.

"I sliced my thumb cutting up the veggies for the quiche," he continued to whisper. "She doesn't want the milk. I kept trying to put the teat in her mouth but she keeps going for my thumb!"

Holy shit! OMG! Nooo!

I felt sick to my stomach. I turned to Charlie for support, but he had this look of resignation on his face. I wasn't sure if I could accept what we were both now knew.

Our daughter is a baby sucker!

Sign up for news on the Suckers Trilogy at
www.suckerstrilogy.wordpress.com.

'Suckers – Book 3. Killing A Vampire'

The third book of the Suckers trilogy is in the process of being conceived.

Sasha is released from prison... and she is out for revenge!

Sign up for news on the Suckers Trilogy at
www.suckerstrilogy.wordpress.com.

Acknowledgements

First of all, I would like to thank my children who encouraged me to write down my dream, the root of this story. Without them, I would not have started writing and would not have known the enjoyment it gives me. I also thank them for putting up with me since I started this writing journey, sitting behind my computer for hours on end. Love you guys!

I would like to thank Ruth Morris, who helped by proofreading the first chapters and pointing out to me that there are no 'pound stores' in America. She made me realize the story needed to happen in a proper American setting, instead of a mismatch of a European, American and Australian setting, using equally mismatching language. I would also like to thank my friends Suzie, Bob, Chris and of course my mother, who all proofread my first draft, and encouraged me to keep writing.

I couldn't have delivered the first version without my proofreader, Dr. Chloe Alexander, Academic Skills Adviser (Academic Writing) at the University of Aberdeen. She did me a great favor by taking on my proofreading request and teaching me a lot about the

English language. Even though English is not my first language, I thought I was pretty good at it. It appears I still have a lot to learn...

I would like to thank all my friends at the One Stop Fiction Authors Resource Facebook Group. They have been a tremendous help and encouragement, keeping me sane through the past few months. I am so glad I know I am not alone! I particularly thank those who have done the beta reading for me, giving me honest feedback.

This second version would not have been what it is today without the special help of my friends Colin and Stephanie. Your adjustments and suggestions have been invaluable. I thank Colin in particular for helping me take a step closer to writing in the proper tense. I need to thank Stephanie for making me think like a normal person and not being afraid to tell me when my writing was alien ☺.

Last but not least I couldn't have done any of this without the perpetual tolerance and love of my husband. As I am embarking on yet another hobby, he puts up with my minimal (renovation) activity in our house, my dismal cooking efforts and little attention to his needs. Your never-fading belief in me is inspiring. I love you.

Jacky Dahlhaus